COLLISION COURSE

COLLISION COURSE

Matt Hilton

SEVERN
HOUSE

First world edition published 2020
in Great Britain and the USA by
SEVERN HOUSE PUBLISHERS LTD of
Eardley House, 4 Uxbridge Street, London W8 7SY.
Trade paperback edition first published
in Great Britain and the USA 2021 by
Severn House, an imprint of Canongate Books Ltd,
14 High Street, Edinburgh EH1 1TE.

British Library Cataloguing in Publication Data
A CIP catalogue record for this title is available from the British Library.

ISBN-13: 978-0-7278-9046-7 (cased)
ISBN-13: 978-1-78029-729-3 (trade paper)
ISBN-13: 978-1-4483-0450-9 (e-book)

All Severn House titles are printed on acid-free paper.

Severn House Publishers support the Forest Stewardship Council™ [FSC™],
the leading international forest certification organisation.
All our titles that are printed on FSC certified paper carry the FSC logo.

Typeset by Palimpsest Book Production Ltd.,
Falkirk, Stirlingshire, Scotland.
Printed and bound in Great Britain by
TJ Books Limited, Padstow, Cornwall.

ONE

P unching a person's head with a closed fist is never advisable. The human hand is brittle in comparison to the skull, and is prone to breaking on impact. As only a few years earlier her fist had almost been severed from the wrist it was not only a stupid idea but also a reckless one. Tess Grey knew from the unarmed combat training she'd completed when she was a sheriff's deputy not to pound her knuckles into an assailant's skull, but like most things absorbed in training it gave way to instinct during highly stressful encounters. Actually, it was never her idea to punch Nathan Doyle; it was a knee-jerk response to the fact he was about to kick her fiancé, Nicolas 'Po' Villere, in the face. Po, grappling on the ground with Nathan's brother Adrian, in an effort to free an axe from his hands, wasn't in an ideal position to defend against a sneak kick from his sibling.

Tess lunged in and swung for him. Despite the wrongness of her punch, and of the situation that had devolved rapidly from a curt exchange of words to Adrian picking up the axe, it had an extraordinary effect. Caught poised on one leg, his mouth open in a wordless shout as he aimed for Po's face, Tess's fist impacted with Nathan's jaw. This was the first time she'd person-ally witnessed anyone having their lights knocked out for real. It was certainly the first time she'd ever stopped an assailant with a single blow. Nathan collapsed, dropped clean, with one foot still in the air. He shuddered on his back, his outstretched leg twitching in response to the shock to his nervous system. Tess stared down at him, stunned also by the finality of her punch.

Po and Adrian had also paused in their tussle. Po had gained dominancy, kneeling astride Adrian's chest, with his left heel forcing down the hand wielding the axe. Astounded, Po blinked once at Tess, then he grabbed for the weapon. He plucked it out of Adrian's grasp and slung it away, while his other palm was jammed against the other man's face. Adrian no longer wished to fight; he was more concerned with his brother's wellbeing than carrying on. He attempted to crane his head, to see past Po to where Nathan rasped in an effort to breathe. He struggled to rise, but Po pinned him in place.

Po coiled his fist and shook it an inch from Adrian's nose. 'Quit strugglin', bra, or you'll be next to go to sleep.'

'My brother!' Adrian was too concerned for Nathan to take heed of a threat. 'You have to help him!'

Tess stooped at Nathan's side. His labored breathing was a result of his positioning. Unconscious, everything relaxed, including the soft tissue at the rear of his throat: the rattling was due to his epiglottis vibrating with each intake and exhalation. She eased him onto his side, placing him in the recovery position and immediately his breathing calmed. She touched fingertips to his carotid pulse: it was strong and even. He'd awaken shortly with a sore jaw and a loss of dignity, but otherwise he'd be fine. She caught Adrian's eye. 'He's going to be OK; now do as you're told and you'll be fine too.'

Adrian relaxed, relieved that Nathan was going to recover.

Po stood, leaving Adrian flat on his back. Both men exchanged looks. Po's mouth formed a tight line. 'You expect me to kick you when you're down? Don't. S'long as you don't go crazy on me again, you can get up.'

Adrian glanced at Tess. After she'd knocked his brother unconscious he was possibly wondering if she was the one to be most wary of. She shook her head in disbelief, gesturing for him to stand.

'Things didn't have to get to *this*,' she reminded him. 'We only came here with a few questions; you were the one that got all uppity and picked up a weapon.'

'Yeah,' Po growled, 'about *that*.'

'I'd never have used it on you,' Adrian whined, showing the palms of his hands as he rose. 'I mean, whaddaya think I am?'

'I don't take too kindly to anyone wavin' a hatchet in my face. Certainly don't wait till it's planted in my skull before decidin' if the threat's real or not.'

'I overreacted, man. Look, I'm sorry. Uh . . . is it OK for me to help my brother?'

Already Nathan was stirring. His legs jerked a couple of times, and then he had his right knee under him and he pushed up onto his braced arms. His head hung and he shook it like a dog dislodging a bug from its ear; he'd no idea where he was. Adrian stooped, patting him on his shoulders as he cajoled some lucidity back into his brother. Po and Tess exchanged a look. The situation had gone from naught to sixty in a few seconds, and it had reversed equally fast.

While Adrian cared for his brother, Tess rubbed her wrist. It wasn't sore; the action was an unconscious habit. Remarkably her knuckles didn't hurt either, but things might have gone horribly wrong if her blow had landed a few inches higher on Nathan's head, or, worst case scenario, had struck him in the teeth. An ex-colleague of Tess's had once punched an aggressive felon in the mouth, splitting his hand open. He'd contracted a raging infection from the mouth's bacteria and almost lost his hand: he'd undergone a series of surgical procedures but to this day he couldn't form a fist and had lost feeling and mobility in two fingers. Unlike she, whose injury had forced her resignation from the Cumberland County Sheriff's Department, he now worked as a dispatcher, hanging in there for his pension. Since leaving the sheriff's, Tess's latest work choice was due to a series of events that had led her from compiling family trees as a genealogist to licensed private investigator, while her life choices had also seen Po transcend from reluctant hired guide to best friend and lover, and – if all went well – to future husband. She checked on Po.

He was dressed in high-topped boots, jeans, T-shirt and a black collarless leather bomber jacket. His knees were dusty and his short greying hair tussled, but otherwise he'd taken no harm from his brief scuffle with Adrian Doyle. If anything it had placed sparks of amusement in his turquoise eyes. When he caught her checking, he returned her gaze and she saw the lights didn't diminish, and his lips pulled up at one corner. 'You musta got him right on the sweet spot, Tess. I'm impressed.'

She was torn. She was mildly embarrassed by her uncouth actions, but couldn't shake a touch of pride that she'd taken down a guy standing six inches taller, and who outweighed her by at least seventy pounds, with one punch. 'Resorting to violence is nothing to be proud of,' she scolded him, but couldn't avoid a brief quirk of her own lips. Po grinned unabashedly.

'There's a time and place for it, f'sure,' he countered. 'Y'ask me, the Doyle brothers are gonna be more amenable to our questions from now on.' He turned his attention to the siblings. 'Hey, guys, how's about we start again from the beginnin'' and you tell us where to find Jacob?'

Nathan wouldn't look at Po, due mainly to concealing his shame from Tess. Not only at being knocked flat by a woman, but that it had happened during his cowardly attack on Po. He placed his face in his hands, massaging his jaw, but also hiding behind his fingers. Adrian, the older of the two, continued patting his brother's shoulders, but he also returned Po's stare. 'We're Jacob's brothers, man, you can't expect us to rat him out to the law.'

'Do I look like the law to you?' Po set his jaw.

Adrian flapped a hand at Tess.

'I'm not a cop either, and you should thank your stars I'm not.' She nodded at the discarded hatchet. 'If I were, you'd both be in cuffs and on your way to jail.'

Adrian hadn't actually tried to strike Po with the axe. Whether it was his intention or not, Po hadn't hung around. He'd pounced on him and grappled for the weapon the instant Adrian yanked it out of the old tree stump he employed as a chopping block. It mattered not though; there were few police officers that'd be as lenient as Tess was prepared to be. She tilted her head, offering a sympathetic grimace to Nathan, and reiterated her earlier words. 'Like I said, things didn't have to get to this. How about we all take a deep breath and try again, in a more civilized manner this time?'

'If you're not cops, who are you?' asked Adrian.

'I'm Tess Grey, I'm a private investigator—'

'So you're as bad as a cop in my book. No good's ever come of any investigator showing up around here.'

'Here' was the front yard of the Doyle family house, a split-level timber structure just outside Standish, about fifteen miles west of Portland, Maine. The property backed onto a swathe of orchards, comprised of different varieties of apple trees; a destination for families who made a fun day out of 'picking their own' and picnicking under the leafy canopy. The Doyles weren't involved in the fruit growing business. In fact, Tess had no idea how the brothers made a living, but judging by the decrepit look of their home it wasn't lucrative. She wondered if they were involved in petty crime to bolster their existence, which would explain their distrust of investigators.

'Jacob isn't in any trouble,' Tess reassured him.

'Why are you so keen on finding him then?'

'He can help us with another case we're looking into.'

'How's that?'

'I can't tell you. Client confidentiality.'

'What's with all the secrecy? You're not an attorney and your buddy over there sure isn't a priest.'

Po had stepped away to give Tess room, but not too distant; staying close in case the conversation disintegrated into anger again. He leaned his hips against the chopping block, arms folded across his chest. He raised his head and gave Adrian a tight smile.

Tess said, 'Let's just say I'm bound by my word. Besides, I'm not in the mood for sharing if you're not going to help.'

'Jacob's a good kid. I can't think how he'd be involved in anything you might be investigating.'

'Perhaps he isn't. In fact, I'm sure he isn't involved. But he might be able to give us the location of someone that is.'

'Who?' Adrian checked with Nathan that he wasn't overstepping a sibling boundary with his question: Nathan was more interested in nursing his jaw. 'We're a close family, we share friends; maybe we know whoever it is you're interested in finding.'

Tess mulled his suggestion over and decided to hell with it. Once they found Jacob, he'd likely inform his brothers who she was looking for. 'What do you know about a girl called Hayley Cameron?'

He grunted. 'Yeah, we know that no good bitch! Jacob ran around with her a few months ago, acting like a lovesick fool. We warned him she was just stringing him along, using him, but he wouldn't listen. She was, too; she used him right up until the moment she dumped his penniless ass.'

'How did Jacob take being dumped?'

'Well, he wasn't crying into his beer, if that's what you mean. He realized we'd been right about her, put her down to a bad experience and moved on. Good riddance to garbage, y'know?'

'Jacob didn't see her after they broke up?'

'If he did he didn't tell us, 'cause we'd have hauled him out here in the yard and knocked some sense into him.'

'Maybe,' Po interjected from his perch, 'he kept schtum because he didn't want you two lunkheads wailin' on him like you tried with us.'

Adrian looked suitably abashed. 'Maybe, man, but I don't think so. Hayley was trash, and now Jacob's seeing another girl, a nice girl. He's got no reason to have anything to do with Hayley again. If ever he goes near her again I'll—'

Tess's somber expression halted him.

It dawned on him why a private investigator might be seeking Hayley.

'It's her who's in trouble, right? Doesn't surprise me. What's she gone and gotten herself into now?'

'She,' Tess said, 'has simply *gone* and I need to find her.'

TWO

P o drove them towards Portland in his vintage Ford Mustang. The muscle car was uniform black, sleek and powerful. The car suited Po, but seated in the passenger seat Tess often felt self-conscious. The nature of her employment meant she preferred to keep a low profile, while the Mustang was guaranteed to draw attention – particularly when Po drove it as if they were in a street race, contesting for ownership slips. Though he always drove as if he was trying to beat a clock, it was with skill and control, so it wasn't his manner of driving that caught attention; she had to admit, to certain tastes the car was a beauty to behold. While the car got appreciative looks, she usually kept her head down and averted, hiding her face behind her blonde locks. On the trip back to Portland her face was averted in the opposite direction, to conceal her blushing cheeks from Po. He had retold her David versus Goliath moment twice now already and wasn't finished glorifying the details. He was impressed, and also grateful that she'd saved him from a mouthful of boot leather, but she wished he'd drop the subject. Like she'd told him, resorting to violence was nothing to be proud of, but she had to admit to experiencing a fresh shiver of adrenalin each time he'd brought up the knockout blow. She should be horrified but was secretly proud, and that was rather unbecoming of her.

'OK, Po, let's drop the subject, shall we, and concentrate on finding Hayley?'

'Sure thing,' he agreed, but with a snarky grin. 'Where d'you wanna try now, Rocky?'

They'd already done the rounds of Hayley's neighbors, past workmates and closest friends, none of whom knew where the girl had gotten to, but who had led them to Jacob Doyle. 'We may as well hit up Cooper's.'

Cooper's Bar was on Middle Street, in Portland's entertainment district, mid-point between Congress and Fore Streets. According to his siblings, Jacob had taken a job bussing tables

at an establishment that couldn't decide if it was an Irish-style
tavern or an English-style fish 'n' chips restaurant: its type of
clientele depended mostly on the time of day, the diners and
drinkers rarely mixing.

'Makes sense. Then we can swing by and collect Pinky. I can't
wait to tell him how you knocked Nathan Doyle on his ass.'

'Po, please don't. You know what Pinky's like . . . I'll never
hear the last of it.'

Jerome 'Pinky' Leclerc was once Po's cellmate during their
incarceration at Angola, the Louisiana State Penitentiary. For
most of his adult life, the flamboyant Pinky had been a career
criminal in and around Baton Rouge, until Tess and Po's first
job together had reconnected the two men. Since then Pinky had
regularly assisted them with their activities, putting his life on
the line for them on more than one occasion, and growing to
be their best friend. Through his involvement – in his words – on
the side of the angels, he'd suffered a paradigm shift in his
mentality. Tess sometimes cringed when Pinky held her up as
his idea of a paragon of virtue, a shining example he wished to
emulate. He'd glorify her act of knocking out Nathan Doyle
to save Po as proof of her righteousness! A few months ago he'd
abandoned his old life, fled north with a bounty on his head and
taken up residence in Tess's vacant home above an antiques shop
on Cumberland Avenue, a hearty stone's throw from Cooper's
Bar.

'Maybe we should go collect Pinky first,' Po suggested with
a grin. 'Should you need to knock out Jacob Doyle; I'd hate for
him to miss the show a second time.'

Tess backhanded his shoulder, and Po laughed. 'Hey! Maybe
you're gettin' too handy with those fists. I thought you said that
resorting to violence was nothin' to be proud of?'

'Keep it up,' she warned, 'and you'll be the one getting knocked
out, *Nicolas*.'

'Uh-oh, I know when I hear my given name you mean
business.'

'You'd better believe it,' she agreed. They both laughed.

Thankfully, Po changed the subject.

'Jacob's brothers painted a damning picture of Hayley. You
think there's truth in it?'

'I prefer to reserve judgment and make up my mind after meeting someone.'

'I'm with you. There are two sides to every story, maybe more. It'll be interesting hearin' Jacob's take on the tale.'

Tess understood where he was leading. If Hayley Cameron was the type of girl Adrian Doyle had described then she might have attracted trouble from someone that had forced her to lie low. Jacob had supposedly learned his lesson after being used by her and he'd moved on; maybe there was somebody else in her life that wasn't as forgiving. But Tess wasn't about to prejudge her. A couple of years ago, Tess had been hired to find Jasmine Reed: if she'd believed half the stories circulating about Jazz's lifestyle she might not have thrown herself into discovering the young woman's whereabouts, and Jazz would have died along with her murderous abductor's other victims. Jazz's supposed promiscuity had turned out to be lies spread by his rich parents to protect their rapist son. Jazz was a good and decent young woman, who now, as it happened, helped run Po's retro bar-diner *Bar-Lesque*.

Po found a parking spot as close to Cooper's Bar as possible, but it still meant a short walk in light rain. The weather had come in off the north Atlantic, lowering the temperature by several degrees. The raindrops hitting her cheeks felt like ice shavings. Tess hunched against the shower, but Po walked with his usual languid stride while finishing a cigarette. He'd waited to feed his nicotine habit until they were out of the Mustang, more for Tess's sake than for the integrity of his car's interior. At Cooper's he flicked the stub into a curbside drain and it rode the trickle of water sluicing off the road.

'How'd you want to play this?' he asked.

Patting raindrops from her hair, Tess said, 'Nice and easy. We don't want a repeat performance of what happened earlier.'

'Speak for yourself.' He smiled at her creased brow, held open the door for her. The aroma of deep-fried batter washed over them. Po wrinkled his nose, but Tess's stomach gurgled.

'We should kill two birds,' she suggested, 'and get something to eat while we're here.'

'I'm good, but knock yourself out.'

Again Tess frowned at him, unsure if he was still poking fun at her earlier escapades with the play on words. Apparently it was only a figure of speech though, because he returned her look with one of confusion. 'Seriously,' he said, 'I'm not hungry. But if you want I'll grab some fries so you don't have to dine alone.'

'If that's all you want, fine, but no picking off my plate.' She showed him her bunched fist.

A young woman dressed in a green tabard and black trousers greeted them. She announced herself as 'Stacey' and that she'd be their server. It would've been rude to immediately ask for Jacob in case she misconstrued their meaning. The restaurant was busy. They allowed Stacey to lead them to a free table, where she indicated cutlery folded in napkins, and helpfully laid out menus before them. 'Can I get you started with some drinks?' she asked.

'Iced water will be fine,' said Tess, while Po hit her up for an Americano. While Stacey poured water into Tess's glass from a jug, Tess thanked her, and asked if Jacob Doyle was around.

'Jacob?' Stacey scanned the bustling restaurant, but must've come up short. 'Hmm, I don't see him, but I know he was here only minutes ago. Let me go check for you and I'll be right back to take your order.'

Once the server was out of earshot, Po said, 'Y'ask me, one of his brothers has given him a head's up and he's booked outta here.'

If one of his siblings had telephoned ahead of their arrival, Jacob hadn't run away. However, when he emerged from the kitchen area, and Stacey indicated them, all color flooded from his features and he immediately grew jittery. Perhaps he too suffered the intrinsic distrust of investigators that his brothers did. He approached, waxy with cold sweat, and he ran his fingers through black curly hair. He wore the company uniform of green tabard and black trousers.

'Umm, I believe y'all were asking about me?' Jacob didn't clarify if the first he'd heard about them was via their server or by other means.

'There's nothing to worry about,' Tess reassured him. 'We only want to speak with you about your girlfriend, Hayley Cameron.'

'Ex,' he said quickly. 'Hayley's my *ex*-girlfriend.'

'My mistake.' Tess hid her lie with a smile.

'What do you want with Hayley . . . are you guys cops?'

'Your brothers didn't already explain?' Po countered.

Jacob looked genuinely confused.

Tess explained. 'We visited your home first; your brothers told us where you worked. We wondered if they called to let you know we were coming.'

'I'm not allowed to carry my cellphone at work.' An electronic tablet on which food orders were recorded already encumbered him. Whilst serving and clearing tables he stored it in a pouch in his tabard; his clothing lacked other pockets. His explanation rang true. It didn't exclude his brothers ringing the restaurant directly, but Tess trusted they hadn't. He looked back at Stacey, who'd waited a respectful distant behind him. 'Umm, Stacey says she still needs to take your order. I'm about to take my break, if you'd rather . . .'

'Our food can wait,' said Tess. 'We'll try to take up as little of your break as possible.'

Jacob nodded in the general direction of the kitchens. 'I usually take my breaks out in the back yard.'

Po got his meaning first, and took a pack of Marlboros from his shirt pocket and shook them enticingly. Jacob gave the pack a brief glance, but in that moment he was filled with avarice. Perhaps his waxy appearance had nothing to do with a distrust of investigators and everything with his need for feeding his habit.

'I'll see you guys in the yard in two minutes,' he promised, and strode away, head down and avoiding eye contact with any of the patrons. Stacey approached their table, an open question hanging over her.

'Can I get my coffee to go?' asked Po.

THREE

J acob physically resembled his brothers, but he lacked the pent-up aggression they'd displayed when first greeted by Tess and Po in their front yard. In fact, as they exited a fire door into the back yard behind Cooper's he looked relieved to see them. Jacob hadn't tallied. By the time Stacey had filled a take-out cup with coffee and Po had tipped her generously, the young man had thrown a jacket over his uniform and gotten himself seated in his favorite spot. He was perched on an upturned crate, under an overhang formed by an upper-story extension later added to the building. It served to keep the rain off him. A small bucket served as an ashtray, overflowing with dead butts and crumpled Lucky Strikes packets. Tess moved in alongside him, while Po stood stoic against the elements, raindrops pattering on his shoulders. Jacob ignored Tess, staring plaintively at Po as a reminder. Po handed off his coffee to Tess and pulled out his cigarettes. Jacob's fingers trembled as he accepted one and fed it to his mouth: he had his own disposable lighter ready for action. Po's Marlboro wasn't his favorite brand but he struck a flame and inhaled gratefully as the nicotine-laden smoke invaded his lungs. Po also lit up, before accepting his coffee back.

Finally, Jacob acknowledged Tess, allowing smoke to leak from between his clenched teeth.

'Does this bother you?' He held up his cigarette.

She squinted through the blue-tinged cloud at him. Often those most fervent about how filthy a habit smoking is are those that have given it up; Tess used to smoke, but she was around Po enough that she sometimes felt she was still feeding her craving through passive inhalation. Somebody smoking in her vicinity didn't normally bother her but in such close confines her eyes tingled and she suspected her hair and clothing would stink after. She must accept her lot or she must take the rain as Po did. She stayed put.

'Knock yourself out,' she said, and avoided looking at Po.

Now that Jacob was more settled, and amenable to questioning, she wanted to get down to business. It was probably best for now that Jacob was kept unaware she'd knocked one of his older brothers on his ass.

'So you're looking for Hayley, huh?'

His question was rhetorical, so Tess answered obliquely. 'I'm hoping you can point us in her direction.'

'Why?'

'Because we need to find her.'

'I meant why do you need to find her. Is she in some kind of trouble?'

'Would it surprise you to find she were?'

He pondered her question while drawing in more tobacco smoke. 'Depends,' he decided, 'on what you deem trouble. I'm guessing that being hunted by a couple of private eyes means she's done something worse than shoplifting a lipstick.'

'Is that the kind of stuff she got up to when she was with you?'

'I plead the Fifth,' Jacob said.

'Don't worry, Jacob, we're not looking for her because of nonpayment of a restitution order over some petty theft. It's, well, let's just say the situation's more serious than that.'

'When you find her will she be sent to prison?'

'If that were the case it'd be the cops looking for her, not us.'

'So how can the *situation* be so *serious*?'

Tess had refused his siblings any of the specific details concerning her case, but she saw no harm in giving them to Jacob. If he was going to help them he needed to understand the full implication of locating Hayley.

'When you were together, did Hayley ever tell you about her father?'

'Sure she did. She said he died a hero.'

'Yeah, well that was untrue.'

'She lied?' His features screwed up in bafflement. 'Why would she? She told me her dad was killed on active service in Afghanistan.'

'The truth is she was lied to, and was only repeating what she had been led to believe.'

'Why would her mom lie to her like that?'

'Evidently Hayley didn't share everything with you, Jacob. Are you unaware she was adopted?'

'Jeez, I hadn't a clue. So Jessie's not her real mom?'

'Jessie Cameron raised her; that makes her Hayley's mom in my book. But as far as being her birth mother, the answer's no. After her father abandoned them, her birth mother sought solace in alcohol but it didn't help. She was unable to care fully for a newborn baby and Child Services had to step in. Losing both her partner and her little girl proved too much for Hayley's mom, she took her own life . . . a cocktail of booze and antidepressants.'

Stunned, Jacob stared between his feet. Even his half-smoked cigarette was forgotten as he absorbed the details of Hayley's early childhood. It hung loosely between his fingers, a curl of smoke writhing up his forearm. He finally looked up, and his eyes were moist: Tess had been correct in assuming that Jacob still had feelings for Hayley, despite what his brothers claimed to the contrary.

'Her dad abandoned her as a baby?' Tess nodded in answer and Jacob went on. 'He didn't die in Afghanistan? Was he even in the military?'

Tess shook her head. Beyond her, Po muttered under his breath. 'He's a no-good waste of crap is what he is.'

Tess understood his feelings. As a teenager, Po's life had been ripped apart by his mother abandoning him when she left for a man who'd been his father's best friend. His mother's betrayal had sparked a blood feud that led to his dad's murder and a spell of fourteen years in Louisiana State Penitentiary for Po after he sought equally violent vengeance. The Villere v. Chatard war had only ended a couple of years ago following his mom's death-bed confession that he was not the youngest of his family line, and Po had needed to band with his former enemies to save his younger sister Emilia's life. He had a good excuse for disliking the notion of absent parenting, but she didn't want it getting in the way of her search for Hayley.

'It was a fantasy concocted by Jessie Cameron to make things easier on Hayley, to explain why she didn't have a daddy. Better that she believed her dad was some kind of war hero than an abusive drunk who abandoned her at birth. She claims she intended coming clean with Hayley, at some point, but as Hayley aged she found it tougher finding a way that wouldn't hurt her. The truth is that Jessie's brother died in Afghanistan, so she knew all about grief: it was a story she found she could sell to the girl.'

'You asked if I was unaware of her adoption; are you telling me that Hayley has recently learned the truth? If she did she didn't tell me.'

'It's the reason her mom, Jessie, thinks she has gone into hiding. The truth must've come as a shock to the girl, it's hardly surprising that she has rebelled and is avoiding all her mom's efforts at reconciliation.'

'I haven't seen Hayley in a couple of weeks. I'm dating another girl now . . . uh . . . you met her already. Stacey, your server?' Jacob waited for her to acknowledge his announcement before sucking greedily on the last remnants of his cigarette. When it was down to the filter he flicked it on the floor and ground out the embers underfoot. 'Last I saw Hayley she seemed her same old self. She must've learned her life was a lie after that, right?'

'Yes, but maybe within a day or so. She stopped all correspondence with her mom, and with everyone else we've spoken with up until now, ten days ago.'

'Have you checked her social media?'

Tess only offered a tight smile.

'Yeah, that was probably your first move,' Jacob said. 'If she has been inactive on the social networks it's . . . well, Hayley has a lot of followers and recorded every minute of her day on one site or another.'

'All the platforms she used have been de-activated,' Tess confirmed. 'Which is worrying.'

'Maybe not,' said Jacob with more than a hint of hope, or maybe even guile. 'Perhaps after learning her life was a lie, she realized everything she'd posted online only reflected those lies and she prefers to put that part of her life behind her and move on. Y'know, with a fresh start? Maybe she's still on there but under a different identity.'

Again, from behind her, Tess caught Po's response, a grunt this time. She too had found Jacob's words strange, but chose not to challenge him on them.

'Why aren't the cops looking for her?' Jacob asked.

'Hayley's twenty-one – in the eyes of the law she's an adult. There's no sign of foul play. Besides, Jessie hasn't filed a missing persons report; she only thinks that Hayley is avoiding her. She only wants a chance to explain everything to Hayley and for her to come home. It's why she asked us to find her daughter rather than involve the police.'

Jacob nodded. 'I wish I could help you.'

'We do too.'

He held up his open palms, mouth set in a grimace. 'I'd best get back to work. Uh, are you guys still eating? I'll have Stacey take your order.'

Tess shook her head and backed out into the rain. She'd lost her appetite.

FOUR

'He's hiding something from us,' said Po. They had returned to his car to make the short drive to collect Pinky, though Po was yet to start it moving. The showers had grown heavier, raindrops battering on the shell of the car and rolling down the windshield in waves.

'Of course he is,' said Tess.

'That stuff about Hayley learning her life was a lie and deletin' her past sounded as if he'd practiced it in front of a mirror.'

'Yeah. As if he knew exactly what she'd done, because Hayley told him so.'

They eyed each other. Po's mouth quirked. 'Do I have that same fool expression on my face when I talk about you?'

'Most people find you harder to read than a brick wall, Po. I saw what you meant with Jacob though.'

'He's still carryin' a torch for Hayley Cameron. He got all gooey-eyed every time he mentioned her name, but talked about his latest girl as if she was just part of the furniture.'

Poor Stacey. It was obvious to Tess that she was a simple convenience to Jacob, and that he was still clinging to his feelings for Hayley. Perhaps Stacey meant no more to Jacob than part of the barricade he'd helped pile up to conceal Hayley. It could be assumed Stacey was cover for him too, because seemingly busy with a new girlfriend he could plead ignorant to what had become of his ex. It was apparent that his brothers had given him a hard time over his relationship before, and he was dangling Stacey before them to both convince them he'd moved on and to avoid a front yard smackdown.

'He couldn't help himself,' Tess said, only for Po to crease his brow in response. Tess explained. 'I said it was worrying that she'd de-activated her social media accounts, but Jacob was unconcerned. He couldn't help offering the reason for that like he'd practiced it, or for going one step further and blurting out a clue . . .'

'Maybe she's still on there but under a different identity,' Po recited *ad verbum*. He started the car, waited for a gap in the traffic and pulled out into the rain-washed street.

'Exactly. She's using a fake profile on one or other of the social media platforms, through which she can keep in touch with him.' Tess had taken out her cellphone before she'd finished speaking and though it would be almost impossible to randomly identify Hayley's new identity, she had a shortcut in mind. She searched for Jacob's profile instead. Unfortunately she came up blank using his actual name. She switched to a page dedicated to Cooper's Bar, and in short order found comments added by Stacey Mitchum. Following Stacey's comments back, she found the profile of the girl who'd recently attempted to serve them at their table, and as girls these days often did, she'd shared dozens of photographs of her and her new boyfriend, tagged in the photos as Jakey D. Swiftly. Tess brought up Jakey's profile and checked out his list of contacts: unfortunately her delving ended there as the site would only display mutual friends Tess shared with Jacob . . . of which there were none. It didn't perturb her; she had access to programs that'd circumvent that problem once she was back at her computer. For now she was happy that she'd found her way to Jacob's profile, from where she could dig deeper. She was confident she'd soon have Hayley's pseudonym, and soon after a location where she was hiding.

Po brought the Mustang to a halt outside Tess's previous home. Since Pinky had moved in, her old apartment hadn't changed externally, and for the briefest of moments Tess felt homesick. The major difference was that drawn up on the sloping driveway along-side the steps that gave access to the upper-story apartment, was a huge Volvo SUV. Prior to this her diminutive Prius would have taken pride of place. The presence of Pinky's ride was enough to remind her that they'd all moved on, and home for her was now Po's ranch-style property north of town near Presumpscot Falls.

'Want me to go get him?' Tess offered.

'Unnecessary.' Po leaned on the car's horn.

Below Pinky's apartment, Anne Ridgeway kept shop. When Tess lived there Mrs Ridgeway had acted as her unofficial gate-keeper, alert to the comings and goings of visitors to Tess's house. It appeared that since Pinky had taken up tenancy her role hadn't changed. She was elderly, small of stature, almost as fragile as a bird to look at, but she was also a force to be reckoned with. She appeared at the door to her antiques and curios store, mouth pinched and eyes magnified by the spectacles she held up to better see the culprit who'd shattered her peace. Her disdain lasted only a second before affection flooded over her features and she waved in greeting. It shamed Tess that on previous occasions she'd tried to sneak past Mrs Ridgeway, because once she began talking she sometimes forgot to stop. It mattered not if Tess was investigating private or sensitive matters because the old woman couldn't help prying. In reality Mrs Ridgeway had been looking out for her, and all she'd desired in return was a little company. It surprised Tess to realize she'd missed their chitchats. She made a mental note to return to visit Mrs Ridgeway, but now wasn't the time. She waved in return, gestured at the rain and grimaced. Mrs Ridgeway held up both hands, and gave a nod to the deserted shop – business was slow – but then she retrieved a paperback novel she'd been reading and indicated all was not bad.

'I'll come see you soon,' Tess mouthed, and received a smile and a thumbs up, before the old woman retreated back to her reading nook.

Pinky stuck his head out of the upper-story door. His dark features spilt in a grin, before he grew aware of the rain pattering on his forehead, which swiftly received a derisory scowl. The inclement weather didn't deter him much; he closed the door behind him and danced down the steps with a grace that belied his girth. Tess held her breath until he'd alighted the bottom step – they could be treacherous when slick – and was safely at the bottom of the ramp. He graced them both with a beaming smile and his usual gregarious and idiosyncratic manner. 'I'm pleased to see you guys, I was going stir-crazy up there, me.'

Getting wet again didn't appeal to Tess. She made room, squeezing between the seats onto the rear bench seat. Pinky accepted her vacated seat up front alongside Po, the car rocking on its chassis as he clambered in.

'So what's the job?' he asked. 'Something interesting, I hope.'

'Just your run-of-the-mill locate-a-person-who-doesn't-want-located case,' Tess said. 'Bread and butter stuff, really.'

'Aww, man, I was hoping for something that'd get my heart pumping, me.'

'You missed all the excitement earlier,' Po said, and Tess leaned forward to menace him if he took the story any further. Of course, he wouldn't be put off. She sat back heavily in her seat: Po may as well get it off his chest, they could have a laugh and pull her leg but at least it'd be over with. Po, however, could be infuriating at times. 'I'll tell you later, Pinky.'

'Oh?' Po's reticence piqued Pinky's interest more. 'Do tell, you.'

Po glimpsed Tess's glowering visage in the rearview mirror. 'Nah, best we wait, brother.'

'I knocked out a guy,' Tess blurted. 'It's no big deal. Can we move on now?'

'Say what?' Pinky howled.

'You heard right, Pinky,' Po crowed. 'One punch in the mug and down he went. An' was I grateful; I'd've been tastin' his boot leather otherwise.'

'Some dude tried to kick you in the head, Nicolas?'

'Pardon the pun,' Tess said before Po launched into a blow-by-blow account of the fight, 'but things just got off on the wrong foot. It was due to a misunderstanding which was swiftly rectified.'

'Very swiftly,' Po added. 'Wham and down he went like a sack of—'

Pinky threw his hands in the air, finishing Po's exclamation with the desired profanity. In the back seat, Tess shook her head in mock dismay. She gave Po a harder than usual tap on the shoulder to chivvy him on and he got the Mustang moving. He and Pinky relived the fight, laughing and hooting at the siblings' comeuppance, before sobering slightly at how things might've turned out much worse had Po been alone at the time. It occurred to Tess that they were paying a compliment to her judicious intervention, but if she hadn't taken Po to the Doyle house then the fight probably wouldn't have happened. But life and its consequences – for good and bad – were deemed by a series of random choices, right? She shut out Po and Pinky's voices, closed her eyes and relaxed into the plush leather seat. Rain drummed on the car's roof while she contemplated where her next move might take them.

FIVE

The prevailing winds pushed bands of rain towards shore. They followed one after the other with metronomic regularity, timed by each surge of the ocean. Out on Penobscot Bay visibility was so poor that both the Rockland Breakwater Lighthouse and Owls Head Lighthouse had been activated. The lights would've helped steer the returning fishing fleet into Rockland harbor except they were largely invisible beyond the curtains of steadily falling rain. These days, commercial fishermen didn't rely on beacons the way sailors of an earlier age had; their boats were equipped with sonar and GPS navigation, but that only went for the skipper at the helm. Those on deck still sought recognizable landmarks as they headed for home. Of the mainland nothing could be defined yet.

Mike Toner braced his feet and rode the swell as the prow of the boat lifted skyward. In the next instant the prow dipped and he leaned backwards, fighting gravity. Nearby, another fisherman staggered against the gunwales, cursing. His voice was immediately snatched from his throat and carried away on the wind, but Toner could read the frustration on the man's bearded face. As he rode the next swell out, he saw the other man shamble, bent over towards where the ropes tethering the catch pots had come undone. The fisherman skidded on the deck and fell hard. He struggled up, face reddened with effort, pain or humiliation. Toner should've offered help, but his thoughts were elsewhere. He only wished to have land beneath his feet again, and the less he had to do with this boat and crew the better. He feigned ignorance to the man's plight, grasping the rails and staring ahead, searching for signs of the coast.

Working on the boat hauling lobster pots, was never his choice of career. It was difficult, dangerous, exhausting work, all facets of a job Toner was averse to. This, he'd already decided, would be his final time out with the fleet. Fishing and the harvesting of lobster was Rockland's oldest commercial enterprise, dating back centuries, and continued to play a significant role in this modern age. From now on, Toner was determined it was an industry that'd continue without his input. Why work his knuckles raw when there was money – good money – to be had without the physical toil and little risk? He'd come late to this understanding, prompted by one much younger but with greater vision than he'd ever had.

Through the billowing gusts of rain he finally caught sight of the first pinpricks of light denoting the mainland. The boat had already crept around the breakwater, though it had done little to calm the surging waves yet. The skipper turned the boat towards the harbor's Municipal Fish Pier, as much by familiarity and experience as guided by his instruments. Toner glanced back at his crewmate, to share his joy at spotting terra firma, but the other fisherman was still lashing down equipment, swearing furiously. Another six men crewed this boat, but aside from the skipper and the cursing man Toner had no idea where they'd gotten to and didn't care. There wasn't one amongst them he cared for; he certainly wouldn't miss them after he walked away from the boat this final time. In fact, to hell with it, he wasn't even going to wait for their catch to be unloaded and the wages of their labor shared out. His take from the haul would amount to a couple of hundred bucks at most, while through his new direction he could make easily twenty times that much with a few keystrokes. Actually, he didn't even have to hit the keys when his partner would do that for him.

He spat over the side into the brine. He had no personal disliking of the sea, only that he preferred it to be blue and calm, fringed by white sandy beaches and palm trees. In short order he was about to amass wealth that'd let him pick and choose where next he took to the ocean and it'd be on a vessel more salubrious than this old junker. The engine roared and diesel fumes wafted over him. The smell was as loathsome to him now as the stench of fish guts and he couldn't wait to get far away from it. From inland came the clang of a bell, and the distant shouts of workers whose day wasn't over despite the teeming rain. The skipper powered down and edged towards a pier at the posted speed limit. Toner readied to leap overboard and tie off the boat as soon as they arrived. Except that, he realized, tying off was an old habit. Let one of the others secure the boat: if they didn't and it drifted out to sea it would be no loss to him. He was poised to leave, and he wouldn't look back.

There was a cessation of the wind and the docks and wharfs of Rockland loomed into view, all painted in the dreary shades of the pouring rain. Light switches had been thrown to combat the unexpected dimness, and pale halos surrounded the windows and open doors of the nearest buildings. Further back the streetlights were on timers and remained dark, but the town had come alive with the headlights of vehicles. He was home, though his time spent in Rockland would be brief, only as long as it took to grab his few belongings and throw them in his truck. He'd be gone, and the only view of Rockland he cared to see after that was the one that'd be in his rearview mirror. A rush of anticipation went through him; he shivered in almost orgasmic pleasure at the thought of leaving behind the crappy life he'd been stuck with until now.

The boat bumped against the pier, muffled thumps that he felt through the deck as much as heard. Behind him his crewmates spilled from below deck, heading to their prescribed stations as they prepared to unload their catch. Toner glanced once over his shoulder, offering a sour grin at the men bustling about, they were already drenched through despite their oilskins. He flicked them a sharp salute, then clambered over the side onto the pier. 'Take it easy, losers,' he grunted as he strode away.

If anyone noticed him leave they didn't bother hailing him. It showed his worthlessness to them, but that was OK because he cared as little for them in return. Maybe if anyone had noticed him abandon the boat they hoped he'd keep walking, because then their percentage of the takings would rise. Toner could imagine their greedy snatching hands as the skipper divvied out his wages to the others.

He laughed aloud.

There were other people on the piers. Dockworkers were as hardy as those that put to sea and a little rain wouldn't slow them. He caught a quizzical glance or two, but nobody chose to ask why he was so happy. He must look insane, chortling away to himself but wasn't deterred from laughing harder. A man stepped from under an awning and aimed a sharp nod at him.

He was tall, with fair hair neatly groomed, and a severe, almost
ascetic face to match his wiry build. When Toner didn't immediately respond, the man pulled open the front of his jacket to
show the pistol holstered below his armpit. He crooked a "come
hither" finger at Toner. Then Toner's laughter caught in his throat
and he faltered in his step. He darted a look each side and saw
the sea to his right, and the wall of a warehouse to his left. He
could retreat, but sooner or later he'd run out of pier and his
options would be to dive in the sea or do as the man commanded.
The man was a stranger to him, but Toner guessed what he was.
He wasn't carrying that pistol for show.

Toner touched his chest, opened his mouth, in a silent 'Who
me?'

The gunman stepped back under shelter, indicating with
another sharp nod that Toner should join him.

To hell with him! Toner wasn't about to do the bidding of an
armed stranger, just because of a threat. If the guy meant business, he'd have taken out his gun but hadn't. Toner felt for the
knife he kept strapped to his belt: it was used for shucking
seashells, but could as easily lay open a would-be mugger. It
wasn't very accessible with his coat zipped, but if it came to
it he could draw it in seconds. The gunman wasn't going to shoot
him where there were so many potential witnesses. Right?

His thoughts of refusal and rebellion followed instantly, one
on the back of the other. But they were merely illogical responses
to the gunman's appearance. Instinct in such cases usually took
one of very few forms: under threat a person would run, fight or
freeze. Though he'd considered fighting back, it was because he
was static by shock. Immediately all thoughts of resistance trickled
out of him, along with any spine he had for a confrontation, and
the only remaining reaction took hold of him. Now that the gunman
had stepped back under shelter, he had a free run past him, to
where he could seek protection from a bunch of dockworkers
clustered near the Municipal offices. He took a clumping step
forward.

From behind a hand grasped his left elbow, and something
hard was shoved against his ribs. Toner blinked in dismay at the
bearded face looming alongside his. A second stranger had moved
in on him, probably having followed him along the pier after he

left the boat. The guy was large, with a thick neck and broad shoulders, with the mark of a brawler scrawled all over his face. For the briefest of seconds he wondered if this was some kind of retribution organized by the skipper, but no. The skipper had no idea of his intention to leave his crew, so couldn't have gotten these thugs in place. This was something else. Something worse!

'Do as you're told or you'll be hurt,' the man growled in Toner's ear. To emphasize his point he jabbed the muzzle of his gun deeper into Toner's armpit. 'Get moving.'

'What's going on, man? What do you want with me?'

'I ain't asking twice.' The man stuck tight to his side, steering Toner for the doorway from where the first gunman eyed him somberly. Toner glanced around, hoping somebody else had spotted his abduction, but everyone's heads were averted against the weather. He could shout, try to escape, but any notion he'd had of fighting back had burst with the wet bubble of phlegm in the back of his throat.

He was propelled towards the door, and the first gunman stepped aside so he could be shoved inside. Toner found he was in a boat shed. Apart from the upturned hull of a rowboat under repair, and an assortment of joists, pulleys and tools, the workshop was otherwise empty. He wondered who owned the shed. Neither of the men who'd grabbed him struck him as sailors. They'd simply chosen to use this shed because it was deserted. They pressed him on, aiming towards a door at the far end.

'Look guys,' Toner tried, 'if you're after cash you're outta luck! I haven't been paid, and I'm up to my ass in debt.'

'We know about your debts, Mike,' said the first gunman. He was also stating he knew exactly who Toner was, and that this wasn't a random mugging. 'One of them's why you're coming with us.'

'Which one?' Toner demanded. 'Is that it? You're some kind of debt collectors or something?'

The two gunmen exchanged a knowing sneer. 'We're more like debt enablers. The debt is the one you're about to owe our employer,' the first gunman said, totally enigmatic, totally sinister.

'Uh, what are you talking about?'

The bearded gunman opened the door, and parked directly outside it was a panel van, the side door already open and the engine running. A third member of the abduction team sat in the driver's seat. It was a woman, as lean as a long distance runner with a dusky complexion, her hair woven in cornrows.

'Get inside,' said the first man.

'Why? Where are you taking me?'

'You're going to meet your new employer. *He's* the one you'll owe for allowing your daughter to live another day.'

SIX

While Po and Pinky laughed and joked over some freshly brewed coffees in the kitchen, Tess took her cup through to the spare bedroom they'd converted into a home office. She sat at her desk. Two computers were running, one of them patched into Emma Clancy's intranet system, through which she could access programs usually unavailable to the public. Emma Clancy, besides being her brother Alex's fiancée, was also Tess's main source of employment. Tess subcontracted jobs from Clancy's specialist inquiry firm, which in turn was tied closely to the Portland District Attorney's Office. Usually the jobs shoved in Tess's direction through Clancy required adequate distance from the DA. Considering her partner and their best friend were both ex-convicts, and didn't always obey the laws of the land in order to get the necessary results, it was prudent. Tess always tried to stay within lawful boundaries, though she wasn't averse to stretching their limits on occasion. For instance, accessing Clancy's programs to invade another person's privacy might be morally questionable to some, but Tess considered it as for the greater good.

She brought up Jacob 'Jakey' Doyle's social media accounts as before and with a few deft keystrokes had opened a secret gateway that allowed her to interrogate the metadata contained within his pages. She was no computer hacker, but she didn't need to be as the program she set to analyze the data did the work for her. Before long it began streaming out strings of code that were fed back through the system in order to decode the previously blocked information she'd been refused access to. She interrogated Jacob's contact lists but found nobody that jumped out as a possible pseudonym of Hayley Cameron. She switched focus to his messages and again found nothing that'd lead her to her quarry. It was possible that Jacob and Hayley were conversing via one of the private messaging boards of any number of sites they could access via the Internet, but without physically getting her hands on Jacob's phone or computer she didn't have the ability to find out.

She went over Jacob's contact lists a second time. He was a popular guy, and determining if any of the hundreds of contacts was Hayley in disguise could take forever. Tess thought about Stacey. How would she feel if she discovered her boyfriend was still communicating with his ex? Not very happy, Tess would bet. So, it stood to reason that Jacob might conceal his activity from her, by having Hayley listed under a name that wouldn't rouse suspicion should Stacey catch sight of it. With this in mind, she did away with all fully named contacts and concentrated instead on those with nicknames or user ID handles. One in particular caught her attention. It was registered simply as INS, and when she checked against the metadata she found that Jacob and INS had communicated at regular intervals over the past few weeks.

'Who are you, INS?' she wondered aloud.

Tess opened a search engine on the second computer and typed in the initials. The results threw up various examples of what the acronym could stand for – everything from International News Service through Immigration and Naturalization Service to an abbreviation for a computer's insert key – none of which were helpful.

She stood from the desk, knuckling her lower back as she stared at the screen, hoping for enlightenment but receiving none. Sometimes technology wasn't the answer. Good old-fashioned detective work involved putting your feet on the ground, knocking on doors and speaking with people. Tess had no intention of causing trouble for Jacob, but she was certain he'd lied to her, which meant if she had to press him harder for the truth, she wouldn't hold back. Still, she didn't wish to do so while the youth was at work. He might clam up for fear of incrimination if in possible earshot of Stacey.

Carrying her coffee, she wandered through to the kitchen. Pinky was seated at the table while Po had struck a regular pose, his hips against the breakfast counter, ankles crossed, arms folded on his chest. His sleeves were rolled up and old puncture wounds on his forearms shone silver against his duskier skin. They'd both fallen silent at her approach.

'My ears are burning,' she announced.

'Sorry pretty Tess, but your pugilistic escapades are old news,' Pinky announced. 'We've moved on, us.'

'I'm glad to hear it. So what are you two plotting?'

Po stirred, settling his feet, but otherwise didn't move far. 'We were just kickin' back, waitin' for you, Tess. You get anythin' we can act on?'

She shook her head. 'I've managed to dig up some activity between Jacob and someone listed as INS, but have come to a dead end identifying what it means.'

'Insurance,' said Pinky, the word tripping off his tongue unbidden. When Tess looked at him, he shrugged his sloping shoulders. 'I'm lazy, me. When I enter names into my cell I use abbreviations. I use "ins" as a shortcut to my insurance provider.'

'D'you even abbreviate my name?' Po had a snarky twist to his mouth.

'You are no exception, Nicolas.' Pinky still fully hadn't come to terms with Po's nickname, a derivation of Po'boy, given to him when he'd first relocated to the north by those who'd demean his Cajun heritage. 'You I have listed as BUB. It stands for "Big Uncouth Brute", but you already know that's what I think of you.'

'I daren't repeat what I have you listed as in my cell,' said Po.

Her guys were happiest when disparaging each other, something that Tess was fully used to by now. It was testament to their depth of friendship that even the snarkiest of insults brought forth laughter and swiftly an equally stinging rejoinder. To most they were the epitome of chalk versus cheese: a white, heterosexual, deep southern Alpha-male, was the best of pals with a black, flamboyant and decidedly eccentric homosexual with chronic health difficulties. They'd formed the inseparable bond as inmates at Louisiana State Penitentiary after Po had taken the young Jerome Leclerc under his protection from the resident white supremacists that would've otherwise made his life hell. Po had physically defended Pinky's life, and Pinky had reciprocated in more recent years. They were more than friends, as close as brothers, and it occasionally surprised her that either man had room in their hearts for her, but they did. She loved them both, for differing reasons of course.

She had to wonder if Pinky was onto something important. Perhaps INS was a shortcut for Jacob; perhaps it had nothing at all to do with Hayley Cameron though. She relegated the conflicting notions to the back of her mind. 'I've decided I need to speak with Jacob again.'

'I tried being good cop last time,' said Po, 'want me to twist his ear this time?'

'Yeah,' Pinky joined in. 'I could twist his other ear and we'd have him squealing like a piglet in no time.'

Tess clucked her tongue. 'Yeah, good idea, guys. Why not put him in a burlap sack and drag him behind the car for a few miles while we're at it?'

Pinky laughed, clapping his hands, and Po said, 'It's great to see she's comin' around to our way of thinkin' at last!'

With unvoiced consent, coffee cups were set aside, and after donning jackets, the three returned to Po's Mustang. Before setting off to Cooper's Bar, Tess explained her desire to get Jacob alone, where there was no fear of him being overheard by Stacey and might be more forthcoming with the truth. As they drove into town Po noticed they had picked up a tail. Through the steady downpour, it was difficult defining anything of its occupants beyond the beating windshield wipers of the truck, but two dim forms could be made out. Tess had to wonder if those following them were as a direct result of her previous discussion with Jacob, or his brothers. Or maybe this was because of something else.

SEVEN

Mike Toner was shoved down into a chair. His coat was rucked up around his ears, and a hot waft of air expelled from the collar. His face was fire hydrant red, and sweat trickled from his hairline. He shifted uncomfortably, the leather squeaking beneath him as he glanced around. In his bulky, stained waterproof clothing he was totally out of kilter with his plush surroundings. At least, in his estimation they were plush, despite the layers of dust: although mostly devoid of furniture it reminded him of one of those Gentlemen's smoking rooms sometimes featured in old black and white movies.

His male abductors from the van stood either side of him, as silent and menacing as they'd been during the drive here . . . wherever here was. He had no idea, because the instant he'd been pushed inside the panel van, the bearded man had yanked a bag over Toner's head, effectively blinding him. He'd been forced belly down while he was searched. His knife was taken away, plus his wallet and a few loose coins and the keys to his truck from his trouser pockets. The woman with the cornrows had gotten the van moving, but other than it leaving the harbor front Toner had no clue where he had been driven since. It seemed an eternity while he'd laid belly down, gasping for air and terrified, but perhaps his confinement in the van had really been for minutes at most. He wasn't confident he was still in Rockland, but again could be wrong. Still wearing the bag over his head, he'd been pulled from the van and ushered through a door. He'd been manhandled up a narrow flight of stairs and through some kind of workroom, a short hallway and then into here, where he was jostled to a halt. The bearded man took command of the bag. Blinking in surprise as it was wrenched off, Toner wasn't given a second to orient himself before he was pushed into the chair.

His first instinct was to take in his surroundings, checking exits, seeking a way to make a bolt for his life. There were no windows in the room, only panels of some rich wood, on which were hung paintings so dark in hue they must be centuries old. Placed around the walls were a couple of low leather couches and tables and little else. The only door he was aware of was the one he'd entered by, and that was behind him. There was no chance of getting past his guards before being brought down. He searched the face of the person directly in front of him. An antique table separated them. The person rested their elbows on the table and their chin in their hands as they returned Toner's scrutiny. Toner was surprised to find a pleasant looking woman staring back. Having caught his attention, she flicked him a smile, then sat back, adjusting her body for comfort in a ladder-backed leather-cushioned seat not unlike the one he was seated on. Her fingers spread on the table, and Toner noticed her long nails were immaculately shaped and polished, in keeping with the rest of her appearance. It would be a few years since the flush of youth had left her, but neither was she old, maybe fifty at most. Her hair was light red, streaked with blonde to blend with the natural incursion of grey. Faint wrinkles surrounded her lips and eyes, but her cheeks were plump, and set off her twinkling blue eyes. She was dressed, he supposed, in a corporate style – a pristine lilac colored blouse, open at the neck displayed a thin gold chain, but whatever else she wore remained a mystery, concealed by the table – and he could imagine her as the head of human resources at a reasonably sized blue-collar company. He had no idea who she was, but he wasn't fooled by her pleasant demeanor.

'What the fuck do you want from me?' he demanded in a voice he barely recognized as his own.

The woman tilted her head on one side, admonishing him with an equally lopsided twist of her mouth. She ignored his question, instead turning her attention to the guards behind him. She shook her head as if now scolding them. 'I hope you obeyed my instructions and treated Mr Toner with due respect?'

Toner answered for them, his voice strident. 'They jammed a bag over my head and made me lie face down in the back of a fucking van!'

She cocked her head to the opposite side. Then she raised a single finger from the tabletop. Without warning a fist slammed Toner's jaw. A flash of agony exploded in his skull, and blackness followed. Before it could completely enfold him, he was shaken and a rough palm slapped lucidity back into him. He blinked in dismay at the architect of his misery: her smile had returned.

'Due respect,' the woman stated once she was confident she had his attention, 'is a matter of perspective. I don't believe you're exhibiting the respect due to me, hence your punishment. Act like a potty-mouthed lout and you will be punished further. Do we understand each other, Mr Toner?'

Toner touched fingers to his mouth. They came away bloody. His teeth however all felt in place. He was fortunate that the unexpected blow had been dealt without much power – he'd received a short jab from the first man that'd showed on the pier. He was weirdly thankful that the man hadn't wound up his arm and smashed him with full force. Through lips that were beginning to swell, Toner said, 'Please, there's no need for violence. I . . . I don't know what's going on, or what you want from me.' He glanced back at the one who'd punched him, and received a nonplussed expression. 'All I was told was I was being offered a new job and it'd—'

'Save your daughter's life?' the woman finished for him. She again held up a finger, and Toner flinched, anticipating another blow. But this time her raised finger wasn't a command, but to clarify a point. 'Let's get this straight from the get go. It was never an *offer* of employment; there is no negotiation, you *will* take the job. Refuse and the next person in the back of the van will be your daughter. She won't, of course, be brought here to these comfortable surroundings. I can assure you of that.'

Toner's mind was a heaving whirl of emotions and confusion. What in hell was going on? Who were these people? What kind of job demanded death threats to ensure he'd take it? Why were they threatening his daughter? How did they even know about his daughter? He was both horrified and perplexed. Toner had never been the bravest of souls; in fact he was aware of his own cowardice and though it shamed him he couldn't change his nature, though he tried. Faced with these questions unanswered, he responded with a level of outrage he could rarely muster.

He thrust up to his feet, stabbing a finger at the woman. 'This is bullshit! You've no right to treat me like this, and no fucking right to threaten my child! So here's what's going to happen, y'hear? You can take your job and go fuck yourself with it.'

Before he was halfway through his tirade, hands were on him, grasping at his elbows and forcing him down into the seat again. His final shout was delivered with a spray of exhaled saliva. Opposite him the woman hadn't moved, though she lost some of her cool when dabbing a droplet of spit off her cheek. Toner, held in check by his guards, glared at her, shivering with the endorphins rushing through him. She returned the look, her glare icy. The tableau held for protracted seconds. Finally the woman leaned forward and spread her fingers on the tabletop again; she drummed a staccato beat with her fingernails while coming to a decision.

'It seems to me that Mr Toner isn't taking this situation seriously enough,' she announced, as if he wasn't in her hearing. 'I'm going to step out of the room. When I return I want him fully on board with the plan.'

She stood, moved around the table. Toner watched her closely, almost as if she was the one about to deliver punishment. She wore tailored trousers, and pumps. She wasn't tall, and she carried a few extra pounds on her hips. She was unremarkable, but undeniably she frightened him. More so than his surly abductors had done so, because he knew they were only dogs obeying their sadistic mistress's commands. He wondered briefly what she held over them that they obeyed her without question, if they had children imperiled by her too. He couldn't bring himself to hate either man, even as they loomed over him, bunching their fists.

EIGHT

'Are they still behind us?' Deliberately – after one seemingly nonchalant check earlier – Tess had avoided turning to look again, and from her position in the rear of the car she had no view of the mirrors.

'Yup,' said Po, nonplussed.

The most direct route from Presumpscot Falls into downtown Portland encompassed several leafy suburbs before reaching any of the busier highways around Back Cove. They were on Allen Avenue, approaching North Deering. The downpour meant there were few vehicles on the roads. It had been a simple task for Po to spot their tail, but not to easily shake it without making the attempt obvious.

'They're keepin' their distance,' he added after a moment, 'and seem content to follow wherever we're goin'.'

'That truck,' Tess pondered, 'I didn't notice it earlier when we were at the Doyle place.'

'Wasn't there.' Po had obviously given more attention to the siblings' cars than she had. He glanced at Pinky for clarity.

'If they're after me, I haven't spotted them before now,' he said. 'Besides, if it's me they're interested in, wouldn't we have noticed them back at Cumberland Avenue, us?'

Proclaiming there might be some interest in him wasn't due to ego or paranoia. Only months before Pinky had slipped out of Baton Rouge with a price on his head after abandoning his previous life as an illegal arms trader. Some of his criminal contemporaries didn't want to see him go, many were more determined he would never return. Before he'd gotten his feet under the table in Tess's old home, hired gunmen, Frank and Carlo Lombardi, had come after Pinky. Ironically the pair of cousins dispatched to end his life had fallen into the midst of Tess's latest case involving a rogue DEA agent and violent mercenaries. Faced with greater enemies, and after his younger cousin was murdered, Frank's loyalties changed and he'd become a valued ally. That wasn't to say that different hitmen hadn't been sent after Pinky since.

'These guys are amateurs,' Po decided. Which didn't go far to allay any fears they might be hired guns . . . not every would-be assassin was a slick, highly trained ex-spy. Po halted the Mustang. 'Nobody get out,' he cautioned.

Behind them the truck came to a shuddering standstill as the driver reacted to the unexpected stop. It was still distant enough that the occupants were largely invisible.

Po threw the Mustang into reverse. 'Let's see how they want to play things, shall we?'

He hit the gas and the muscle car powered backwards, briefly fishtailing on the flooded street. He hit the brakes. The car stopped with bare inches to spare between the vehicles' fenders. Tess checked out those within the truck's cab. She saw two men, both of them unshaven, one whose beard was more established though he looked more a hipster than a mountain man. Both men wore looks of momentary panic at Po's unexpected maneuver: neither face was familiar to Tess. The hipster in the passenger side was talking, his hands gesticulating, and she guessed he was exhorting the driver to get them out of there.

Po saved them the trouble. He took off, tires spinning for traction, and showered the truck's windshield with a deluge of dirty water and fallen leaves from the curbside gutter. If those in the truck intended to pursue, he didn't give them an opportunity. He took the next left turn at speed, streaked along a residential street lined with trees and within seconds cut to the left again. The road they were on was an elongated crescent, and looped back to join Allen Avenue, but at a point behind the truck. Po pulled into the oncoming lane and crept the Mustang to the intersection, staying back just far enough that the roadside shrubbery hid them.

'They still haven't moved,' he said.

The truck was where they'd left it less than a minute ago, barely a hundred paces away. Tess figured the occupants were still trying to come to terms with what had just happened, and they were undecided on how they should respond. Who were those guys, and what was their purpose in following her? As a cop, and more recently as a private investigator, Tess had conducted surveillance on various people; it was an uncomfortable sensation when the shoe was on the other foot.

'What do you think they're up to?' she wondered.

'Probably still checking their shorts for stains, them,' said Pinky. To Po he added, 'For a second there even I believed you were about to ram them off the street.'

'That was my intention,' Po admitted. 'I just wanted to gauge their response; they ain't givin' me much to go on.'

'I got a look at their faces, but didn't recognize either of them. You didn't give me time to read their tags before you took off again.' Tess craned for a better view of the truck. She couldn't distinguish the detail of the license plate other than that it was local to Maine with the Vacationland slogan and pine forest silhouette.

'I've a suggestion,' said Po. 'Let's go an' ask them who they are and what the hell they want.'

Her interest was piqued enough that Tess wasn't averse to his idea, except for one thing. 'Missed our opportunity. They're moving.'

The truck pulled away slowly, and didn't exactly build up a head of steam as it trundled down Allen Avenue. The driver was proceeding with some trepidation, she guessed. He didn't take the left turn as Po had earlier, so it was apparent there was no intention to try to pick up their trail again. Without any debate, Po followed. He stayed back far enough that the Mustang would be indistinguishable behind its headlights, matching the truck's slow progress. Unlike Po had earlier, those in the truck didn't think to check who was behind them. As far as they knew, Tess and friends were probably miles away by now.

'Get us in close enough so I can read their tags,' said Tess.

'I can do better than that.'

Po hit the gas and the Mustang rocketed. Within seconds they were gaining on the truck, and as he got within a couple of car lengths Po repeatedly flashed his high beam and then peeled around the truck. He cut tight towards the curb, forcing, for the second time, the truck to shudder to a halt. Before those in the truck could respond he was out of the Mustang and marching towards the driver's window. He rapped his knuckles on the glass, and when he didn't get the reaction he wanted, he yanked open the door, leaned in past the driver's shoulder and whipped the keys out of the ignition. By then, Pinky was on the opposite side and glowering through the rain-streaked glass at the passenger. Almost as bewildered as the men in the truck, Tess clambered out to join Po. She danced through water almost topping the sides of her shoes even as Po tugged the driver out to join them in the rain.

'Tell me what business you have followin' us or you and me are gonna have a problem,' Po growled.

'You won't get any problems from me, pal. I'm only doing my buddy a favor.' The driver was burlier than Po, though not as tall. He had the thick forearms and neck of one used to heavy manual labor, but he also had a fleshy, soft appearance to his face and gut. If he took umbrage at Po's threat he didn't react with violence. He held up both palms in surrender, and glanced frequently at his passenger to intervene on his behalf. Tess and Po exchanged glances too, before Po shoved the driver aside, with a command to stay put.

Tess bent inside the cab so she could see the passenger clearly. He was the one with the hipster beard. She was alert to him going for some kind of concealed weapon, or indeed launching at her, but he was held in flux at the sudden turn of events. He blinked in confusion at her. 'Want to explain yourself?' she asked.

'I don't know what—'

'Don't lie. You were following us and we want to know why.'

Pinky rapped on the side window. When he wished, he could make his usually jovial features appear sinister. He mouthed something at the guy – a warning he'd better do as he was told – and the man looked again at Tess, dry swallowing as he tried to dredge up the correct words.

'Let's start at the beginning. What's your name?' Tess prompted.

'I'm, uh, I'm . . .' he dug his fingers through his beard, tugging on it as if it were a memory aid. 'I'm Jeffrey Lorton. I'm, uh—'

'You're Hayley Cameron's biological father.' Tess had learned from Jessie Cameron that Hayley's birth dad was allegedly an abusive drunkard who'd abandoned his partner and child, and in her mind she'd formed an image of him. She'd conjured a florid-faced thug, wearing a beer-stained wife-beater tank top. Jeffrey

Lorton didn't fit the cliché. But then, she knew from past experience that looks could be deceptive, and even the mildest looking person could be a monster towards somebody under their control.

Lorton nodded glumly, as if ashamed to admit it. 'Not that I've been much of a dad to her,' he added.

Tess frowned. Thinking furiously. Lorton's appearance here threw cold water on a theory she'd been considering for Hayley's disappearance. 'Why follow us?'

'I heard you guys had been hired to find Hayley by her adoptive mom . . . I hoped by sticking close, I might finally get an opportunity to see and speak with her after so many wasted years.'

Tess exhaled slowly. She'd wondered if Hayley's disappearance was due to hooking up again with her father. It wasn't unknown for adopted or fostered children to later seek out their birth parents. Occasionally it wasn't unknown for such kids to abandon their adoptive family and return to their original roots, for some only as long as it took to find the grass really wasn't greener. Partly she'd expected Hayley to return with her tail between her legs. And yet, according to Lorton, they hadn't yet met in person. Knowing Hayley's biological father was back on the scene, and that he might know where Hayley was, Tess had planned seeking him out; in a fashion events had cut to the chase. However, she hadn't planned speaking with Lorton in the middle of the street, soaked through by battering rain.

'Following us around like this wasn't your wisest move,' she said. She looked to where the driver was silently being menaced by Po, although her partner had gotten the gist of the situation. Pinky also wore a grimace as rain dripped off his eyebrows and the tip of his nose.

'I didn't know what else to do,' Lorton admitted. 'If I'd've contacted you directly, you wouldn't have given me anything, not when you've been engaged by Jessie Cameron. I thought that by shadowing you, I'd be able to make my own approach to Hayley once you'd found her. Bob over there' – he indicated his driver – 'he's innocent in all this. He's just an old buddy trying to do me a good turn by driving me around. I, uh, don't hold a driver's license these days.'

'Why's it so important you get to speak with Hayley now?' Tess asked.

Lorton frowned. 'Isn't it obvious?'

'I wouldn't have asked if it were.'

Tears shone in Lorton's eyes. His voice warbled as he spoke. 'I've finally gotten my act together. I'm making no excuses. Back when Hayley was born, I was a mess, a drunken mess and no kind of father to her. I booked out on her and her mom, but you have to believe me, I've regretted it every sober minute of my life since. Now I'm in a better place, well, I hoped to try to make up for lost time. You understand?'

Tess caught the shake of Po's head. He didn't buy Lorton's wheedling excuse, but he'd a bitter sentiment regarding parents who abandoned their children. Tess thought that Lorton's words were genuine and heartfelt. 'I'm making no promises, and it's finally down to Hayley whether she agrees to see you or not, but if you give me your contact details I'll drop you a message when I've found her.' She waited for Lorton to nod in agreement, then fished in her jacket pocket for a business card. She aimed it at him. 'In return, you must do two things for me. First, if you learn where she is or of anything that can help me find her, you must let me know immediately. Second, you don't follow me around or interfere in my search again.'

'Sure, I, uh, think that's probably for the best.'

'It is. We got off on the wrong foot just now. Things could've gone much worse.' She pushed her business card towards him. 'On there's my cell number. Drop me a message so I have your contact details.'

As Lorton nodded in agreement, Tess backed out from under shelter, and she was again assaulted by the full power of the downpour. Po's hair was flattened to his skull, making his features more ascetic than usual. The unnecessary soaking didn't faze him. He dangled the truck's keys before the driver. 'Git goin', Bob,' he warned, 'and don't let me catch you in my rear-view again.'

Before she was fully ensconced again in the dry interior of the Mustang Tess heard a ping from her cellphone, and knew that Lorton had come through on her instructions. As she clambered in the back, Pinky reclaimed the passenger seat with much huffing and puffing. He shook droplets off his hands, then wiped his face and forehead. Po's hair dripped on his collar, and his leather jacket glistened wetly. He stared momentarily in his mirror, checking out Lorton and Bob, who were yet to get moving.

'You think Lorton was sincere?' he asked without turning to Tess.

'I've no reason not to.'

'According to Jessie, he was violent and abusive towards Hayley's mom; who's to say he isn't still that person now? What if we've got this wrong and Hayley's gone into hiding to keep outta his way? You recall why Jazz ran away, right?'

Jasmine Reed had left town to avoid the man who'd once raped her. Though history accused Jeffrey Lorton of being an abusive alcoholic, Hayley had gone into the system after her mother's suicide, not as a result of her absent father's alleged behavior. In adulthood Hayley had never met her father, but she could have formed a maligned impression of him – the way that Tess previously had – so could indeed be fearful of coming face to face with him again. It was possible Lorton's return was responsible for her going into hiding, even if for the wrong reason. However, Jacob Doyle had given no hint that Hayley feared her father. No, Hayley going incognito was for reasons yet unknown, and possibly for her own benefit. Tess shouldn't discount the other Doyle brothers' character assassination of Hayley, whose opinions made her out to be selfish, and manipulative, at the best.

Judge as you find, Tess cautioned herself. Good advice, but she must find Hayley first.

NINE

Expecting a beating, Mike Toner had steeled for the first of numerous blows, so it was all the more shocking when his captors employed a subtler approach to ensure his compliance. The bearded one was grudgingly subordinate to the first man Toner had spotted on the pier. He stood aside as the other moved in close and bent close to Toner's face.

'Do yourself a favor, Toner, and listen to what you're being told without any argument.' Up close, the man's eyes were glassy, showing weariness with no appetite for a prolonged debate.

'That's the problem: I don't know what's expected of me. There's no need to threaten my daughter's life without even giving me an idea of what I'm supposed to agree to.'

'You love your daughter, right?'

'Yes, of course I do?' Toner beseeched him. 'Are you a father? Even if you're not, you must still understand the importance of a child to any parent?'

'My parental status isn't the one in discussion here. If you care for her as much as you say, you should show it by protecting her. The only way you'll do that is to do exactly as asked.'

'Asked *what*?' Again Toner's voice grew strident. Frustration warred with fear for dominance. 'I still don't know what you people want from me.'

'Due respect,' said the man. 'This has been stressed more than once. It appears the concept's taking some sinking in with you.'

While they'd talked, Toner had grown unaware of the bearded man's position. He'd moved back, out of Toner's peripheral vision, and he'd collected the sack Toner had worn during the drive here. Without warning he yanked it down over Toner's head, though not this time as an impromptu blindfold. He dragged Toner backwards against the chair's headrest and he gathered the open end of the sack tightly around Toner's throat, strangling him. In the same instant the first guard snatched down on Toner's flailing wrists, forcing them down on the armrests. He squeezed in, his knees between Toner's so he couldn't be kicked.

Toner struggled, but it was only a fight for oxygen. The throttling didn't relent, and agonizing pressure built in his straining lungs. They felt as if they were withering in his chest, even as his brain expanded, threatening to burst from his earholes in the next few seconds.

The pressure was released, from throat and wrists, and Toner buckled forward, retching to clear his windpipe. In the next moment he reared back, gasping for air. The bag stayed put over his head: panic made him reach for it, to get rid of it so he could breathe unimpeded. His hands were slapped down. Behind him, the bearded man grunted a question, and having gotten a response he dragged off the bag. Toner's eyes streamed and bloody saliva hung from his lips. The man in charge asked, 'Was that unpleasant? Believe me, Toner, we can make things much worse for you. Imagine if it was your daughter sitting where you are; if Dom squeezed her neck that hard her head would tear right off her shoulders.'

'If you hurt her in any way I'll—'

'Do not make idle threats.'

The bag returned without warning, and once more Toner flailed in desperation as he was throttled. This time it was as though Dom used more strength to prove the point, and to Toner it felt as if his head was about to be separated from his vertebrae . . . Lord help her if it were Madison they tortured.

He must have blacked out. When next he was aware of his surroundings the bag had been removed. His neck ached, but he must have gotten past the bout of hacking coughs that'd helped rouse him. His eyeballs felt too large and mucus dripped from both nostrils. Saliva had gone cold on his chin. Shamefully, he could feel damp warmth at his crotch and the seat of his pants: he'd pissed himself. When he looked again at his guards it was in abject dismay.

Both men had moved aside, no longer threatening him. It was apparent they'd concluded their job. Toner had to agree. He would be nothing but compliant from now on.

The woman returned to the room.

She walked past Toner, one eyebrow raised, asking an unvoiced question. Toner lowered his gaze and heard her laugh.

'That was quick, Arlen,' she said, a note of congratulations aimed at the first guard. Toner now had the first names of two of his abusers – Dom, the bearded one, and Arlen, his superior – but the woman's identity remained a mystery. He wondered who she was working for; when first he'd been grabbed Arlen told him he was going to meet his new employer. '*He's* the one you'll owe for allowing your daughter to live another day,' Arlen had said, stressing the male gender. Had the woman left the room in order to communicate her progress with her mysterious boss, or because she didn't have an appetite for the torture she knew was coming? No, though he'd first thought her pleasant looking, it was only skin deep: from her nasty laughter he could tell she delighted in other people's pain.

She sat primly at the far side of the table. Her silence added further disquiet. Finally Toner couldn't resist looking. As his eyelids flickered and he raised his head, she appraised him with the same half-smile as before. 'So, you accept that you now work for us?'

Toner nodded, because that was expected of him.

'Good. Let me be the first to welcome you to our company.' The woman reached across the table, extending her hand. Her manicured fingernails looked sharp enough to pierce skin. Toner was tentative. He lifted his right hand in response, but was unsure what her game was. Was this some introduction to further torture? Dom sniffed, shifted his weight, and it was enough for Toner. He reached and accepted the woman's hand. He was tempted to squeeze it with all his might, break every damn bone in her hand, but retribution would be swift. Her skin was cool to the touch, soft . . . and it made his hide crawl.

As the woman withdrew her hand, she indicated her lieutenant. 'Arlen will answer any further technical questions you have after I'm finished here. Know this: you will continue with the scheme dreamed up by Madison; do so and you'll continue unmolested as if we never met. At the end of each week you will transfer fifty percent of your net takings to us. This figure is non-negotiable. In return you will be treated as an employee of our organization and afforded necessary protection and security. I need not repeat what will happen should you try to renege on your commitment to us. You are now in our debt, Mr Toner, to the tune of both yours and your daughter's lives: it'd be unwise to default. We got wind of your decision to leave your former employer, in the same manner in which we cottoned on to Madison's scheme . . . we have eyes and ears everywhere, and our reach is very long. You are permitted to leave Rockland, take up wherever it was you planned to in Bangor, any further than that – without permission – and we'll be forced to call in your debt.'

She allowed her terms to sink in. Toner could say nothing; his thought processes had all but closed down. The woman stood and left the room.

Arlen grasped Toner's shoulder. His automatic flinch served to bring his mind into focus. 'Is she for real?' he asked at what he hoped was a respectful whisper.

'She's deadly serious,' said Arlen and tugged Toner up out of his seat. 'Come on, I'll have you driven back to your truck. You're going in the back of the van. Get your piss on her van seats and Temperance will rub your nose in it. That's if she doesn't slit your throat.'

TEN

Stacey Mitchum appeared beaten down on their return to Cooper's Bar. Her cheeks were flushed, her throat blotchy, her smile forced as she greeted diners at their tables. She took their orders, tapping away at her electronic menu, before trudging to the service hatch to fetch food and drinks. It wasn't because she was under pressure of work – there were other servers on duty capable of handling the diminished afternoon crowd – she simply seemed crushed by some personal issue. When she spotted Tess and Po had returned with a friend, her eyes grew glassy and her first response was to feign no recognition, and attempt to scurry for cover without speaking with them. Tess felt a pang of guilt, suspecting why Stacey appeared upset. Jacob Doyle was conspicuous by his absence. She offered the girl a conciliatory smile and beckoned Stacey over. Stacey was undecided for a moment, until Tess left Po and Pinky standing and gestured the girl to join her in a more private location near the restrooms.

'If you're looking for Jacob again, he's gone.'

'By gone I'm guessing you don't just mean his shift has ended?'

Stacey bit her bottom lip, on the verge of tears. 'Gone. Period. It wasn't long after you left here earlier. He took me to one side, said "Sorry, I can't do this anymore. We're over, Stacey," and that was it. No other explanation. He just took off his tabard, collected his jacket, told the boss he'd quit and left.'

'I'm sorry,' said Tess, and she was. But only partly. Stacey might not thank her right then, but she'd possibly been saved from worse heartache if Jacob had kept on stringing her along.

'What have you to be sorry about?' Stacey asked, barely concealing a bitter undertone. 'I'm not an idiot. I'm intelligent enough to figure out that Jacob was forced into making a fast decision after speaking with you earlier. But I don't blame you. He was trying to keep a secret from me, even though I knew exactly what it was – no, *who it is*. This is about Hayley Cameron, right?'

Tess's silence was the acknowledgement Stacey needed.

'I knew it. You're looking for Hayley, aren't you?'

'I'm a private investigator hired by her mom to locate her.'

'Jacob knows exactly where she's hiding. He thinks he was so clever, keeping her a secret, but I had him figured out.' Though the girl was adamant, Tess wasn't as sure. She probably had a suspicion that her boyfriend wasn't being totally loyal to her, but it had taken him abruptly dumping her to crystalize the thought in her mind. 'All those secretive phone calls, those times he stood me up and spoiled our plans. I should've dumped his cheating ass and not given him the satisfaction of doing it to me.'

Stacey made an over-the-shoulder check of the restaurant. Her other workmates were beavering away. She squeezed out a grimace. 'I really should get back to work . . .'

There were few customers now. The downpours had put paid to passing custom as the sidewalks were deserted. It looked as if the rain would continue for the foreseeable future, and those who'd held out against leaving had decided that there was nothing else for it. Even as Tess watched a young couple left the premises, bent over, trying to shield under one umbrella as they rushed for their parked car. Po and Pinky had been seated at a table: Po gave her a knowing smile.

'I promise I won't take up much more of your time,' said Tess. 'You said that Jacob knows exactly where Hayley's hiding. He didn't give you any idea where that is, did he?'

'No, but I can guess. Do you know Hayley? Personally, I mean.'

'We've never met.'

Stacey cleared her throat. She wanted to say something harsher. 'She's one of those self-righteous, privileged girls. She thinks the world should revolve around her and isn't happy when it doesn't . . . I don't know what Jacob sees in the selfish bitch.' Self-consciously she stood a little taller, pulled in her stomach and tucked a stray lock of greasy hair behind her ear. Tess had seen plenty photographs of Hayley and she was undeniably beau-tiful – she could tell why a smitten guy would moon over her, and why a plain, homely girl like Stacey might be envious. Stacey went on: 'You know how like attracts like, yeah? Well, sure as hell, Hayley won't be making do. She expects the best and will get it, and she won't care how.'

Without explaining why, Tess asked, 'Do the initials INS mean anything to you?'

Stacey thought about it for a few seconds, but she shook her head. 'Why do you ask?'

'It's unimportant. Just something I'm following up on.'

'Involving Jacob?'

'It came up in my inquiries.' She wasn't about to admit to the method she'd used to reach those initials. 'Probably unrelated, though.'

'You should look at Hayley's friends for where she is now.'

'I have already.'

'I don't mean those here in Portland. She has a clique of other friends from when she went to college in Bangor.'

Tess was already aware that Hayley had completed a two years undergraduate program at Eastern Maine Community College in Bangor, but during her discussions with Jessie Cameron it'd never occurred to ask if she'd kept in touch with her fellow students after her return to Portland. It was an error; to an alleged girl like Hayley, friends made at college would probably trump those left behind from high school.

She'd barely given Tess two minutes of her time, but already Stacey was conscious she was shirking her duties. She adjusted her tabard and took out her electronic ordering pad as a signal she must return to work. Tess wouldn't keep her any longer than necessary. She asked, 'You wouldn't happen to know any names of her college friends?'

'Jacob mentioned one a couple of times when Hayley's name came up. Maddie something-or-other . . . I don't remember.' Her jawline tightened. 'You see, I wasn't really interested in hearing about my boyfriend's ex or any of her bitchy friends.'

Stacey scuttled away, heading for the serving hatch. Tess joined Po and Pinky at the table they'd sat at. Po said, 'We done here?'

'How do you feel about driving up to Bangor in this weather?'

'Sounds like I need to get my coffee to go again,' he said, and beckoned to a different server.

ELEVEN

Taking the I-95, it was approximately one hundred and thirty miles, and a two-hour drive from Portland to Bangor. Po shaved fifteen minutes off that time, driving with an economy of motion that saw him make progress where other road users were dictated to by the pace of the traffic flow. At times the rain grew so heavy visibility was poor, and some drivers took it carefully, slowing Po's forward momentum but he still made good time. They reached the exit onto Hammond Street, and drove east towards central Bangor. Tess was no stranger to Bangor; she'd graduated from Husson University so knew the town well. They could have continued further northeast along the I-95 if their destination was the community college, but it wasn't. Tess had been busy on the drive up, speaking with Jessie Cameron on her cellphone and identifying who Maddie was. She'd learned that Hayley's college friend was named Madison Toner, and her last known address was a converted loft on Broad Street, near where the tributary Kenduskeag Stream spilled into the Penobscot River.

Tess directed Po in and within minutes they had parked on a riverside lot adjacent to Maddie's apartment. Without getting out of the Mustang, all eyes turned to regard the uppermost floor of a three-story building, converted from a metal fabricators' workshop if the faded signs on the brickwork were to go by. The windows were shuttered, and due to the unusual dimness of the day, internal lights had been illuminated. Shadows moved behind the blinds, indicating somebody was home. Whether or not it was Madison remained to be seen.

Tess shifted, an indication of her intent. 'Maybe I should go up myself,' she suggested. Presented by three strangers, two of them guys, Maddie might not be too keen on opening her door to them.

'Your call,' Po said, although he wasn't comfortable with the arrangement. There was no need to fear reprisals from Maddie

Toner, or from Hayley, if they were home, but after what had gone down during their visit to the Doyle house earlier, Po was cautious.

Pinky reached to open his door, in order for Tess to slip out once he'd vacated his seat, but Po beat him to it. 'I wanna smoke,' Po said.

Tess recognized his words as a concession to staying behind. At least if he were out of the car, he could respond faster should she call for help. There was a brief lull in the rain, though the atmosphere was pregnant with moisture. The breeze caught up tiny droplets and threw them at her as Tess climbed out of the car. Po moved aside, seeking shelter under the hanging branches of a tree at the edge of the parking lot. Heavy droplets audibly impacted on the shoulders of his jacket before he was under cover. He lit up a Marlboro, nodded at Tess. *I've got your back*, his gesture said.

Tess studied the building, searching for a way inside. A railway track ran parallel to Broad Street, close enough that passing trains must rattle Maddie's bed at night. To access the building there was a designated crossing. At the front the first floor sported two steel roller shutters. When the building was remodeled part of the workshop had been transformed to accommodate off-street parking. Tess assumed one of the shuttered garages belonged to whoever lived on the second floor, the other to Maddie. It hadn't passed her notice that a realtor's sign was fixed to the far end of the building at the second story, advertising a vacancy, meaning Maddie was the single current tenant. Tess moved to go left, where it was most likely that a side entrance gave access to the upper-floor apartment. She'd barely taken three paces when she came to a halt. A truck approached along Broad Street, giving her pause. Her mind was thrown back a couple of hours to the incident with a similar truck, and she wondered if Jeffrey Lorton had ignored her warning to leave the search for his daughter to her. Her concern was passing, because it was instantly apparent that it was a different truck, with a single driver aboard. However, her pause in step was long enough to allow the truck to slow, and its flashing blinkers announced the truck was about to turn. Tess waited.

The truck cut across the tracks and nosed in towards Maddie's building, and a few seconds later a rumble announced the opening of the furthest left shutter. The truck rolled into the garage and stopped. From her place alongside Po's Mustang, Tess watched a man get out of the cab. She'd no idea who he was but his demeanor gave her a sudden hike of adrenalin. As he closed the door, he leaned into it with his cheek pressed against the window, and his knees almost gave out. He struggled to maintain his balance, one arm clutching across his chest, and for a second Tess feared he was in cardiac arrest. She glanced once at Po, and then started forward.

She halted again after a rushed few paces.

The man had turned towards her footsteps, and he stared at her blankly, his mouth open in question. She knew his unvoiced question wasn't aimed at her but inward. His mouth was swollen and bloody, and being on the verge of collapse was to do with his battered state. Spotting her, anger, then something else – fear? – flashed across his features and he stumbled forward and hit a button next to the open shutter. It began to unfurl, concealing him from view.

'Maybe I should accompany you, after all.'

As the shutter clunked shut Po had moved alongside Tess.

'What did you make of him?' she asked.

'Dude looks as if he's just fought ten rounds with a junkyard dog. Also looks to me as if he's got business at the same apartment you have. When he gets home I'm bettin' emotions are gonna be high. I'm comin' up with you, Tess. No argument.'

She shrugged. 'You'll get no argument from me.'

Po flicked aside his partly smoked cigarette.

Pinky hailed them in an exaggerated stage whisper. 'You want me to come up, you?'

'We'll be fine,' Tess assured him, even as some silent instructions danced back and forth between the men folk. If things turned dicey upstairs Pinky would be seconds behind them. For now he was contented to remain in the dry comfort of the car. In fairness, Tess wasn't as happy about going up to the apartment as she'd made out. As Po had said, emotions would be high when the man's beaten state was discovered, and it'd probably take precedence over anything Tess wanted to talk to Maddie about. She said to Po, 'Unless we leave things for now and come back later?'

'We're here, we may as well get it over with.' He wouldn't admit it but Po was as intrigued as she at what they'd stumbled across. When the man got out of his pickup truck he had been wearing dungarees, a thick woolen pullover and gumboots. He looked as if he'd just returned from sea, and Tess wondered if his bloody mouth was down to some accident out on the water, perhaps due to the boat being caught up in the sudden squalls. Though she thought Po was closer to the truth; he looked as if he'd been on the losing end of a fistfight. Seeing her had alarmed him: maybe he thought he was in trouble because of the fight. All speculation, she cautioned, and unhelpful to discovering Hayley's whereabouts.

'You're right. Let's do this.'

There was an entrance at the left side as Tess had expected. There the building had been beautified with a fresh lick of paint and hanging plants decorated the window ledges. A small garden had been formed adjacent to the entrance, but it hadn't been cared for lately, and was almost bare with only a few straggly plants sitting among the weeds around a single tree. An accumulation of discarded cigarette butts and packets formed a drift against the stones edging the garden. Someone, it appeared, regularly used the tree for shelter having been chased outside Maddie's no-smoking apartment. Tess had a flashback image of Jacob Doyle, hunkered down on one of the edging stones, holding aloft his cigarette and asking: 'Does this bother you?'

Alongside the door there was a keypad, and also an intercom button, so the residents of either of the upper apartments could be hailed. However, due probably to Maddie being the current sole occupant, she'd allowed the security measures to slip, the same way she had maintaining the small garden. The door was propped open, allowing access to an interior stairwell. There were two doors either side of the stairs, and it took no figuring out that they gave access to the first-floor garages. If they'd crossed over the road a little sooner, they'd have probably met the beaten man as he exited the garage, or at least heard him trudging up the stairs. As it were, he had already made the climb. By unspoken agreement, Po led the way up, Tess only two steps behind him.

Voices sang out from overhead, one high-pitched and female,

the other desultory and male. That wasn't to say there were only two people inside Maddie's apartment, others could be there but respectfully staying out of the drama. As they progressed upward, the female's voice grew more questioning, and it sounded concerned. Then the man's voice rose in response to make his point: unfortunately their actual words couldn't be made out. Tess exchanged a glance with her partner; Po had predicted high emotions and he was right. They hit the first landing and passed the door of the vacant apartment, the voices still rang out from above.

At the top of the stairs Po halted and waited for Tess to arrive. They were on a landing that stretched the width of the building, and were faced by a door to Maddie's rooms. At the back corner, another more utilitarian door offered access up to the roof. That door looked as if it hadn't been opened in years. Po strode over and checked the bolt was snug in its bracket. Not that an ambush was expected, but it paid to cover all bases. Tess waited until he'd returned before reaching for the doorbell. Po's hand intercepted hers.

'Can you make out what they're arguin' about?' he asked.

Tess couldn't. The couple had moved towards the far end of the apartment, their voices muffled by distance and intervening walls. She pressed the bell. The corresponding chime made a musical tinkle that was at odds with the abrasive atmosphere inside. Both voices fell silent.

They waited.

Tess pressed the bell again.

There was a scuff of shoes on concrete, but it had come from below: Pinky had left the shelter of the car to back them up should they need him.

Tess pressed the doorbell a third time; less patient, Po knuckled the door, rapping hard twice.

This time the corresponding shuffle of feet was from the other side of the door; whispers were exchanged. There was no spy hole through which visitors could be observed – the security measures were at ground level – and no CCTV camera apparent. Tess straightened up, adjusting her jacket and the handbag over her shoulder so she presented a more professional first impression. The door opened a slither and Tess opened her mouth to introduce herself. Before she got a chance a man's voice barked, 'Whaddaya want from me now? I agreed to your goddamn terms, didn't I? What are you doing here . . . making more threats?'

The man didn't wait for an answer; he yanked the door wide, and rushed at Tess forcing her backwards towards the safety railing.

TWELVE

I t took an instant before her attacker grew aware of Po looming at Tess's side, and an instant more for genuine alarm to register. By then Tess had begun a pivot to avoid falling headlong off the landing, and Po also swiveled, one hand slapping down on the crown of the man's skull, the other pinching his pullover at the ribs. Po didn't halt the man's forward momentum; he aided it, dragging the lunging man fully out of the apartment and onto the safety rail at the head of the stairs. For a moment the man teetered dangerously, bent at the waist, head and torso over the open stairwell.

'Quit your struggling, you sumbitch, or you'll be taking a dive.' Po need only give him an extra shove and the man would make a hard fall to the next landing. As the man reared back in panic, Po again utilized his weight against him, this time slamming him backwards against the doorjamb.

A young woman hurtled out, clawing at Po, but Tess grasped her and forced her aside. The woman squirmed like an eel, trying to break free, her fingernails raking at Tess. Tess's only recourse was to wrap her arms around her and cram the girl against the wall on the opposite side of the door to avoid having her face scratched raw. 'Calm down,' Tess rasped. 'We aren't here to hurt you.'

Her words didn't penetrate the young woman's mind; she'd already concluded wrongly why they were there.

'Get off him you bastard!' she screeched at Po. 'Haven't you already done enough?'

Po's captive wasn't fighting. Po's left palm was flat against his chest. He had flattened himself against the wall, eyelids squeezed tightly, face turned away . . . he exhaled an elongated hiss of pain courtesy of his spine hitting the doorjamb. Blood was on his lips but not from anything Po had done to him.

Still screeching, the young woman struggled against Tess again, but Tess kept her jammed against the wall. 'Maddie?' she asked, her tone brusque. 'Are you Madison Toner?'

Hearing her name spoken, something clicked in Maddie's
brain, and she stopped struggling to gawp instead at Po. He gave
her a lopsided smile before turning a sterner frown, and a few
words of warning, on the man. Maddie exchanged looks with
Tess. 'Have I got your attention?' Tess demanded. 'Good. Now
chill out. If you calm down I'll let you go, OK?'

'Tell him to get his hands off my dad,' Maddie responded
curtly.

'My friend's only making sure that nobody gets hurt. I promise
you, Maddie, we're not here to hurt you or your dad.'

'You already hurt him, you bastards!'

'He was stopped from making a stupid and misguided attack,'
Tess corrected her. 'He'd have fallen over the railings, possibly
taking me with him if my friend hadn't intervened.'

'What are you talking about?' That was not how Maddie had
perceived the brief but telling scuffle. To her, she, and more so
her father, were the injured party. She again wrenched to get
free. Maddie was still wrapped by Tess's arms; their faces were
too close for either of their comfort. If she wished, Maddie could
sink her teeth into Tess's cheek. Tess released her hold, putting
some distance between them. She mirrored Po's stance, her left
palm to Maddie's chest, forcing her to stand against the wall.

'Everything fine up there?' Pinky's voice boomed up the stairwell. Maddie's eyes grew large at the realization there was a
third stranger to contend with.

'Everything's under control, Pinky,' Tess called down. 'We've
got this. Now that a slight misunderstanding's been cleared up.'

'Good good, I'll go back to the car, me.'

'There's no misunderstanding,' Maddie snapped, 'you hurt my
dad and now you've come back for more.'

'Maddie,' said Tess slowly, 'I don't know who you think we
are, but you've got things all wrong.'

'Bullshit! You followed dad back just so you can force your
point. Well, you can go back where you came from and tell
your bitch boss I'm not easily frightened.'

'Maddie . . . hush now,' said her father, but Tess got the sense
it wasn't to halt her defense of him, but that she might say
something she shouldn't. He, quicker than Maddie, had obviously
realized he'd mistaken her and Po for somebody else. What kind

of trouble had the Toners invited? Tess knew that one of an investigator's greatest tools was silence, allowing the other person to fill the information void. She didn't say a word, only stared at the young woman.

'No! I'm not going to hush, I'm not doing anything these bastards demand.' Maddie yanked to one side, free of Tess's control, and then she threw up both arms, gesturing aggressively, inviting Tess to try taking hold of her again. 'Try me and see.'

Finally Tess said, 'We're not who you're afraid of.'

'Do I look afraid of *you*?' Maddie postured. It was all for show. Yes she was afraid, but saying so would invite another display of fake bravado.

'If you're in some kind of trouble, being threatened to do something against your will, you should call the police,' Tess said.

Her words gave Maddie pause. Tess wanted her to ask herself if anyone threatening her father would actively encourage her to call the police? Then again she might think Tess's encouragement some kind of double bluff or veiled warning of what would happen if she did, but Tess didn't mind confusing her. It'd make Maddie more inquisitive, and by that process, more manageable.

'You know we can't call the goddamn cops,' Maddie sneered.

'Maddie, hush.' Her dad's voice was strident. He glanced between Po and then his daughter, and concluded he wasn't about to be struck for speaking. 'Don't say another thing. I . . . I'll handle this. You just go back inside now.'

'Sorry, bra,' Po said. 'I know you've good intentions, but we didn't come here to speak with you.'

'So what do you want?'

Po gave Tess the go ahead to explain. Ignoring the father, she eyed Maddie steadily. 'Like I said, we're not who you think. We're private investigators, hired by her mom to locate Hayley Cameron.'

Maddie stood, mouth open. Her dad hung his head, muttering at his rash stupidity. Sensing that the prospects for further violence had ended, Po relaxed, lowering his hands and taking a step away from the man.

'You're only looking for Hayley?' Maddie sought unnecessary confirmation. The truth was taking a little time to sink in.

Tess said, 'It's bad timing, I guess. You seem to have your own troubles to contend with, and probably aren't interested in ours. So, how's about you just answer a few quick questions, and we'll get out of your hair?'

'Is Hayley in some kind of trouble too?'

'Not unless you know something about her that we don't.'

Daughter and father exchanged glances. Maddie elected to spill only half-truths. 'No. Hayley has nothing to do with this . . . uh, this is personal stuff, uh, family stuff.'

'Then she isn't in trouble,' said Tess. 'Her mom needs to speak with her, that's all, but Hayley has gone off grid. All we need is to see her, confirm she's safe, and ask her to return her mom's calls. Do you know where she is, Maddie?'

Her response was to shake her head.

Po said, 'We spoke with Jacob Doyle earlier and were told Hayley was staying here with you.' He wasn't exactly lying; he'd pieced together Jacob's lies, mixed it with Stacey's supposition, and come up with a plausible take on Hayley's whereabouts.

'I don't know who that is,' said Maddie.

'That's funny,' Po continued. 'Seeing as he's the one been smokin' outside your door and leavin' all those Lucky Strike butt ends lyin' around.' It was a jump but another plausible conclusion that Jacob had been visiting Hayley here, and Po's delivery sold it.

'Oh, yeah, *him*,' Maddie said, caught in a lie, but she quickly glossed over Jacob with what was another lie. 'Hayley finished with him weeks ago. Hayley hasn't been here in—'

'Where is she now?' Tess butted in, before the girl could concoct another fabrication. 'Like I said, we only want to put her in touch with her mom.'

'She doesn't want to speak with her. Jessie isn't even her real mom.'

'We know. That's why Jessie wants to speak, to explain things to Hayley, so there's no more animosity between them.' Tess purposefully brought in the father again. 'I can tell that you guys are close, the way you stuck up for each other just now. We'd like to give both Jessie and Hayley another opportunity to be a family again.'

'Hayley's stubborn,' said Maddie.

The father squinted at his daughter: yeah, he knew the stubborn type too. 'Maddie can ask Hayley to get in touch but we can't promise she will. You got a name and a number Maddie can give her?'

'If you give me her number I'll contact her directly,' Tess suggested.

'Uh, no.' Again Maddie and her father exchanged glances and barely visible shakes of their heads. Maddie said, 'Hayley's my friend, I'm not betraying her confidence. I'll tell her you're looking for her and why, but if she doesn't want to be found . . .'

Tess conceded. She dug again for a business card, but had given the last in her bag to Jeffrey Lorton earlier. She found a pen and piece of paper and scribbled down her cellphone number, and her name. Hayley took it from her and studied it.

'Tess Grey?' she asked in confirmation.

'That's right.'

Po elected not to give his name. Instead he gave the father some advice. 'You should get your mouth looked at, you've a couple of loose teeth there.'

As if reminded of his previous injury, the man touched tremulous fingertips to his lips. He flinched. But then shrugged off any concern. 'I'll be fine.'

'Hope you got your licks in with the fella who did that to you,' Po went on. The man lowered his gaze, ashamed, so Po let the subject drop. However Tess wasn't finished. She said, 'By the way you flew at us, you thought we were the people that hurt you already. If you're expecting them to come back, you really should do as I suggested and call the police.'

'No, no, I overreacted. I've no reason to think they'll come after me again. They've no need.' The man stirred uncomfortably, again exchanging furtive looks with Maddie, almost as if his last statement was to convince her. He dabbed at his bloody lips to make a point. 'Look, if we're done here, I really need to get cleaned up. Maddie, you gonna help me?'

Maddie moved to enter her apartment but Tess blocked the way. 'You'll pass on my details to Hayley, right? We aren't from Bangor; if you don't want us hanging around here it'll be in your favor to call Hayley soon.'

'Yeah, right, OK. Will do.' Maddie understood the concession

Tess had offered her. 'I'll try to get in touch with her as soon as my dad's patched up.'

'Great.' Tess smiled. The Toners scuttled back inside and the door closed resolutely in her face. Father and daughter whispered conspiratorially as they headed deeper into the apartment.

Tess turned to appraise Po. 'What is it with today and people flying off the handle as soon as I show my face?'

'Beats me, Tess, yours is a nice face to me.'

'Must be you who's the problem then,' she said with the ghost of a smile, and he grunted in laughter.

She went downstairs ahead of him.

Pinky, despite announcing he'd return to the car was where she expected him, sheltering in the entrance lobby. 'Nobody needed knocking out this time, then?'

'Dude up there came close to being punched,' said Po, 'but somebody already beat us to it. Whaddaya think, Tess: we just stumbled across somethin' we shouldn't't've? There was somethin' inside that apartment they didn't want us to see and it wasn't Hayley Cameron.'

'We sure weren't invited in for milk and cookies.'

'So I guess we're on stakeout, huh?'

THIRTEEN

He stood in the bathroom long enough that the motion-activated lights went out. He stood a while longer, breathing slowly, until his vision adapted to the dimness. It wasn't completely dark: a glow etched the door in its frame, and traveled far enough inside the small room to paint the left side of his features in a sickly yellow hue. In the mirror above the washbasin he stared at his reflection and did not recognize it as his own. He chose to think that it was the poisoned man beyond the glass who carried out the sickening demands of his employers, and that he was the innocent reflection of those deeds.

He blinked, realizing it was wishful thinking, and with that he rocked on his heels.

It was enough movement to trip the lights and they flickered on, causing the man in the mirror to strobe also. The flare of stark white light was painful, and he squinted, muttering in discomfort. The mirror-man was gone and only Arlen Sampson remained. He leaned forward, resting his knuckles on the counter surrounding the washbasin. 'Are you proud of yourself?' he challenged his reflection. In response, he formed a globule of saliva under his tongue then allowed it to dribble into the sink: his gaze never left the eyes reflected in the mirror.

The door banged open, and he turned his head to regard Dominick Burgess. His bearded companion peered at him, wondering what the hell he was doing bent over the washbasin. The string of drool still hung from his lips.

'You OK, Arlen?'

Sampson straightened up, using the back of his hand to dash the saliva off his chin. 'Totally.'

'Thought you were sick for a minute.'

'Dom, I'm sick all of the fucking time. Aren't you?'

Dom shrugged at Sampson's rhetoric. His allegiance hadn't been bought the way that Sampson's had. Plus, their work didn't trouble him the way it did Sampson: Dom was a different kind of man, and he was being paid for doing something he was good at. What had he to complain about?

'I'm OK,' Sampson reiterated. 'I'm not physically being sick if that's what you mean? You can leave me be now.'

Dom shook his head. 'She wants you.'

Exhaling noisily, Sampson threw up both hands. 'I need a minute. Tell her I'm coming, will you?'

'She wants you now, man. You'd best get a move on.'

'In a minute.'

Without waiting for an answer, he reached and twisted on the faucet. Hot water gushed. He scrubbed at the string of saliva on the back of his hand, then cupped and splashed water over his face. Behind him, Dom left the room and the door swung shut. Sampson yanked paper towels from a dispenser and rubbed his face vigorously. The towel disintegrated in patches, forming rolls of compacted paper that scraped painfully: it was penance and he didn't let up until his skin smarted. He tossed the wad in the trash. Turned towards the door. Washing and drying had taken more than a couple of minutes, twice the time he'd told Dominick he needed, and it gave him a moment's smug satisfaction. Fuck her if she thought he would jump when she said frog!

His small act of rebellion was as far as he was prepared to go for now. He exited the bathroom and found Dom returning to fetch him a second time. 'Relax, Dom, I'm coming.'

'Good, she's about to crap a lemon cause you've made her wait.'

'You're right, it is good.'

They passed the room where Mike Toner had suffered. Temperance Jolie was inside, and not too impressed. She wore latex gloves and had cloths and a bucket of soapy water. The task of cleaning up Toner's piss and blood had been handed down the chain to her. A thin layer of perspiration glistened on her forehead – more to do with subdued outrage than through effort, Sampson thought. He offered a conciliatory wink. She returned the sentiment with a raised middle finger and a mouthed curse. She was such a sweet mannered girl.

Actually, to him, she was quite the opposite. Her first name was synonymous with an act of virtue, meaning moderation of action, thought or emotion, and most often given as 'restraint.'

From what he'd experienced, Temperance struggled with all the meanings of her name, and restraint was never in her mind unless it had to do with physically obstructing a person's freedom. She was subordinate to Sampson and Dom, and as the latter did, sometimes enjoyed her work; the task of driving her van when required was never cause for complaint. But she hated the menial tasks she was forced to complete, and often raised the racist or sexist card when her Caucasian male superiors sidestepped the dirtier graft. She despised white men – some may argue with good reason – and Sampson hadn't been exaggerating when he'd warned Toner she'd slit his throat if he angered her.

Sampson still preferred Temperance to Dominick. His thuggish second was a grade-one asshole. Dominick had once been a cop in some shit-heel backwater Alabama town before losing his job over a scandal involving alleged 'police brutality.' He was a white supremacist with a badge back then, and he still swaggered around with his superiority complex intact even though he was no more than a servant. Dom was a bully, a sadist, and claimed he got off on the fact he was being paid to inflict terror, but he was also a liar. Sampson knew there was a hold over Dom as there was over Temperance and him. They were all servile attack dogs on leashes jerked by Kelly Ambrose, who was almost certainly a vassal to her husband Blake.

Sampson held no pity for Kelly's similar plight. She was an evil bitch who'd happily usurp her husband's power, the same way that Dom would gladly step on Sampson at first opportunity.

Dom waited outside in the hall.

'Hi, Kelly. You wanted to see me?' Sampson asked as he entered her temporary office. It commanded a view south over Lermond Cove and on a clear day she could watch the Rockland ferry service come and go to Vinalhaven Island. As a second storm front had pushed in over West Penobscot Bay the service had been suspended.

Kelly stood with her back to him, apparently staring out the window at the deluge washing over Rockland Harbor, but Sampson wasn't fooled. She was watching for his reflection in the glass. Briefly his gaze struck and held hers, and he suffered the same uncanny sensation he had in the bathroom: Kelly's mirror form was hazy, laced by runnels and beaded with raindrops, and infinitely evil. She turned and graced him with a smile that held no warmth.

'Blake called. His flight out of Chicago O'Hare was delayed so he has rescheduled for tomorrow morning. He asks that you see me home and you wait with me until his return. Temperance can collect him from the airport in the morning.'

Sampson scowled.

'You don't look happy with Blake's instructions.' Kelly moved towards him and placed two fingernails against his chest. The sharp tips pricked despite his several layers of clothing. It wasn't only Blake's order he was averse to, more what Blake's wife saw as her opportunity.

'I had plans for this evening,' he said.

'Plans can be changed,' she said, allowing her fingers to walk up his chest and onto the bare skin of his neck. 'Oh, you mean personal plans? Do these plans include Caroline?'

Sampson's lips grew dry. He resisted licking them because it would show she'd pricked him worse at mention of his wife's name than with her manicured claws. 'Just some stuff I have to do,' he said, his voice hoarse.

'Just some stuff.' Kelly sniffed in disdain and turned from him. Her raincoat was folded over the back of a chair. She picked it up, readying to leave. 'Caroline is unaware of the nature of our arrangement . . . need she learn the finer details?'

'Let's not start up with that again, huh? Can't Dom take you home? I'm sure he'll be happy to.'

'I'm sure he would. But Blake has given Dom and Temperance a different task.' Kelly held out her coat to him, the command unvoiced but apparent. He arranged it so that she could work her arms into the sleeves. Again, facing away, she observed his reflection in the window. This time he didn't meet her reflected gaze. She turned, and began buttoning the coat, emphasizing the swell of her breasts as she did so. Sampson stared at the floor. 'There was a time,' she sneered, 'when you jumped at the chance to take me home.'

Yeah, Sampson thought. *Back then I was young and naïve . . . and I didn't know you were a fucking cruel bitch. Back then I wasn't married to a woman I love and who's a thousand times the woman you are.*

'It's growing complicated, Kelly. There are only so many excuses I can come up with without Caroline suspecting.'

'There'll be no need for suspicion if I decide to tell her *everything.*'

Sampson wasn't too concerned about Kelly telling Caroline the details of their long-term adultery, not when it'd mean Blake learning about it too. Caroline would be hurt, likely furious, at their infidelity, but Blake would have them both skinned alive. It wasn't in Kelly's favor for their secret to come out. Their affair was not what Kelly meant though, the reason she'd stressed telling everything. She had the power to destroy Sampson with the dropping of another woman's name: Mary Rhodes. Should Caroline learn about Mary, both of their lives would spiral into wreck and ruin. Worse than that, if it became known about Sampson's involvement with Mary Rhodes, it would threaten Blake and Kelly Ambrose's liberty, so Kelly would ensure that once Caroline learned the truth, both she and her husband would be silenced. Refusing Kelly was akin to a death sentence for both he and Caroline.

Sampson held up his left palm. 'Just let me think for a minute; I need to come up with a believable excuse.'

'Do what you must, Arlen. I'll see you at the car in two minutes. I'll speak with Temperance on my way past about collecting Blake tomorrow.'

'You said Dom and Tempe have another task tonight? I'm supposed to be in charge of them, I should check they know what they're doing.'

'They know exactly what's expected of them. As do you now, I'm happy to see.' She smiled in victory. It was the same cheery smile that lit up her eyes and dimpled her cheeks that she'd graced Mike Toner with after he'd been forced into acquiescing to her demands.

FOURTEEN

'At least the rain's dying down,' Tess observed.

Po powered down his window. The rain had slanted against the Mustang, whirling on billows above the Presumpscot River and across the parking lot, forcing him to keep the windows shut till now. Fresh air invaded the confines of the car, forced inside on a guttering breeze. Tess was relieved. The glass was fogged with condensation; Tess's clothing felt damp, and the air had grown stale and unpleasant. The fish and chips lunch she'd fancied earlier had never transpired, and she had grown hungry. Pinky had volunteered to brave the rain and head out on foot in search of sustenance for them. He'd returned twenty minutes later, soaked through to the skin, with the best he could find: a soggy box of Dunkin' Donuts and take-out coffee. He'd grinned at Tess's disappointment. 'Hey, I thought you'd feel nostalgic, you. Isn't this what you ate on stakeout when you were a cop?'

The donuts were stodgy and the coffee bitter, but she'd surprised herself by downing three donuts, her coffee and the half a cup that Po was about to pour away. Now she needed desperately to pee, but kept her discomfort private. It was her who'd suggested they wait and see if Hayley responded to Maddie's call before they left Bangor, and had suggested they stay put to add urgency to Maddie, who'd want nothing more than them gone. Twice already she'd spotted someone standing close to a shuttered window on the top floor, peeping out through the slats to check if they were still there. Perhaps they'd been checked on more than Tess was aware of, because her view of the building was limited from the back seat.

'I'd love a poke around inside that apartment,' Po said, surprising Tess as it sounded as if he'd spoken a thought out loud.

'We aren't here because of what the Toners are up to,' Tess cautioned. 'Our job's to locate Hayley.'

'Yeah,' he intoned. 'I hear ya.'

But of course she was as intrigued as he was. Whatever they'd stumbled into was a far more interesting prospect than simply reuniting a recalcitrant girl with her adoptive mom. Some clues to the desperate nature of the Toners' situation had been dropped during the brief discourse at the top of the stairs. It went without saying that the father had taken a beating, and it was to ensure not only his but also his daughter's cooperation. People generally didn't get beaten up to ensure something lawful and above board happened. Reading between the lines, Toner had been roughed up, but it was a warning to Maddie to toe the line. Maddie, being hotheaded over her father's treatment, had made it clear she'd no intention of complying with any demands made by a 'bitch boss.'

Tess owed Maddie nothing. In fact, if the young woman was involved in some kind of criminal activity, then she'd invited the trouble she was now in and the blame for her father's beating should rest heavily on her conscience. Tess shouldn't feel any concern for them. Toner had barreled out of that apartment intent on having a showdown with Tess, and who knew to what extent he might have gone if Po hadn't intervened? She hadn't been kidding when claiming Toner could have taken them both over the railing in his mad rush. In the seconds following, Maddie had launched at Po, and would have scratched the flesh from his face if Tess hadn't grabbed her: the girl had jostled and fought too, and if she could have hurt Tess she would've. No, she shouldn't feel any concern for them whatsoever.

But therein lay the rub.

She was concerned.

Although Maddie had been fired up, it was through fear that her injured father was about to be set upon again. Attacking Po, and fighting to free herself from Tess, was due to trying to defend her dad. Tess, for one, didn't hold that against her; she would fight tooth and nail for her loved ones too. When first he'd arrived home and parked his truck in the garage, almost collapsing after he got out, he'd spotted Tess approaching the building and concluded wrongly who she was. Toner was frightened and confused, and tried only to defend his daughter; she'd already forgiven him his behavior.

Before Maddie or her father there was Hayley Cameron's welfare to consider.

'Those cigarette butts you spoke about,' she ventured with Po, 'how'd you know they belonged to Jacob?'

'I didn't, it was just a wild guess. He took a Marlboro from me, but his favorite brand is Lucky Strike. They matched the butts at the scene.' Po shrugged. 'From the little I could see through her open door, Maddie keeps a clean house, and probably doesn't welcome smokers.'

'You're a regular Sherlock Holmes, you,' said Pinky.

'Maddie didn't exactly confirm it,' Po replied, 'but neither did she say I was wrong.'

'Would you say some of those butts looked freshly smoked?' Tess asked.

'Couldn't say. It's too wet out. If you're askin' if I think Jacob's been here since we spoke to him this morning, again I couldn't say.'

'I'm only wondering if he came up here after he quit his job, and if he's with Hayley now.' She could kick herself for not asking for a contact number from him. She'd interrogated his social media platforms, and even gotten into his contacts list but without logging his cell number . . . stupid mistake. If she had a way of calling him she would, and ask outright to speak with Hayley. It'd save waiting around here any longer than they had to.

Tess took out her cell and opened the web browser. She looked up Cooper's Bar and hit the contact hyperlink and chose the telephone icon: down in Portland a landline began ringing.

'Cooper's,' answered an older male voice. 'How can I be of assistance?'

'Could I please speak with Stacey Mitchum?' Tess asked.

'Who's asking?'

'My name's Tess Grey, Stacey was my server earlier today.'

Immediately the voice grew guarded. 'If you'd like to make a complaint, I'd rather you spoke with me. I'm Ben Wishaw, I'm the duty manager.'

'Oh, it's nothing like that,' Tess reassured him, 'it's more a private matter.'

'Then, sorry, I don't allow my staff to take personal calls. You'll have to get her at home after she's gone off shift.'

'Look, maybe you can dispense with company protocol this one time? It's important that I speak with her, and I don't have another contact number.'

'Hey, wait a minute!' Suddenly the voice dropped any pretense at professional manners. 'Are you the same woman who kept Stacey away from her tables earlier on? You're some kind of private eye, right? Well . . . I don't know what you said to her, but you upset Stacey, and it's affected her work all afternoon. Seems I've also got you to blame for one of my other servers walking out. Nah, I'm not going to dispense with protocol, in fact I'd prefer if you didn't call again, or show your face in my bar. Goodbye.' He hung up.

'Wow! Just *wow*.' Tess glared at the 'call ended' message on her phone.

'That didn't go too well, pretty Tess,' said Pinky, as he poised an iced donut before his lips.

'I'm beginning to feel like the least popular kid in school,' she said. Not that she took Ben Wishaw's words personally. You had to have a thick skin if you hoped to make it as a private investigator: ruffling feathers and reaping the comebacks was all part of the job. She only felt that Wishaw's ire was misguided . . . if he should be pissed at anyone it should be at Jacob Doyle. No, that wasn't entirely true, not when Hayley was manipulating the lovesick fool. Suddenly Tess experienced a prickle of disliking for the girl, and again had to caution against forming an injudicious opinion: judge as you find, Tess.

'It'll be dark soon,' Po pointed out.

'Let's give it another hour, if Hayley hasn't made contact by then we'll head on back to Portland, yeah?'

'Let's not wait till dark, I've a better idea.' Po drove off the lot, taking Broad Street towards the underpass of the nearby river bridge. He wasn't leaving the area, just repositioning. After swinging around he tucked in at curbside beneath the bridge, the Mustang hidden in shadow. Their presence at the parking lot hadn't galvanized a response from Hayley, maybe their absence would.

FIFTEEN

Hayley Cameron showed up at Maddie Toner's place within twenty minutes of Po pulling the disappearing act. It surprised nobody when she arrived at the converted building escorted by Jacob Doyle. The young man drove a twelve-year-old Chrysler with a faded paint job, scratched fenders and mismatched wheel trims; to listen to other people's opinions of her, Tess expected the girl to demand no less than a carriage worth multiples of tens of thousands of dollars, not the old junker that Jacob owned.

Jacob actually drove past where they waited at curbside in the bridge's underpass. He hadn't seen Po's Mustang that morning, and Maddie mustn't have described it when she summoned Hayley to her apartment after they seemingly gave up and left. Neither did he recognize Po behind the wheel when he glanced at the parked car, but that was probably due to Pinky mostly concealing him. Pinky gave Jacob the rheumy eye. Jacob glimpsed at the large black man, and quickly averted his gaze, in case his interest was misconstrued and he attracted trouble. Sometimes racial stereotyping could work in their favor. In the back seat of the Mustang, Tess was hidden from view, but she strained to see past Po's shoulder as the Chrysler rolled by and into the shallow bend after the bridge. She recognized Jacob and saw enough of Hayley's profile to identify the girl. She tapped the back of Po's seat in her urgency.

Po started the engine, and pulled out from under the bridge. Rain assaulted them, having returned after the recent quiet spell. Po's wipers struggled to fight the deluge. As he drove around the bend, the Chrysler was already across the railway track and moving towards the roller shutter. Jacob parked on the hard base in front of the garage, possibly already informed that Maddie's dad's truck was inside. Jacob got out and danced past the hood of the car gibbon-like, arms flung overhead against the downpour until he reached the passenger side. He opened the door for

Hayley as if he was her personal chauffeur. She got out, small in stature, but with curves bordering on plump. She was dressed in a silver bomber jacket, jeans turned up to expose her bare ankles and sneakers. To a casual observer they might take her to be a high-school kid, but Tess knew she was twenty-one years old. The girl clutched a large purse to her abdomen, but passed off another satchel-type bag to Jacob. Preparing to go around the building to the side door, Hayley held her bag aloft so it acted as a shield, protecting her short dyed purple hair against the rain. Tess didn't want Hayley sequestered inside the apartment. 'Cut them off,' she told Po.

He was already on it. He hit the gas and the Mustang lurched forward. Seconds later he braked in controlled compressions of the pedal, decelerating safely and avoiding skidding on the slick road. He swung the car in off the street, bumped over the railway track and pulled in so that the Mustang's front fender was an inch from the Chrysler's rear. Hayley and Jacob were blocked from making a run for it to the side entrance. They could scarper away along the length of the building, and back onto the street towards the underpass, but they didn't. Both were caught in shock, Jacob slightly behind Hayley: nearest them was Pinky. Tess wondered if Jacob thought Pinky had chased them here after Jacob had the nerve to glance at him while passing under the bridge. Or if the fear on his face was due to a different perceived threat. However, having been warned they were in the area, it soon dawned on Hayley who they were. Her blanched features bloomed in color, eyes widening, nostrils pinching. She lowered the bag, forgetful of the rain pattering down.

Po stepped out of the car, allowing Tess to clamber out. Hayley was already heading around the car, her stride determined. She tried to swerve past Tess, with a curt, 'Leave me the hell alone.'

Tess got in front of her, backpedaling as Hayley continued towards the side of the building.

'Get out of my goddamn way,' Hayley snarled.

Tess didn't. She set her heels and held out both palms. Hayley again tried swerving past, but Tess adjusted her footing, blocking her again. 'Hayley, just let me explain, will you?'

Hayley swore at her.

Maybe opinions of the girl's nature were true after all.

Tess grasped Hayley's elbow, and she dragged the girl to a halt. 'If you just listen to me for one minute, I'll have done my job and can leave you be. It's up to you, Hayley.'

'I told you what to do. Fuck off. And get your hands off me or I'll sue you for assault.'

'Really?' Tess demanded. 'You want to involve the police? Fine. Here, I'll call them for you if you like?'

Hayley's face was livid. The last thing she wanted was police involvement, confirming that Maddie and her dad were up to something illegal, something which Hayley and Jacob had become part of.

'I didn't think so,' said Tess.

Behind them, Po was in a similar vociferous discussion with Jacob Doyle, although the youth wasn't as outwardly hostile . . . maybe by now he'd learned of what went down at his family home when his brothers had tried to get heavy with Tess and Po. Tess gave them no heed; getting Hayley to listen was her priority. She didn't release her grasp, if anything she tightened it. 'Hear me out. I'm assuming Maddie called you and let you know why I'm looking for you. All I need do is check you're OK, give you a message from your mom, and then it's completely up to you with what happens next.'

Hayley wrenched to get free, but Tess's grasp tightened again. The girl faced her. 'I don't want to speak with her. Why should I? She's nothing but a goddamn liar.'

Tess nodded along with Hayley, a ploy to get her onside. 'Like I said, it's down to you whether or not you get in touch. I've been hired to find you and pass on Jessie's request, that's all. Your mom only wants to explain things to you regarding your adoption in the hope that you can reconcile your differences.'

'OK, you've done what you had to. Now get your hands off me.'

This time when Hayley wrenched her arm, Tess released it. From the car, Pinky videoed the meeting on Tess's cellphone as she'd requested: proof of locating Hayley to show Jessie Cameron. Jessie might expect more from her investigator for her money. 'You really should give your mom a chance, Hayley. She only wants the best for you. She regrets not telling you the whole truth before but she was only trying to protect you.'

'No, she lied because it was easier for *her*.'

'Just give your mom a call. Straighten things out. It can't hurt you, right?'

'I don't want to speak to her. I don't want to see her. Tell her from me to back off and leave me the hell alone.'

'I spoke with your father earlier and—'

'What? How, he's . . .' Hayley faltered.

'He's back in Portland. Take that information how you see fit. But he'd also like to speak with you, to explain—'

'Why the fuck he ran off and left me with a suicidal whacko? Yeah, like I want to hear his fucking excuses!'

With that Hayley broke away, rushing for the side entrance. Jacob scuttled past Tess, making plaintive gestures of apology with his open hands. Tess scowled at him. It wasn't for her to advise him he was on the wrong path, or that he'd lost a good thing when he dumped Stacey in favor of this petulant child. Hopefully Po had put a word or two of wisdom in his ear while she'd been otherwise engaged.

Tess had completed her task. She'd located Hayley, personally spoken to her and passed on Jessie's request, and as a result ensured that she was fit and well. She'd always cautioned Jessie that she could not force Hayley into complying with her request, or that she could physically compel the girl to return home. Her side of the bargain had been delivered, and yet a sense of failure stung her. She watched Jacob disappear around the building, calling out to Hayley to wait for him. Tess felt she should follow, perhaps try again to convince Hayley to call her mom.

'Job's done,' Po announced from behind her shoulder.

She appraised him. He looked back, his turquoise eyes seemingly peering into her mind. 'You're unhappy with the way things went?' he asked.

'Is it so obvious, Po?'

'You did what you were hired to do. What's to be unhappy about?'

She didn't reply. He knew that, for her, the perfect end to the day would've been coordinating a happy reunion between mother and daughter. Well it wasn't going to happen.

'C'mon, let's get outta this darn rain,' he suggested.

Tess looked up. Maddie's window shutters remained resolutely closed. 'Maybe I should go up and try again.'

'That girl's dug her heels in deeper than a tick. You'll only be wastin' your time and breath, Tess, with nothin' more to show for it at the end. Guarantee ya; you'll only feel the worse for it. C'mon, you've delivered Jessie's request, best we can do now is get on down the road and let her know Hayley's safe and sound.'

From the confines of the Mustang Pinky waggled her cellphone at her. 'I've got all the proof you need on here, pretty Tess. I'm a veritable Spielberg, me.'

She gave Pinky a brief smile of acknowledgement, but her mind was on Po's words. 'Is she though?' she asked. 'After what happened to Maddie's dad, are any of them safe and sound?'

'That's not for you to concern yourself with. C'mon, let's go. We've aways to drive and I'd prefer if we were off the road before this storm really hits.'

Unlike Portland, Bangor was a good twenty miles inland, so was more protected from the storms that roared in off the North Atlantic to lash the coast. Judging by the charcoal grey of the eastern sky, which was lit occasionally by jagged lightning bolts, it wouldn't be spared the fury of the incoming weather front though. The drive home could prove hair-raising if they didn't depart soon. Tess hurried for the car, every second saved was a second they didn't have to spend at the mercy of the coming storm. She clambered inside behind Po's seat and then he slid in. He started the engine.

'Who're these bozos?' he wondered.

Tess twisted around to check.

Parked on Broad Street, a panel van blocked their passage over the railway lines. From the driver's position a mixed-race woman stared back at Tess. The woman's hair was styled in tight cornrows, and elaborate silver earrings decorated with feathers hung almost to her shoulders. Beyond her a man strained to see the occupants of the Mustang. He had a shaved head, countered by a full beard and moustache. His styling was fashionable, but his didn't appear the result of a trend, the dome of his head was puckered white, his temples darker, a sign he'd inherited male pattern baldness. As she'd found that day, Tess was again returning the stares of persons unknown to her.

The van idled parallel to the crossing. It stopped Po from reversing onto the road. The bearded guy leaned further across so he could see more of the Mustang. He was reading Po's license plate. He snapped his gaze up and sneered at Tess, apparently unimpressed.

'Want me to go ask what they want?' Pinky offered.

Inside the car there was a tangible buzz of energy: it smelled of testosterone to Tess.

'Let's just give it a moment longer,' she suggested.

Her words heralded a decision by those in the van. The woman pulled away from the railway crossing and headed along to where Broad Street merged with Front Street, where the van continued along the riverside drive. It was doubtful it would be the last they'd see of it.

'What do you say?' Tess asked. 'Those were the guys that Mr Toner mistook us for?'

Po said, 'I guess we won't be leavin' Bangor any time soon, huh?'

SIXTEEN

'**N**icolas Villere?' Dominick grunted, unimpressed. 'He sounds like some kinda Euro-trash faggot to me.'

Temperance had stopped the van at the furthest reaches of a public parking lot, on park ground alongside the Presumpscot River. There were riverside trails and views downstream towards a sprawling casino hotel that boasted its own harness racetrack, and a famous Paul Bunyan statue. On nicer days, the park would be the domain of young families, dog walkers and fitness enthusiasts, but in the teeming rain they had it to themselves. As soon as she'd stopped the van she'd gone for her cellphone.

Kelly Ambrose boasted to Mike Toner that her reach was long, and she'd eyes and ears everywhere. It was an exaggeration for effect, but that wasn't to say she didn't have certain resources her subordinates could pull on when necessary. Temperance rang Kelly's contact in the DMV who ran the Mustang's tags through the system. The car came back as owned by Villere, the owner's address given as an autoshop in Portland, Maine. It was enough detail to get going with. She threw his name through a web search engine.

'Maybe you shouldn't take him lightly, Dom,' Temperance cautioned. Villere's name had come back attached to various news reports over the past few years. He'd been partly instrumental in stopping a cartel assassin and on another occasion a serial killer, and other stories hinted at his involvement in solving other high-stakes criminal cases alongside his employer, private investigator, Teresa Grey.

'She's the blonde that gave us the stink-eye back there?' Dom asked.

'We can assume it was her.'

'What about the nigger?'

Temperance snapped a look of sheer hatred on him. 'Are you for fucking real, Dom? You still use that horrible word around me?'

He shrugged. 'Why not? I have to be true to myself, right? Besides, it goes to prove I see you in a different way than I do others.'

'If you tell me you don't see my color no more, I swear to God I'll—'

'Chill out, girl. I still see your color, and it ain't black. You're mulatto, right, your daddy was white?'

'No, you son of a bitch, my mother's rapist was a fucking whip cracker like you!'

Dom stared at her coolly as he scratched his bearded chin. Her teeth were clenched, eyes bolting from their sockets. Her right hand crept to her side.

'Draw that knife, Tempe, and you'd better be prepared to use it,' he warned.

His words took the steam out of her. Her fingers withdrew from the blade she kept sheathed at her hip. 'One of these days you're going to go too far,' she said.

'Thought you'd be used to me by now. You're getting too sensitive for your own good, Temperance.'

'Just think about what you're going to say before you open your mouth in future. We might not like it, but we have to work together, and it needn't be unpleasant the whole time.'

'I quite enjoy our times together. Mind you' – he aimed a lascivious wink and a nod at her long legs – 'I prefer to watch you leave.'

He'd turned from racism in favor of sexism. Temperance shook her head in frustration. Trying to change Dom was an exercise in futility. She concentrated on searching for details of Teresa Grey on her phone. Cross-breezes buffeted the van, and the rain was a constant drumroll on its shell.

'What've you got?' Dom prompted after a moment's pause.

'She used to be a cop. Sergeant with the Cumberland County Sheriff's Department before being injured in the line of duty. Since then she's been making a living poking around in other people's business.' Temperance's eyes widened a fraction more. 'Villere's not the only one we should worry about. Remember a few years ago when Albert Sower's outfit was broken, and his brother Hector was killed? That was down to Grey.'

Until a few years earlier the Sower siblings' name had been

synonymous with organized crime in Maine. Dom being a late-comer to the state hadn't a clue about them, but the gravitas Temperance gave them hinted they'd been hot shits before meeting Teresa Grey and her sidekick. He said, 'Do I look worried?'

'What interest has a private investigator got with Mike Toner's daughter?' Temperance prompted. 'He was warned what'd happen if he called the cops. You don't think Toner disobeyed his instructions and called in help?'

'You had to clean up his piss. Do you really think he's gonna disobey?'

'His daughter must've called them then?'

'You have to think about the timescale, Temperance. Do you really believe that during his drive over from Rockland, Toner telephoned Madison, he told her everything that happened and she called in the cavalry from Portland? They wouldn't have made it here already. It doesn't add up.'

It irked admitting that Dom was right. 'So they must be here over some unrelated matter. Do you think they got wind of Madison's scheme the way that Blake and Kelly did?'

'Beats me,' he said. Drunk one night in a Rockland bar, Mike Toner had mentioned to another drinker that his days hauling lobster pots was coming to an end, that he'd soon be rolling in cash through a scheme his daughter had thought up. The drinker was in debt to Blake and Kelly Ambrose. Thinking he'd earn himself some leniency from Blake and Kelly's 'debt collectors' he'd pointed them at Toner as a sure-fire source of income. 'You saw that other car, right? Some old model Chrysler. Looked to me as if they'd blocked it in the way we did with them. Maybe their business is with whoever the car belongs to.'

'There's only Madison living in the apartment block just now. Has to be her car.'

'On the money she's making? If she's splashed out on some new wheels it won't be on a shit heap like that.'

'Maybe she's being careful and not advertising the fact she's suddenly earning a packet.'

'Speculation's getting us nowhere. Let's do another drive-by; if it's all clear we'll go visit Toner like we were told.'

'You want to do this while there's a PI sniffing around?'

'I sure as hell don't want to be out in this storm all night. Let's get this done, Temperance. If Grey or Villere get in our way, I've got it covered.' He touched his holstered gun for emphasis.

After another brief check of her phone screen, Temperance shut it down and started the van. She cut a rapid turn, and headed back towards Madison's apartment building. By then the wind was roaring out of the east. Leaves stripped from the riverside trees made a green and gold blizzard, while airborne trash added flashes of different colors. Otherwise everything was grey or silvered by the rain. Lightning cut jagged streaks on the far side of the Presumpscot. Though she was unhappy about Dom's plan, she was in agreement with the part about getting out of the storm.

It was a minute's drive back to Madison's place. Temperance slowed the van as they drew adjacent with the railway crossing, but didn't stop. The Mustang was gone, but the Chrysler was where they'd last seen it. 'Make a note of those tags,' she told Dom. 'I want to know who might be inside there before we go in.'

She drove until sheltered beneath the underpass, where she again rang Kelly Ambrose's DMV contact. Dom called out the license plate number when prompted, and then she waited a moment until the details returned.

'You sure about that?' she asked the woman on the other end of the line. She listened again. 'All right, then. If that's what it says, I'll take your word for it. Your discretion about this is appreciated.' Temperance ended the call and looked across at Dom. 'Interesting. The Chrysler threw up a red flag just now. Keeper details come back to a Jacob Doyle, a kid from Standish, but hear this, Herbert Wetherby, a sixty-eight-year-old retiree from Wiscasset, holds the insurance details. You know what that means, right?'

Dom grunted in comprehension.

'One of Madison's disgruntled customers has come calling,' he said, 'or the stupid bitch has used her system to save her boyfriend Jacob a few bucks. Either way, it's a problem we'll have to sort or we'll be collecting fifty percent of *fucking zero*.'

SEVENTEEN

Tess stood buffeted by the wind, soaked through, hair whipping across her face, regretting her plan. There was no shelter from the storm on the exposed roof of Maddie's apartment building. She waited, leaning with her ear against the roof access door – the same one she'd noted earlier when Po checked it was bolted from within. She'd considered calling the local police to warn them of possible impending trouble, but hadn't. What could she tell them? With no firm facts concerning the nature of the 'possible' trouble the police response would be marginal at best, and could quite possibly cause further problems for the Toners down the line. It was apparent that those in the van were connected to the people that Toner was fearful of. Tess had no timescale to go on. The van might return within minutes or hours, but she was confident it'd be back and she wanted to know why. Po was of a similar opinion, while Pinky was only happy to be out in the field with them once again . . . or he was earlier. Now he looked miserable.

Pinky hunched behind her, rain battering on his shoulders and washing over his screwed features. Ordinarily he'd be large enough for Tess to shelter behind, but the whipping gusts had a way of finding egress to every nook and cranny, delivering payloads of raindrops equally on her as on Pinky. She glanced at him, saw him blow frothy water from between his lips. He shivered constantly, moving his feet so that his limbs didn't lock up. 'Welcome to the glorious side of being a gumshoe,' she whispered.

He flashed her a grin of supreme irony. Then leaned close so she could hear. 'Nicolas warned me there'd be good times, but also when I'd be verging on hypothermia and bursting for a leak. I guess this is one of those latter times, me.'

Tess nodded in shared desperation. Her bladder was also threatening to explode; she should have made do with drinking her coffee and not downed Po's too. 'At least you can turn your back and relieve yourself,' she pointed out. 'I don't have that luxury.'

'Uh, no, pretty Tess. Don't you know the definition of getting your own back, you? That's right: it's pissing into the wind.'

She grunted in mirth. Pinky's immature humor could occasionally be trying but there were times, like now, when he lifted her spirits. Above them the wind roared and without warning lightning streaked a ragged fork through the boiling clouds. Tess huddled in anticipation of what was coming. The roar of wind was drowned beneath the tremendous rumble of thunder. As a child she used to count the seconds between the crack of lightning and the boom of thunder that followed, to determine if the storm was nearing or moving away. In the last few minutes she'd swear that the storm had remained static almost overhead to add to her misery. She cringed as the tumult faded, knowing that it would be followed in no time at all. Thunder and lightning didn't usually frighten her but exposed on top of the building they were in real peril of being fried. If that damn van didn't arrive soon she'd call off her plan.

'I hope Nicolas is dry and warm,' Pinky said without conviction.

Po was below them in the building, though where he'd hidden was unknown to them. There were few options that Tess had noticed on the way up the stairwell. Thankfully, Maddie hadn't learned from their earlier incursion of the building, neglecting again to lock the entrance door: maybe it remained open in order for Jacob to take his smoking breaks. She wondered if Po had gotten sequestered somewhere he too could feed his nicotine habit. Her thoughts did him an injustice. Wherever he was, he'd be by her side the instant she needed him.

This, she'd cautioned, was an information-gathering mission. Eavesdropping an unfettered discussion between the Toners and the troublemakers could give her more answers than she could gain from trying to question either party. But she also anticipated events getting out of hand rather quickly, and was torn as to how she should respond. If there were violence for instance, the obvious move would be to call the police. Except she never could stand by waiting for a response, choosing instead to intervene where it meant saving a victim from harm. Hopefully she wouldn't have to get in the middle of things again, but in part she hoped things would grow emotive, with voices raised enough to hear. After that, then who knew?

If the Toners were engaged in illegal activity she should report them. However, she wasn't suffering the storm just so she could finger them to the cops. The Toners had come within the circle of her investigation and she felt – wrongly perhaps – that she was somehow responsible for their safety. She owed them nothing. Mr Toner had almost pushed her over the bannister earlier, and Maddie had been nothing but obstructive in connecting her with Hayley Cameron, so why should she be concerned about them? The answer was simple. She'd judged them as she'd found them, and it wasn't as criminals to be reviled, but ordinary decent people who'd made some wrong decisions that were now coming back to bite them.

And then there was Hayley and Jacob. She felt that they'd gone into hiding in Maddie's apartment as a direct result of Tess being in town. She had placed them in the line of fire, so therefore felt responsible for them too.

There was no way of hearing the van's arrival over the storm, or in fact an ascent of the stairs. Tess's phone vibrated in her pocket and she quickly checked the message from Po.

THEY'RE HERE.

She didn't reply to the message. Instead she tapped Pinky's thigh, alerting him to the arrival of the troublemakers. He squared up his shoulders, but Tess wasn't ready to confront them yet. She held a finger to her lips. They could've jumped up and down singing sea shanties and was unlikely they'd be overheard. She was tempted to crack open the door so she could hear better, but the noise of the storm might alert them and one or the other from the van might investigate the open door. She strained to listen, cringing in the next instant as lightning turned the gloom to midday. She smelled ozone, felt her eardrums compress, and also the corresponding boom of thunder in her insides. Pinky almost went to all fours but thankfully only from surprise. 'Holy crap,' he wheezed.

She'd no idea how distant the lightning struck, but it was too close. Again, she was seriously tempted to abort her mission, but from the other side of the door she heard gruff exclamations. The lightning's near miss had even startled those in the stairwell. As Pinky straightened up, she again cautioned silence, indicating with her hands that the troublemakers had arrived on the landing.

One of them hammered on Maddie's door more forcefully than Po had earlier. The voice that followed carried better than she expected.

'Open up, Mike, I know you're in there.'

Mike, Tess assumed, was Maddie's father's name. The voice that hollered it was male, therefore belonging to the bearded guy who'd sneered at her from inside the van a short time ago.

The guy hammered the door again, but could barely be heard for the cacophony overhead. Tess strained to listen as his female companion said something to him, but it was impossible to hear. The guy was deliberately loud; she ensuring her words didn't carry to those inside.

'I'm going to give you five seconds,' shouted the guy. 'If you don't open up, I'm coming in through this goddamn door. You hear me, Mike?'

Mike Toner must have responded, but it wasn't to the guy's satisfaction. 'You think I'm fucking playing around? Open up, or I swear I'll kick my way inside.'

A muffled response sounded like a plea.

The bearded man kicked the door.

Tess tensed, expecting the splinter and crack of wood. She looked at Pinky for support and he was ready to intervene with her. But Mike Toner must have complied and unlocked the door.

'There!' the bearded man snapped. 'That's more like it. Have you forgotten your damn instructions already, you cowardly piece of crap?'

'I haven't forgotten anything,' Mike Toner responded. 'I just don't know what you're doing here. Kelly said—'

'Kelly changed her mind. She has decided she can't wait till the end of the month. She wants paid now.'

'But, we only just got started a few weeks ago. We haven't made that much yet.'

'Whatever you've made, Kelly wants fifty percent transferred right now.'

Listening from behind the closed door, Tess shivered and it had nothing to do with onset-hypothermia. It was surprising what she could learn from eavesdropping, but everything she heard begged extra questions. Who was Kelly? It was one of those genderless names. The bearded man had referred to her as female but it was still unclear if Kelly's was a given or family name. Tess doubted that Maddie had some sort of cottage industry set up in her apartment, and was not manufacturing tangible goods. Neither did she think Maddie had a pharmacy going where she was cooking crack cocaine or methamphetamine. It stood to reason then that the man demanded half of the cash the Toners had accrued in the past few weeks. How they were making money would have to remain a mystery for now . . . unless it was literal, and they were counterfeiting cash?

'That's impossible,' Mike Toner countered. 'We have over-heads, man! Most of what we made has already been spent.'

'Bullshit. You left your job on the boat today and didn't even wait for your pay. That doesn't sound like somebody with a cash-flow problem to me. I'm coming in. I want to see your books.'

'We don't keep records, Dom. Do you think we're stupid?'

'So I want to see your bank accounts.'

This wasn't about counterfeit currency, Tess decided. She exchanged looks with Pinky, noticing the furling and unfurling of his fists. Things were approaching a head, but she again cautioned patience.

Abruptly Maddie's voice rang out. 'Get the hell out of my apartment. You've got no right barging in like this.'

'Your daddy's told you everything by now,' the bearded man – Dom, Mike Toner had called him – must have entered the apartment because his voice was more muffled than before. 'So you know what's going to happen if you refuse. Do you want to go for a trip in the back of Temperance's van?'

Temperance. Tess had learned another name: she must be the mixed-race woman accompanying Dom. And she also understood the threat that Mike and Maddie Toner were under. Had Toner been bundled into the panel van earlier, to be released later beaten and terrified?

'I don't know who you people think you are but you've no right threatening us like this!' Maddie obviously wasn't taking the threat as seriously as her dad did, but then he'd had first-hand experience.

'Shut it, bitch.' Temperance added to the sense of peril by keeping her warning low-pitched. She must still be on the landing. 'Better do as—'

A clap of thunder momentarily deafened Tess. She felt Pinky moving beside her, and realized she'd missed something important. When she could hear again, curses mingled with shouts of alarm, as Dom and Temperance forced their way inside the apartment. Her tongue caught against the roof of her mouth; if she was going to intervene it should be now. She grabbed at the handle and tried to haul open the door. It resisted her. No, not the door. The force of the wind against it was more powerful than Tess's tug. Pinky lent his bulk, grasping the edge of the door, and together they hauled it wide enough for Tess to pass inside. The scuff of rapid footsteps from below told her Po was already on his way up. Pinky lurched onto the landing: his features were grim, echoing what was going on inside the apartment. Something crashed to the floor, causing frightened exclamations. Hayley and Jacob's voices had joined those of the others as demands and questions rang out. Somebody cried out in pain.

Tess didn't think twice. She rushed through the apartment door and into the middle of a violent struggle. It was the type of fight that could only lead to a fatal outcome for somebody, if not right now, then further down the line. Dom, armed with a pistol, and Temperance with a knife, weren't the ones in mortal danger.

EIGHTEEN

D om had anticipated there being an extra person to contend with inside the apartment, after Temperance had discovered the old Chrysler belonged to one Jacob Doyle of Standish. He hadn't expected another young woman to be there, but from the way the skinny kid moved to protect her Dom understood he'd come to the wrong conclusion that Doyle was Maddie's guy. That Maddie had used her scheme to save her friend's boyfriend some cash was a stupid, amateurish move, and could prove the ruination of the good thing she'd gotten going. He strode down the hall, and the four figures before him had no option except to stumble backwards. There was a babble of voices, mostly tinged with fear but Maddie's was strident with infuriation. Temperance aimed her knife at the young woman with a snarled warning to shut her yap. Nobody paid the knife any attention; all eyes were on Dom's pistol.

He forced them down a narrow hall, past closed doors he took to be concealing bedrooms, and into a large sitting room. Maddie and Mike Toner stayed close, while Doyle and his girl tried to make space between them and their friends by circling around a low couch.

'Watch those punks,' Dom commanded Temperance. He was more interested in the Toners. He grabbed the front of Mike's sweater. Shook him, while waving the gun over at the two youths. 'The fuck are these two doing here, Mike? What part of your instructions about keeping our arrangement between us didn't you understand?'

Toner still suffered from last time Dom had laid hands on him, and was easily cowed again by the man's presence. 'They're just kids, Dom. They're friends of Maddie's. They just—'

Dom struck Toner in the face with the butt of his pistol. A gash an inch wide opened like a third eyelid on Toner's left cheek. Toner gasped in agony, his knees giving way as blood poured down his face and dripped onto his chest. Maddie screeched at her dad's rough treatment and launched at Dom to push him away. Dom dropped Toner on the carpet, he backhanded Maddie away and she collapsed on the floor too, stunned and verging on unconsciousness.

'You might want to take things a bit easier,' Temperance sneered from her side of the room. Stupidly, Doyle tried to shift, to place himself between Temperance and his purple-haired girl-friend. Temperance snatched at his jacket, hauling him almost nose to nose. 'What I just said doesn't make me a soft touch,' she said as she rested the edge of her blade on Doyle's chin. 'Try me and I'll happily cut off your lips. Got it?'

Doyle swallowed hard. 'I've got it.'

Temperance shoved him away and his girl grabbed at him for support. Temperance again graced Dom with a sneer. 'See?'

'Yeah. Fuckers need to know where they stand with us,' Dom responded. But she had a point; his warning wouldn't sink in if it were delivered to deaf ears. He bent and grasped Toner, shaking him to lucidity. 'Get up. I smashed your cheek but you're not a fucking cripple.'

'For god sakes, Dom,' Toner groaned as he pawed at the rent in his cheek. 'I haven't done a thing wrong, and look at the way you're treating me. Jesus, man . . .'

Dom ignored him, staring down at Maddie instead. 'Where's your set-up?'

'I don't care what my dad agreed to,' she croaked, 'you can't force me—'

Dom went down one knee, so that he could shove his pistol under Maddie's chin. 'I can do whatever the hell I want, bitch. Now, show me your fucking set-up.'

Toner aimed bloody fingers at the door to an adjoining room. 'It's in there, Dom. Go on. Take a look for yourself. Check whatever you want to. Then please just go and leave us be.'

Dom stood. He didn't require Maddie to show him the way. He stepped over her legs to approach the room Toner indicated. 'I told you already,' Dom said, 'Kelly wants fifty percent tonight. If you know what's good for you, she'll get it.'

He threw the door open, it swung inward into what amounted to a home office. He saw a couple of desktop computers, printers, an archaic fax machine, mountains of stationery. There were several chairs in the small room. His back was to the hallway. Temperance's attention was on the other couple. They were unaware of the newcomers rushing down the hallway until Maddie howled in warning.

Dom wondered if the girl's warning was for him to shut the door to the room, or if she was warning the private investigators he was armed. Whatever. He snapped around, bringing up his pistol as first Teresa Grey and then her hulking black companion crossed the threshold. Neither of them was armed.

Dom aimed his pistol directly at Grey's chest.

She held out both palms. 'Take it easy,' she said.

The big black guy bit down on his bottom lip. He appeared ready to hurtle at Dom, notwithstanding the gun.

'Move, nigger, and I'll drop you on your fat ass,' Dom snapped.

'The police are coming,' Grey warned him. 'You'd do well to put away that gun and get the hell out of here.'

'Bullshit,' said Dom.

'Why'd you call the police?' Maddie cried plaintively.

'Dom . . . we had no part in this!' Toner also cried.

'Shut up.' Dom thought feverishly. He'd boasted to Temperance that he held no fear of Grey or her partner. He felt only loathing for the black man. But neither was he a complete idiot that was going to stand around and wait for the cops to arrive. He was confident that Toner would keep schtum about what had gone down between them that day, but Maddie was another story. She was going to take more convincing that Blake and Kelly Ambrose weren't making idle threats. Jacob Doyle and his girl couldn't be relied on to stay quiet about his violent invasion of the apartment either. The PI definitely couldn't. 'I should shoot you all and have done with it,' he said aloud, but there was no conviction to his threat. Instead he wagged the gun at Grey. 'What do you suggest happens next?'

'You put away your weapons, you leave, and when the cops get here I'll concoct a tale to explain why Mike Toner's face is split open. Nobody here will mention you were here.'

'And I'm supposed to trust you?'

'You can trust me. Right now, my only concern is for Hayley's safety.' She looked at the purple-haired girl, offering a brief wink of support, before returning her full attention to Dom. 'I have nothing to do with either the Toners, or in your issue with them. That's not to say I can stand aside and watch them get hurt either.'

'You took a big risk running in here like this,' Dom said, 'or you made the stupidest move of your life. What did you think you and your pet nigger could do without a gun between you?'

He'd purposefully been free and loose with *that* word even his subordinate seemed to take umbrage with because it was certain to get a reaction. Its usage wasn't lost on the private investigator. Grey switched attention to Temperance. 'What do *you* say? We fight this out, and the cops arrest you, or you leave quietly like I've offered.'

Dom grunted sourly. 'Doesn't matter what she says, I'm in charge. If there's a deal to be made, it's with me.'

Grey switched attention again, and Dom repaid her gesture by lowering his sidearm. 'So we have a deal?' Grey asked.

There was little else Dom could do. He could shoot them all, but perhaps not without danger to himself or Temperance. As soon as his first bullet left the gun chaos would erupt: by the fearless glare of hatred aimed at him by the black guy, he might go for broke and actually reach Dom before he was taken out of the picture. They might struggle, and still be caught in a death tussle when the cops arrived. If there was shooting to be done, he should ensure the first bullet was into the nigger's skull. And where was Villere, Grey's partner? For all he knew, Villere could be coordinating the police response from a safe distance, or he was keeping back, tooled up and ready should the worst scenario develop. Dom didn't want to be pinned down in the apartment and at the cops' mercy. After killing everyone here, there'd be no walking out alive. He wasn't afraid of dying per se, but he'd prefer it didn't happen tonight. He pushed his gun into the holster below his armpit, and nodded at Temperance to follow suit. She wavered, not yet ready to sheath her knife when Grey and the black man blocked the exit.

'Just go,' said Grey, and she and her friend moved aside.

'We'll go,' said Dom. But he then graced Grey with a fixed sneer. 'You shouldn't have pushed your nose into other people's business, *Teresa*.' He enunciated her name slowly so there was no doubt in her mind that he knew who she was . . . and where to find her.

'I told you,' she replied, 'my business is with Hayley. I don't give a damn about you or your beef with the Toners.'

He apprised Mike Toner, who was staring in disbelief over his cupped palm. Blood still dripped freely. 'This doesn't change a damn thing, y'hear? I still expect what we talked about.'

Toner nodded glumly, and Dom turned to follow Temperance along the hall. Before they were out of the door, he heard Maddie turn her irate screech on Teresa Grey. Apparently her intrusion was about as welcome as Dom and Temperance's had been. There was the slight possibility that the PI had done him a favor, because her appearance had added weight to the situation and the Toners should take the threat more seriously now. He grinned over his shoulder as Maddie swore at Grey.

Temperance stepped out onto the landing.

Dom followed, head still turned.

Temperance croaked in warning, but it was too late.

Something sharp pricked the hollow beneath Dom's left ear. His hands came up, but only so that Nicolas Villere could reach under and unsnap the pistol from his holster. Villere didn't remove his knife; using one hand he ejected the magazine from the gun, then the cartridge from the firing chamber. The empty gun clattered noisily down the stairs. 'You can pick up that piece of shit on your way out,' Villere rasped. 'Thank your stars you get to live to do so.'

Villere withdrew the knife and stepped away.

Dom also gained some strategic space between them and turned to face him. Temperance scowled and her hand twitched as if she should go for her weapon. Villere only raised an eyebrow at her and turned his blade so that it caught the overhead lights.

'Leave it, Tempe,' Dom cautioned. He knew she was good with a blade, but he suspected that the rangy-built Villere was better.

'Good advice,' said Villere. He aimed the knife at Dom. 'That way we all live to meet another day.'

'We'll meet again, sure enough,' Dom confirmed.

'You can bet on it. Coupla things you said to my friend in there that are unforgivable. I'd like to cut out your tongue, bra, but I'm not the impatient type.'

'Judging by your accent you're a southerner too. Wouldn't have taken you for a nigger lover.'

'That's three strikes I owe you.' Villere dipped and secreted his knife in a boot sheath. As he stood, he folded his arms across his chest. 'Now, you'd best git. I can hear sirens coming.'

On the landing, Dom couldn't hear much above the roar of the storm outside. Maybe Villere's ears were sharper than his. Temperance had taken Villere's word for it, and had already begun a quick descent of the stairs. He held Villere's gaze a moment longer, feigning unconcern of the imminent arrival of the police or of their promised rematch, then he backed away slowly, turned and went down. He found his pistol at the foot of the stairs – Temperance had deliberately left it for him to discover – and he gathered it up.

The rain assaulted him the instant he was outside. Bent over, pelting raindrops bouncing off his shaved head, he ran for where they'd left the van. Temperance was already in the driver's seat when he dragged open the passenger door.

'Come on,' she urged, 'we've no time to spare.'

'Haven't we?' The wind keened and thunder rolled, but he still didn't get any hint of a police siren.

'I'd rather not risk it. Get in, or you're walking home.' Temperance started the engine and was reversing out across the railway tracks before he was settled in the seat. As they peeled away towards the underpass, Dom strained for a look back over his shoulder at the apartment building, before switching his view to the side mirror. Nicolas Villere had followed them outside to check they left.

'See you soon, asshole,' Dom muttered.

Shrouded by the pouring rain, the tall southerner watched them go. He appeared unmoved by Dom's promise.

NINETEEN

'Who do you think you are, just barging into my place like this?' Tess didn't answer the girl's pointless question. Maddie's face was bleached of color, and there was hardly any strength behind her anger. Really she was in shock, and her brain overwhelmed by what had just occurred. Faced by two separate parties of invaders it was possible she illogically saw them as the same problem. There was more to her rant too; even bewildered, it hadn't escaped her that Tess was on the side of the law and her scheme was in peril of discovery. She tried to pull away from her dad, to go and close the door to her home office.

Pinky got in her way. 'Stop being so ungrateful, you. If we hadn't intervened, who knows what might've happened. Those two weren't playing around here.'

'Nothing would have happened. They were about to leave.'

Pinky rolled down an eyelid. 'You see any green in here, girl?'

She pulled a face at him, not quite understanding his meaning.

'I didn't just fall off a coconut tree,' Pinky went on. 'In other words, I'm not naïve, me. Those computers in there, you've got something illegal going on with them, right, some sort of flim-flam scheme? Which makes you feel like badass criminals. But you're really amateurs, you're the ones who are cabbage green, and you just got visited by *genuine* badass criminals, you. Take a hint from your dad, girl, does he look upset that we intervened when we did?'

Mike Toner required stitches. Blood painted an expanding Rorschach design on the front of his sweater where he kept wiping his hands. He was as shocked as his daughter, but also relieved that no further harm had been done. Across the room Hayley and Jacob were struck dumb.

'Make yourself useful,' Tess snapped at Hayley. 'Go and fetch a wet cloth for Mr Toner. See if you can find something to use as a dressing while you're at it.'

Aghast at the instruction, Hayley shook her head. She apparently viewed herself as a strong, empowered young woman: but her strength trickled from her in the face of so much blood. Her face drained of all color and she verged on falling over. Jacob grabbed at her, steered her around the couch so he could sit her down. Hayley flopped her head between her knees. Tess exhaled in frustration. 'Make sure she's OK,' she told Jacob, then scanned the room for something to use. Another open door led to a kitchen.

She checked that Pinky had the Toners under his control, then moved quickly for the kitchen. Apparently Maddie wasn't much of a homemaker; the kitchen was almost pristine. She dug in drawers and cupboards and found a stack of brand-new tea towels tied in a ribbon. One of them she ran under a faucet, the others she kept dry. She returned to the sitting room, and found the tableau slightly altered.

Hayley was bent over a wastebasket, throwing up, while Jacob fluttered over her . . . if her hair was longer he would have been holding it back as she heaved and spluttered. Mike Toner was still where he'd practically collapsed on the chair but Maddie and Pinky contested over the open door to the office. Maddie was frustrated by Pinky's size; he almost filled the doorway, and she called him a few unkind names. Pinky had heard much worse.

Tess handed over the wet towel to Toner. 'Clean yourself up,' she advised, 'then use one of the dry towels to apply pressure to the cut.'

'Yeah, yeah, I know all about it.' This was the second time Toner had been beaten that day. He'd already made an attempt at cleaning up after his first assault and had changed into fresh jeans. These were now darkened with splotches of his blood.

She left him to it, and approached Maddie. She glanced at Hayley, who was pitifully vomiting still, and caught a look of abstract dismay from Jacob. From his expression he'd fallen into trouble way beyond his expectation and was desperate for a way out.

'The best thing for you two is to get yourselves home to Portland,' she said.

Jacob nodded in agreement. Hayley gurgled and spat, then made a noise of misery that echoed from the wastebasket.

Maddie again tried to force past Pinky, and he merely used his left hip to block her. He was careful about avoiding laying hands on the young woman. Tess wasn't similarly concerned. She grabbed Maddie's arm and pulled her away. Maddie rounded on her, but she saw Tess wasn't in a mood for any more dramatics.

'What is it you don't want us to see in there?' Tess demanded.

'It's none of your business. You just saved us, thanks for that, but you can leave now. Go on. Get out or I'll . . .' Maddie shut up, while she winced furtively towards the hall. Fearfully she glanced over at her dad.

'The police aren't coming,' Tess assured her. 'That was a bluff to get those thugs out of here. But if you prefer, I'll call the police. Let's get them here and we'll tell them you are being extorted by threats and violence to hand over half your takings from your business. Pinky and I are your independent witnesses. The police will have to take your complaint seriously. Of course, they'll also want to know what you've got going on here that makes you a target of those criminals.'

Maddie shook her head in denial. She was not about to spill the details of her scheme. Behind her Pinky had entered the home office, but he only offered Tess a blank expression and shake of his head. Whatever Maddie and her dad were up to, it was a computer-based scheme, and Maddie would be the last person to log on and show them.

'Whatever it is you're up to, you should stop it now,' Tess said.

Maddie snorted.

'It's *wrong*,' Tess stressed. 'In the beginning you probably thought it was easy money. Now you know otherwise. There's no such thing when it's through criminal gain. Somebody always gets hurt.' She drew Maddie's attention to her dad. 'Is it really worth it, Maddie? What about next time when we aren't around to help; will you still think you're onto a good thing when it's you who is scarred for life, or worse?'

'It won't come to that.'

'It could. You have absolutely no control over the matter now. When they return to shake you down again, do you think they're going to be gentle with you . . . after they were made to run away this time?'

In denial, Maddie turned her back and spotted Pinky in her office. 'Hey! Get out of there.'

Pinky complied. There was nothing obvious to see. Maddie pulled the door shut with a resounding bang. She folded her arms and set her face in concrete. Tess turned from her to regard Hayley and Jacob. Red-eyed and miserable, Hayley was again seated on the settee, Jacob's arm around her shoulders. Tess said, 'There's no need for either of you to get further wrapped up in this. Hayley, your best move is to go home. Speak with your mom and straighten out your differences. Stay here and you'll get in too deep. Next time, it could be you who's the target of violence. Such a shame, considering Maddie doesn't care one bit about you. She claims she's your friend, but look at her. All she's interested in is protecting her cash cow.'

'That's a lie!' Maddie snapped.

Hayley gave her friend a pathetic shake of her head. Jacob whispered to her, urging her to listen to Tess.

'I gave you somewhere to stay,' Maddie reminded her. 'I took you in. I've—'

'I . . . I want to go home,' Hayley croaked.

'No. You agreed to help me with—'

'Maddie?' Hayley's voice was a high-pitched plea. 'Tess is right. Those people will be back. Don't you get it? They'll hurt you and for what? So you can hand them half of everything? If you're not hurt you could still go to prison!'

Gawping at her friend, Maddie took a couple of stumbling steps backwards. She threw up her arms to halt Hayley. 'Shut up! Goddamnit, shut up, Hales! In fact, no! Why don't you just blab everything to everyone? Go on. Abandon me when I need you, and while you're at it, make sure I go to jail. It wasn't like that when I—'

'Maddie!' Mike Toner's shout was unexpected, so held more force. He'd pushed up out of the chair, a wadded towel scrunched to his face. He strained forward to add to the impact of his warning. 'You've said enough. Get ahold of yourself and think about things before opening your mouth again. If Hayley wants to go home, *she should.*'

Too incensed to listen though, Maddie continued to bluster and squawk about betrayal of friendship. Her father dropped the bloody towel and grabbed her by both biceps. He shook her, his face close enough that the open wound was directly in her sight. 'Everyone should go back to Portland,' he said, emphasizing his point, 'before those assholes come back.'

His message held double meaning, and finally Maddie got the subtext. She nodded dumbly, then turned to throw a harsh slash of her arm in Hayley's direction. 'Yeah, you should leave. Go home, Hales. Just don't say one word about what I had you doing here.'

'I won't. I promise, Maddie. I'm sorry . . . I hope this isn't an end to our friendship?'

Maddie exhaled sharply and went to her dad. He wrapped a supportive arm around her.

Crestfallen, still shaky and nauseous, Hayley muttered something unintelligible to Tess for Jacob's ears only. He supported her as he steered her towards the hall. They came to a dead stop, Hayley croaking in fright.

It was only Po.

He blocked the doorway from the landing. He looked beyond the youths, seeking Tess. She moved so he could see her, raising her fingers and directing him to stall Hayley and Jacob for a minute.

'Those punks have left in the van,' he called to her. 'I ensured they'll think twice about coming back.'

She nodded, but returned her attention to the Toners. 'We came here looking for Hayley, to get her to go home, and we've done that. If you want, we can help you get out of this mess, but that means you both stopping whatever the hell it is you're up to.'

'We don't want your help.' Maddie pouted. 'Just go.'

Mike Toner though wasn't as certain. 'I don't see how we can give up. Not without attracting worse trouble.'

'Believe me,' Tess warned, with a knowing nod towards Maddie's home office, 'continue down whatever path you're on and it is guaranteed to get rockier. You've got some scam or another on the go. I haven't figured it out yet, and am not sure I really want to know. But it's drawing good cash, otherwise you wouldn't be worth extorting for half of it. You're the parent here and should know better: end it now, Mr Toner, and we'll ensure those people don't trouble you again.'

Toner checked with Maddie, who aimed a sour expression at him. He shrugged at Tess. 'I can't promise anything, but look, once you're out of here I will speak with my daughter and decide what we're going to do next. If things look as if they're getting out of hand, well I'll be in touch.'

'Let's hope,' said Tess gravely, 'that by then it isn't too late for us to help.'

TWENTY

The driving conditions were atrocious, but it had been decided that it would be safer if Hayley and Jacob were returned home to Portland, rather than them having another encounter with the people threatening the Toners. Tess wanted Hayley to travel back in the Mustang with them, but the girl refused, demanding that Jacob be allowed to take her back or not at all. The ulterior motive of Tess's plan was to learn more about what Maddie was up to, because she had more than a feeling in her bones that Mike Toner would be calling for help sooner rather than later. Also, she'd have liked to have spoken with Hayley about her adoptive mom, and further smoothen the way to reuniting them. Hayley, for all it had been made out to Tess was supposedly a bad influence, was in reality as much a pawn of Maddie Toner as Jacob was of his girlfriend. She seriously doubted if Maddie hadn't coaxed her away with promises of easy money, then Hayley's reaction to learning the truth of her adoption wouldn't have been half as dramatic. It was unlikely that Hayley would have left home, and there wouldn't have been any need for Tess to seek her out.

Tess should be happy with the end result. Hayley was going home. She'd more than achieved her end of the bargain agreed with Jessie Cameron, so didn't feel guilt at taking her payment now. It should be a satisfying ending to an otherwise frustrating day, but Tess couldn't help feeling that she'd abandoned those truly in need of her when she left Maddie's apartment. Maddie was too mixed-up to think straight: she was reacting to powerful stimuli – fear, anger, confusion, desperation, greed – each of them vying for dominance, and lashing out in response. Pinky was correct when calling her an amateur criminal, and Tess was even struggling to think of her in those terms. In her opinion, Maddie was like many people who stepped over a line by making a wrong decision, who then found it difficult finding a way back to the straight and narrow. Sometimes a mistake, a slip-up, was enough for an otherwise lawful person to be drawn into the murky word of criminality, after which they next engineered the accident to work in their favor. Soon their transgressions became their norm, and often where cash was concerned, the extra reward their misdeeds brought them became their norm too, and soon after not enough. Greed, avarice and need took over then, and usually it was too late to return to their previous lives because how would they then maintain what they'd grown used to?

Maddie had embroiled her father in her 'get rich scheme', and apparently she'd worked on Hayley to get her on board too, and it was an easy bet that Jacob would've been next to be recruited if Tess hadn't intervened that evening. Maddie was the brains behind the scam, and had likely by now grown used to the extra money and feared giving it up, but hopefully she wasn't beyond redemption yet. Alas, dangerous people had decided she'd now work for them, and once a person fell into that depth of criminality there was rarely a safe way out. Maddie was a defenseless young woman being terrorized, and driving away and leaving her to her fate left Tess feeling nauseous.

Tess asked to travel to Portland in Jacob's Chrysler, but Hayley resisted the idea, so she was again relegated to the back seat of Po's car. It was decided that Jacob should take the lead and Po follow – whether Hayley liked the idea or not – and that Jacob should return directly to Jessie Cameron's house. The storm had passed over Bangor by the time they reached the city limits, but it trailed heavy showers and blustery winds. There was fallen detritus on the roads and the pavement was slick with run-off, and here and there large puddles were traps for the unwary. Jacob drove with the trepidation of inexperience, and the journey took the best part of an hour longer than on the drive up. At no time did Po show any impatience at being forced to crawl along behind the old Chrysler. He and Pinky joked and bantered, told silly stories, and gave Tess time to brood in the back. She really would have liked to have been a fly on the windshield of the Chrysler, and eavesdropped Hayley and Jacob's discussion on the road home, but had to make do with her lot. Reuniting Hayley with her mom was the main thing, she reminded herself, though she knew she'd never be satisfied with that.

Before arriving in her neighborhood, Tess called Jessie's

cellphone and warned her of Hayley's imminent return. Jessie almost went into a state of panic, before devolving into floods of tears. Thankfully her tears were of relief, so Tess doubted there'd be a show of recrimination once Hayley was back in the family fold: she didn't want to deliver Hayley home only for mother and daughter to fight, and the girl to run away again. She had Po flash his headlights, attracting Jacob's attention. Po powered down his window and waved the youth over to the side of the road. Once the two cars were stationary Tess got out and approached Jacob's side. Jacob wound down his window, looked up at her with moon-sized eyes, perhaps expecting another berating. Tess could sense the overheated atmosphere inside the car, and supposed Jacob had been on the receiving end of Hayley's unfair woes most of the drive back from Bangor, and that illogically he'd been deemed responsible for most of them.

'I just wanted to check that we are all still on the same page here,' Tess explained to him. 'Let's not have any childish games and try to lose us once we're nearing Hayley's house, eh? Po won't put up with any nonsense, OK? He'll catch you and force you to stop if it comes to it.'

'I promise it never crossed my mind,' he said, meaning Hayley had been working on him to do just that. That he'd refused earned kudos from Tess, and probably ire from Hayley.

Ignoring the boy, Tess ducked lower so she could see Hayley.

'You'll be feeling nervous and ashamed right about now, and understandably so. You've put your mom through a lot of need-less worry and heartache these last few days. But believe me, Hayley, once she sees you, your mom will forget all about it and be only happy to have you home and safe again. Do me a favor, huh? When you see her, tell her you're sorry and give her a hug. From that moment on, I guarantee, things'll start getting better again.'

Hayley barely acknowledged her. She grunted noncommittally, then averted her gaze. Her reflection on the condensation-streaked window was unclear, but Tess saw her mouth writhing as Hayley muttered under her breath.

'Give her a chance to explain,' Tess went on. 'You've made up your mind about her based upon the wrong emotions. Whatever you think about her she only has your best interests at heart. Your mom loves you, Hayley.'

Jacob reached across and squeezed Hayley's hand.

The girl drew away from him, pushing her fingers through her dyed hair. But Tess noted the lowering of her shoulders as some tension was released. Hayley finally returned her gaze. 'I'll hear her out. But if *Jeffrey* turns up expecting a happy reunion, I'm out of here and I won't be coming back.'

Tess thought of her earlier promise to Jeffrey Lorton about letting him know when she'd located Hayley. Waiting until tomorrow to inform him was soon enough and still fulfilled her promise. Hayley and Jessie could do without the added complication of the estranged father showing up while they were trying to reconcile their differences.

'There's plenty time to hear his side of things,' Tess assured her. 'By the sound of things he's back in Portland for the foreseeable future. Whether you want to reunite with him is totally down to you, Hayley. One baby step at a time, eh? Let's get you home to your mom first.'

Hayley nodded, still without conviction, but she was more open to the idea than before. Tess squeezed Jacob's shoulder, silent thanks for helping. 'Once we arrive, it's best you give them some space, OK?'

'Yeah,' he said. 'I'd best get my own ass home and face the music, too.'

'If those brothers of yours give you any trouble, warn them they'll have me to contend with.' She smiled, offered him a wink and showed her bunched knuckles. She was still unsure if he'd heard yet about the thumping she'd given Nathan.

She jogged back to the Mustang. Once she was inside, Po flashed his lights and Jacob set off.

Jessie was waiting on the front porch when Jacob drew his car to a halt and Po pulled in behind him. The woman, blonde and slim, was only in her early forties: the stress of the last few days had taken a heavy toll on her, mentally and physically. She looked aged by two decades, as she stood rocking side to side and hugging herself tightly. As the car stopped she dropped her hands and took a tentative step forward. Po got out, allowing Tess to join him on the sidewalk. She didn't approach Jessie, only met the woman's gaze and nodded in support. Jessie came down the steps and along the short path even as Hayley slunk out of the Chrysler. Head down, shoulders rounded, hugging her arms across her abdomen, Hayley went to meet her mother. Jessie couldn't contain her joy; she ran the last few steps and wrapped Hayley in her arms. She touched her hair – a recent change to Hayley's image – her cheeks, her chin, and then grabbed her in a full-blown embrace again.

Jacob watched open-mouthed from his car. Maybe he expected Hayley to look back at him, perhaps return for a parting kiss, but she didn't. Tess squeezed him a smile, then raised her chin in a gesture to head on home. He tapped the steering wheel a couple of times, then left without any fuss. By the time she checked again, Jessie had led Hayley back up the path and onto the porch. She invited Hayley to enter first through the open door, and Hayley did so without looking back. Tess was fine with her lack of gratitude; if it were to come it would be at a later date. Jessie did acknowledge her though, mouthing a silent thank you, and then miming calling her on her cell later.

'Another happy customer,' said Po. Tess had forgotten he was at her side. He touched her hand, and she accepted his fingers in hers. 'But you ain't happy, Tess.'

'Nope,' she said. It could've been taken as mockery of his dialect if she wasn't as sincere. 'What are we going to do, Po?'

'We can't help those who don't want helped.'

They dropped Pinky off at Cumberland Avenue, said their goodnights and returned to Po's ranch. Earlier, waiting on the roof of Maddie's building, Tess had desperately needed to urinate. The adrenaline flooding her body when she'd gone to confront the armed invaders had blocked all unnecessary bodily functions, but since then almost three hours had passed. By now she should have burst, but the desire to relieve herself had dissipated; she felt her bladder must have dried up along with the stone her heart had become at the thought of abandoning the Toners to their fate. She retired to bed, and when Po later joined her, he spooned her, pulling her close to his warmth, but she simply felt cold, and the sensation didn't leave her the entire restless night.

She wakened early, and took her coffee outside. She stood on the porch, the sound of the nearby rain-swollen Presumpscot

River somewhat deadened. The storm had passed for now, and the dawn sky was a pale blue sheet. It was calm, pretty, and the warmth of the rising sun was welcome where it caressed her face and hands. Yet she shivered. Her gaze was drawn to the northeast, towards Bangor, where she sensed another potentially violent storm was brewing.

TWENTY-ONE

An hour after dawn Po had rolled over, reaching an arm for Tess, but found the sheets cool. Her absence wasn't cause for alarm; she often rose early when something troubled her mind. He dressed in jeans and T-shirt and padded through the house barefooted. He found her on the swing seat on the porch. The sun cast warm tendrils of light under the porch roof, but it was still cool. Tess had pulled a woolen blanket about her shoulders, sitting there in her pajamas with her bare feet drawn up under her. An empty coffee mug was abandoned on the floor. Without a need for greetings, Po sat alongside her, the seat swaying gently until he planted his soles on the boards.

'You still haven't let it go,' he stated.

'I'm worried about Maddie and her dad,' she admitted.

'They're criminals. Why'd you care?'

He was being ironic. He was a convicted killer, and to others without the full details behind why he'd killed, he might be abhorred. Tess didn't judge him that way; she loved him for the man he was now, and knew his past crimes weren't the sum of his character. Until recently Pinky had traded in illegal firearms – and who knew what other kinds of contraband? His association with Tess and Po had led him to see the light and turn his back on his old ways, but even before his decision, Tess had known he was the best of men at heart. If she could see the truth in them, she could allow the Toners some leeway too.

'They're involved in some criminal act,' she agreed, 'but it doesn't make them bad people.'

'My opinion of Maddie is she's a spoiled brat used to gettin' her own way . . . her father should know better and tell her no now and again.'

'Mike Toner's out of his depth and has lost control, both of his daughter and of the people threatening him. You ask me, Maddie sold him on her get rich scheme the way she did with Hayley. He jumped in to help her, expecting easy money, without ever considering the consequences and now look where it has gotten them. Intervening the way we did might've saved them last night, and you forced those thugs to run with their tails between their legs, but there's no way they're going to let it rest. Dom and Temperance will be back, if they haven't already been. And if not them, others will be sent in their place. I overheard Dom mentioning a name: Kelly. From what I could make out, she's the boss and the one demanding half of Maddie's earnings. Maddie was adamant she'd give Kelly nothing. From the way Dom spoke of her, Kelly doesn't sound the type to let them off scot-free. If not Dom and Temperance, I've a horrible feeling that this Kelly might send somebody more persuasive to change Maddie's mind.'

'So what do you want to do, Tess? Wanna call the cops?'

'And tell them what? We've hardly any idea about what it is Maddie's doing.'

'We could go see Hayley or Jacob and squeeze them a little harder for answers.'

'Maybe with Jacob, but I'm a bit cautious about approaching Hayley too soon. She's mixed up at the moment, and I don't want to do anything that might threaten her reunion with her mom. Besides, what do we do with that knowledge? We find out what Maddie's up to, and we inform the cops? That'll come in time, but that only gets the girl in trouble and doesn't do a thing to stop Kelly. One thing I'm certain of, Maddie's a small fish, she's not the only one being coerced by Kelly, so who knows how many others need our help.'

'So you want to stop Kelly?'

'Ideally, yes,' Tess said, 'but I've no idea who she is or where to find her.'

'So we begin with her lackeys and let them lead us back to her.'

'It should be easy enough finding their whereabouts,' she supposed. 'There could be a few people called Dom living in Maine, but I doubt there are that many named Temperance. Shouldn't take me long to run her name through the system.'

'Or we can do something even quicker.' Without explaining, Po stood and held out his hands to her. She took them and allowed him to steady her as she alighted her unsteady perch. He led her

inside to where he'd hung his leather jacket to dry the night
before. He delved in a pocket and then turned and pressed a
wallet into her hand.

She didn't need enlightening, but Po felt an explanation was
due. Not so much why, but how, he'd appropriated Dom's wallet.
'I frisked him, but the punk was more interested in what I did
with his pistol than anythin' else. He watched me toss the emptied
gun down the stairs, and missed me pickpocketing that. I thought
it wise to get an ID on a guy I was makin' an enemy of.'

Tess's eyebrows arched as she bounced the wallet on her palm.
Po's act – an unlawful search and seizure – was in essence theft,
but so what? His criminal act was for the good. She flipped open
the wallet. One side held a couple hundred bucks worth of bills.
The opposite compartment held various bank and credit cards,
and also a driver's license. 'Dominick Burgess,' she read aloud
from the license, 'current address is in Brunswick, not in Bangor
like I expected.'

'Where he lives and where he works could be two entirely
different places,' Po suggested. 'But if you are right and his boss,
Kelly, has spread her net aways, there's no reason why she can't
be based in Brunswick and still have victims the length and
breadth of the state. Here's how to cross-check.' From memory
he recited the license plate number from Temperance's van. 'Run
her tags, if the van's registered to an address in Brunswick, it's
a fair bet it's our starting out point.'

She leaned and pecked him on the lips. 'I don't know about
that, Po. My first stop's a nice warm shower. I need to work this
cold out of my bones.'

'Want me to join you?' His turquoise eyes twinkled with
promise.

'Do that and we'll get nothing else done the rest of the
morning.' She turned him around and patted him playfully on
the rump. 'You go and get another coffee brewing and I'll be
back with you in no time.'

TWENTY-TWO

A rlen Sampson forced a smile and nod of greeting as he held open the car door for his employer. 'Welcome home, Blake,' he added as the older man extricated his bent frame from the back seat. Rather than in her van, Temperance had collected him from Brunswick Executive Airport for the short drive north of Bath to his home, a sprawling six-bedroom house overlooking the Kennebec River, in a more comfortable saloon car: Blake Ambrose wouldn't lower his standards by traveling in a workman's van. There was some grunting and mild cursing from Blake, and he clung to the frame of the door as he levered up. Sampson studiously avoided lending a hand, because from past experience he knew it was unwelcome. Blake's knees were shot, he was feeling the discomfort of being cooped up on a long-haul flight, and was probably fatigued, but he'd never admit his weaknesses to an underling.

Blake was approaching sixty years old, but could have passed for a decade older. His black thinning hair was scraped back severely from a bulging brow that was at odds with his thin, hooked nose. If he'd large eyes he'd resemble a baby owl, but his were small, recessed raisins. He wore a camel-colored woolen overcoat over a black suit and formal black shoes. Blake barely offered a sniff of acknowledgement to Sampson. Instead he bent down to give Temperance a curt reminder. 'I want to speak to you both. Find Dominick and I'll see you inside.'

Temperance stared dead ahead, hands gripping the steering wheel. 'Right away, Blake,' she replied.

Turning for the front of the house, Blake swept an arm against Sampson to clear his way. 'Fetch my bags,' he instructed.

Temperance popped the trunk and Sampson moved to obey. Kelly was over-exuberant, showing her husband how much she'd missed him. She clapped her hands in delight, squealed like a lovesick teenager and ran down the porch steps and threw herself at him. Her lies sickened Sampson and, judging by Blake's gruff

demand she 'give him a goddamn break,' he wasn't buying her
sincerity either. Unperturbed, because Blake was generally of a
gruff disposition, Kelly continued mooning over him, cajoling
him to return her kiss. Blake relented, but his kiss on her cheek
was perfunctory at best. He groaned as he mounted the porch
stairs. For the briefest moment, Kelly turned and shot Sampson
a conspiratorial look, before following her husband up the steps,
one hand at his lower back to steady him. He allowed her to
touch him, had it been anyone else he'd have slapped the hand
away with a curse.

Sampson grabbed Blake's luggage, one of which was a cumbersome suit bag. His case was heavy. He'd been in northern Europe
on business, and had packed accordingly for the winter weather.
Once Blake was inside the house, Sampson set down the suitcase
and regarded Temperance. Last night, he'd been with Kelly when
Dominick had telephoned with an update, so had heard how
everything had gone to hell at Madison Toner's apartment in
Bangor. 'I pity you both,' he said, without sincerity.

'You should worry about your own ass,' Temperance sneered.
'I saw that look Kelly just gave you; how long d'you think it's
gonna be before Blake recognizes what those sneaky looks mean?'

Sampson neglected to answer. He'd no argument.

'He might come across as a dull, miserable S.O.B., but don't
mistake that for stupidity, or a lack of interest. First thing he
asked when I picked him up was if you were still here with
Kelly.'

'What other option did I have when those were his orders?'

'You don't have to convince me, Arlen.' Temperance shifted
impatiently. 'I'd best get this parked and find where Dom's
gotten to.'

'He's inside already. I left him phoning the banks to cancel
his credit cards; how'd the idiot manage to mess up a simple job
and lose his wallet into the bargain?'

'I don't think he lost it. You hear about this guy, Nicolas
Villere? I think he stole it when he took Dom's gun.'

Sampson snorted. 'Yeah, how'd that happen? One guy with a
knife manages to chase both of you off . . . and Dom armed with
his pistol.'

Slipping her knife from its sheath, Temperance turned it so it caught the light. 'Come here, Arlen, and let me stick this in your ear. Let's see if you can draw your gun before I skewer your brain.'

Again he'd no argument, so he let the issue slide. 'Best get these inside.' He dragged up the case and slung the suit bag over his shoulder and headed for the porch. Temperance drove the saloon car into the four-car garage built cater-corner to the large house.

Entering the house, Sampson was faced by a central staircase to the bedrooms and equal number bathrooms. There were three bedrooms and en suites either side of the head of the stairs, a landing with balustrade forming the arms of a squared-off horse-shoe. A large picture window dominated at the top of the stairs, making use of the space to offer views over the Kennebec River. Ordinarily only Blake, Kelly and their elderly housekeeper, Marianne Perez, were allowed access to the rooms to the right, but last night Sampson had spent several uncomfortable hours in one of them. He tried to block the experience from memory as he struggled upward with the cases. At the top he stood the suitcase upright and folded the suit bag over it: Kelly could take them from there. By the time he was on his way back down, Temperance had entered the front door. Her normally dusky pallor had an insipid caste as she exchanged grimaces with him. She didn't relish her coming talk with Blake. She went to Sampson's right, towards the huge day room where Blake usually directed business. Sampson hadn't been likewise summoned, but he followed behind her. Dom had found his way to the room without her bidding. Blake and Kelly were also in attendance. He had doffed his outer coat and suit jacket, and had loosened his tie, or more likely Kelly had done the undressing for him. He was seated behind his desk, and Kelly stood, mouth pinched and arms folded below her breasts, as Temperance and Dom presented themselves before them. They looked like a pair of school kids sent for punishment from the principal. Sampson stood at the threshold, and when Blake didn't instruct him to leave, he crossed his arms and leaned nonchalantly against the doorframe.

He'd learned most of the details about the mess last night during an early morning call from Kelly, but Blake wanted finer detail. Temperance, being Dom's underling was largely ignored as Blake set his sour gaze on Dom. 'What possessed you to go through with your instructions, knowing full well there was interest in the Toners from a private investigator? Wasn't this investigator already on the scene when you arrived at the girl's apartment? You had Temperance identify her, and still knowing she was a PI, you went back. Do you think it wise drawing the attention of any investigator?'

'I was obeying your instructions,' Dom countered, unfazed by Blake's questions. 'I'm loyal to you Blake, and to Kelly, and wanted to do what you asked me to do. It turned out that the PI wasn't there for the Toners; she was only looking for one of Madison's friends . . . some kid called Hayley. By all appearances the PI had left the scene shortly after we first showed up, and I never expected her to come back. So rather than leave, I decided I should do what was asked of me, and go and demand an immediate payment. I also thought it important to remind Mike Toner what'd happen if he spoke about us to the cops, or to this Teresa Grey woman. I went in under cover of the storm, never expecting the PI and her guys to be waiting in ambush.' Dom swallowed, waiting for Blake to respond, but he didn't. Dom filled the aching silence with more excuses. 'I only wanted to make sure the money was transferred to your account last night. We got rumbled and had to run but we didn't leave entirely. We stayed nearby till we were certain the cops hadn't really been called. Grey and her men left, following Hayley and her boyfriend, and my bet is they went back to Portland where they belong. I think Mike Toner came good on his promise, right? He didn't tell the PI or the cops why we were there, and he paid up?'

'You're correct about the latter,' Kelly interjected. 'The money was transferred late yesterday evening. But we can't be certain about the former.'

'Mike Toner's one of only dozens of people we're squeezing,' Blake went on. 'Why? We've never had a mess like this one before, Dom. Is it because you're not normally the one in command of things? Last night's mess is partially my fault, I guess, because I entrusted Kelly's safety with Arlen. Had Arlen been with you I doubt we'd have this fall-out to clean up this morning. Am I a fool for trusting you to do things without Arlen's guidance?'

Dom squinted over his shoulder at Sampson, his mouth in a

tight grimace, as if Sampson were the one blowing his own trumpet and not Blake. Sampson stared back at him.

Blake's questions were rhetorical. Dom couldn't reply in the affirmative for fear of reprisal, but accepting Blake's words ensured he came across as inept. 'Like I said, Blake, I was doing my very best to follow your instructions, and Toner paid up. Without question you can trust me to do what you ask without Arlen looking over my shoulder.'

'There's no question about your loyalty, Dom.' For the briefest moment, Blake's gaze flicked to Sampson, almost as if he was judging if the same could be said of all his employees, but then his attention returned to Dom and his features grew rigid. 'There's no question about your goddamn stupidity either. Your fuck-up last night could draw unwanted attention to our operation; your fucking stupidity could bring us down. I hear Temperance encouraged caution, but you ignored her and you went back anyway. Of the two of you, Temperance seems to be the one with the wiser head. Maybe,' he wagged a finger between the two, 'the command structure between you is wrong. Maybe I should demote you to driver and make Temperance your superior? Would I still retain your loyalty if I made you bow and scrape to a woman of color, Dom?'

Sampson restrained a sharp laugh. To a misogynistic racist like Dominick Burgess demotion under Temperance would be the cruelest of punishments.

Dom sneered at the woman alongside him, as if she was the source of the idea. Temperance did her best to ignore the hatred radiating off him in almost palpable waves, but couldn't bear it long. She snapped a look at him, promising if he tried to hurt her – verbally or physically – he'd be sorry. Blake laughed nastily.

'No, I don't think my idea would work,' Blake said. 'But your stupidity can't go unpunished, Dom. I can't demote you, and I doubt that docking a fine from your pay would do much to learn you a lesson; it'd only heap misfortune on top of the cash you already lost when you lost your wallet. I think your punishment should be much sharper and swifter: Temperance, punch Dom as hard as you can.'

'Uh, say what?' said Dom. He glanced at Temperance, daring her to try it.

'Dominick, I've given this order. There shall be no reprisal toward Temperance from you; otherwise I'll take it as disloyalty towards me. Accept your punishment. Temperance?'

Dom's brow creased. His mouth fell open, but before he could mount an appeal, Temperance whipped around. Dom flinched in anticipation, his arms coming up to defend himself, but Temperance had foreseen his reaction. Her bunched knuckles drove deep between his legs. A gasp of agony sprayed saliva as Dom folded over her arm, and then he dropped to his knees and bellowed into the floor. Temperance stepped aside. Dom's face screwed in hatred as he peered up at her. A smile jumped on her lips. 'Nothing personal, I only followed orders, Dom,' she said.

'What a cheap shot!' Blake laughed. 'But I suppose I wasn't specific where you should punch him. Thank you, Temperance. Now help Dom up and take him out of here.' Any faux humor evident in Blake faded. 'Now I want a private word with Arlen.'

A tremor went through Sampson. It wasn't fear, more apprehension that his and Kelly's infidelity was about to be called out. But even in this he was torn; a tiny part of him wished that the secret did come out, because then he wouldn't be forced against his will to service Kelly's needs any longer. Of course, being a covetous man, Blake wouldn't see the fault as being Kelly's alone, and Sampson would be punished. A punch in the nuts from Temperance wouldn't be on the cards for him, and it certainly wouldn't be handed over to Dom to inflict punishment . . . guilty of adultery, Sampson could expect worse. Though Blake primarily employed Sampson, Dom and Temperance as the agents of his protection racket, he also had other assets on call, professionals whom Sampson wouldn't see coming but who would ensure his torture was brutal and prolonged.

He stepped forward to face Blake across the breadth of the desk, and avoided looking at Kelly. His reflection was cast back at him from the window behind Blake's hunched form. As he had yesterday in the washroom, Sampson met the eyes of the reflected man, and didn't recognize those peering back. Again he wished that the transgressions he was repeatedly forced into were the load that that stranger was forced to bear. He loved Caroline, betraying his wife tormented him worse than any of the acts of violence he was pushed into. But what choice did he have but to obey their demands when either Ambrose need only dangle Mary Rhodes over him?

'I was a little curt with you outside,' Blake surprised him by saying. 'I was annoyed with Dom and Temperance, and wanted to deal with them first. That's done with for now, so it's time I gave you my thanks, Arlen.'

Sampson was rocked perceptively on his heels. His eyebrows rose towards his hairline.

'My wife suffers a pathological fear of thunder and lightning.' Blake nodded at his own words, in reaction to Sampson's credulous blink. 'Isn't that right, Kelly?'

She neglected to reply. She only closed her eyes and shuddered.

'The same storm that grounded my flight would have terrified her had she been here alone. Thank you for seeing her safely home, Arlen, and for staying here overnight. I appreciate that in doing so your own wife was left alone, to endure the night without you. Perhaps Caroline doesn't fear storms the same as Kelly does, but it's still a measure of your loyalty that you answered my request over the needs of your own wife.'

His loyalty *was* to his wife! Sampson had only acquiesced to Blake's demands to protect Caroline. However, he knew when to keep his mouth shut, and to accept the misguided thanks.

Blake went on: 'Dom is useful to me when I require a blunt instrument, yet he lacks finesse. He is no leader, no tactician. I need someone I can trust to handle this problem for me. Mike Toner is obviously cowed into obedience, but the attendance of a private investigator at his daughter's home is worrying, regardless of why she was there. This girlfriend of the Toner girl, Hayley, isn't it? She was the one that the investigator was looking for; I want to know why, and if it relates in any way to what the Toners are doing for us now. Find out, Arlen, and if she knows anything, then dissuade her from talking, by any means necessary. If by chance you run across this Teresa Grey woman, then she should not be left in any position to interfere with our business either. Make them disappear, if you must, but in a way that does not lead back to us.'

TWENTY-THREE

Tess chose to conduct the hunt for Dominick Burgess and Temperance Jolie from Emma Clancy's office. There she had access to state, county and law enforcement databases, and in no time had confirmed current addresses for both. She threw their details through the systems to identify any known accomplices, cross-referencing names to discover commonality. Living in a small city like Brunswick they shared a number of acquaintances, but that was the nature of such places when everyone knew everyone else. None of the names thrown out related to a person named Kelly. She printed out a list of the most prominent names, with a mind to thin it down later. Next she accessed a restricted system through which she could delve deeper into both of their lives. She discovered how and when they paid their living expenses, their utilities bills, their taxes, and soon had access to their bank accounts and credit card records.

She discovered a common factor. Both were registered as self-employed chauffeurs, though lately they'd driven exclusively for a holdings company based up the coast in Brunswick. She checked out the company – BK-Rose Holdings LLC – and discovered that it existed to acquire, hold and sell various investments in other companies. Their portfolio included holdings throughout Maine and the wider US, and even in England and the Isle of Man, as diverse as retail companies, information technology developers and insurance providers. Tess knew that typically holding companies didn't engage directly in business or in the manufacturing of goods or delivery of services, but apparently BK-Rose also owned a subsidiary company which managed a rather extensive property portfolio. The company directors were listed as Blake and Kelly Ambrose. Online she found the company website, and on the 'About' page photographs of the couple striking imperious poses. Tess decided they were haughtier than anything.

She sat back, staring at Kelly Ambrose. Reddish curly-haired, pale skinned, and with her snub nose in the air, she looked as if she'd just smelled something disagreeable. Kelly's smile barely touched her lips, and might have been described as enigmatic, but Tess thought it was formed more in the secret knowledge that she herself was the source of the bad smell. She disliked the woman immediately.

The door swung open. Clutching a take-out coffee Emma Clancy paused at the threshold, surprised to find Tess behind her desk. Emma always presented a striking image: tall, sleek and athletic, she oozed an aura of power. Her hair and make-up were as immaculate as ever. By comparison, Tess often felt shabby in her presence. Emma looked haughty too; it took a moment before she cracked a smile. 'Tess, I didn't see you come in.'

'I've been here awhile. I'm just doing some background research.' Tess returned the smile. Emma employed her on a freelance basis to conduct investigations on behalf of her specialist inquiry firm. There was a time when her opinion of Clancy was on a level with that she had formed of Kelly Ambrose, but things had changed. The two had fought against the deranged killer Hector Suarez, each prepared to give their life for the other, and only partly because Emma was the girl-friend of Tess's brother Alex. Since then they'd become firm friends, sisters-in-waiting, and Tess got away with more than perhaps any employee should. There was nobody else in the firm that Emma wouldn't scold if she found them using her personal computer. Here she simply let the door close and popped the lid off her coffee.

'If I'd known you were working I'd've fetched you a cup,' she said.

Tess wasn't about to lie to her friend. 'My investigation isn't exactly on the books. More of a personal project.'

Emma moved in close. 'Do tell.'

The photographs of Blake and Kelly were still on-screen. It'd be rude to turn off the computer, and besides, Emma could easily enough check Tess's search history if she wished.

'He looks like a joyful fella. Not. He reminds me of someone . . .' Emma swirled a finger in the air to aid her memory. 'Oh, yeah, did you ever see that old Batman movie, the one with Danny DeVito as the Penguin?'

Tess chuckled. 'Now that you mention it, I see the resemblance.' She hadn't given the husband as much interest as she had Kelly.

'So what's your interest in him?'

Tess wagged a finger between both pictures. 'I stumbled into something last night and think these two could be behind some kind of blackmail and extortion racket.'

'Who are they?'

Tess related the brief details she'd been able to glean about the Ambrose couple, their holdings business and their connection to Dom and Temperance who she, Po and Pinky had chased off. She neglected to mention that the thugs had been armed and that they had previously beaten Mike Toner. For now she didn't wish to involve the police, whereas Emma was bound by duty to report any unlawful behavior.

'They run a successful holdings LLC with international clients,' Emma mused, 'but you think they're running a protection racket? I can only assume they aren't short of a cent or two. Why'd they risk extorting money out of this Toner fella if they already have a healthy income?'

'Greed is a great motivator,' Tess said. 'Besides, if they're blackmailing the Toners, it stands to reason there are other people they're similarly extorting.'

'Maybe it's something the two thugs have going, and it has nothing to do with BK-Rose.'

'I overheard the guy demand fifty percent on Kelly's behalf. That's Kelly.' She indicated the woman's photo.

'She's called Kelly, for sure, but are you certain she's the same Kelly the guy was talking about?'

'I'm reasonably certain.'

Emma didn't press the point. Tess's search had uncovered a name that matched, but there was nothing in her investigation yet to prove that it was the same Kelly Dominick had referred to, or that the director of the holding company was the one also directing a criminal enterprise. Tess understood caution, and wasn't about to rush off and confront the woman with an unfounded accusation. She needed something more concrete than this, but at least she'd a good starting point.

Emma was familiar enough with Tess to read her body language and facial micro-expressions. 'This isn't something you want to involve the police with yet?'

Holding up her palms, Tess said, 'Right now, there isn't anything I can give them. Unless Mike Toner's prepared to make a complaint to the cops there's not a lot I can offer at this stage. He and his daughter have made it clear they don't want me anywhere near them. I only came across them because I was following up on another case.'

'Did you find the Cameron girl?' Emma knew of Tess's latest case, though it had nothing to do with her office: just because she hadn't given Tess the job, it didn't mean she wasn't interested in other work her investigator took on. Emma had to be above reproach. Occasionally she had to distance herself from some of the private tasks that Tess undertook, particularly when Po and Pinky became involved. It was fair that Emma kept abreast of what Tess had going on, if only to protect the integrity of her firm.

'She's home again. I'm not sure how long that will last.'

'You found her at the Toner girl's apartment?' Emma nodded in understanding. She'd easily connected the fact that Hayley Cameron could be involved in similar trouble through her connection with Madison Toner, so to Tess her duty to the girl – and now her friend Maddie – was a long way from over with. 'Leave no one behind, huh? You know something, Tess? There are times when I wonder if you were a US Marine in a past life.'

Tess shrugged at the notion. As a sheriff's deputy she'd followed the same ethos.

'Do you want my *official* help with this?' Emma took a sip of her coffee while Tess considered her offer. She grimaced at its sweetness.

'I've some more groundwork to do before I can present any evidence to the police; maybe once it's done I'll have you check it over and see if it's something the DA might be prepared to act on.'

Emma's smile danced. She knew as well as Tess that, for now, Tess had no intention of involving any law enforcement agency. Tess felt responsible for those girls, and until she'd personally done something to help them she wouldn't hand over the responsibility to anyone else.

'I didn't notice Po's car out front,' Emma prompted. If he accompanied Tess to the office, he usually lounged out in the reception hallway, reading a dog-eared suspense or thriller novel, while she got on with her work. He'd become a semi-regular fixture, and also a signpost to Emma for when Tess was in the building.

'Oh, he has some stuff he needs to do,' Tess said. 'It's been a few days since he's been by either, so wanted to look in on Charley's and Bar-Lesque. He'll be along to pick me up shortly.'

In actuality, Po had gone to Charley's autoshop to swap out his Mustang for something less noticeable, and also large enough to accommodate Pinky so Tess could sit up front.

'You guys, you know, haven't come up with a date yet?' Emma's eyes twinkled, having deftly changed the subject to weddings.

'No more than you and Alex have,' Tess countered.

Emma rocked her head. Due to her public persona, she and Alex were allowing a respectable time delay since Emma's divorce to her previous husband, before tying the knot. Tess and Po weren't similarly constrained.

'You know Po,' Tess explained, with no real need to. 'He's so laid back he's almost horizontal. The same goes for our wedding plans; he's happy with the way things are between us and is in no rush to change things. The way he sees things we're already a couple and that's all that matters. If I'm lucky, I'll legally be Mrs Villere before I'm too old to remember my new name.'

'Give him a jab with something sharp,' Emma suggested, 'and remind him I've already picked out my hat and it's in danger of becoming unfashionable.'

They chuckled at the idea, while Tess vacated Emma's workplace. 'Is there anything you wanted me to do?' Tess asked; after all her job should take priority over her personal project.

'You can take this coffee with you, if you want.' Emma held out the steaming paper cup. It was her way of giving Tess her blessing to get on with her investigation into Blake and Kelly Ambrose.

Tess accepted the drink, said goodbye, and left Emma's office. She was encumbered with the cup, her handbag, tablet, and various sheaths of printed notes. In the outer office, she set down her things in order to take out her cellphone; she'd fully expected Po to return for her by now. Before she could ring him her phone tinkled with an incoming call.

She looked at the unfamiliar number on the screen, before it dawned who was calling.

Yesterday, she'd given out her cellphone number, and though he'd messaged her his contact details, she hadn't yet assigned Jeffrey Lorton as a contact. She cringed inwardly; she'd promised to inform Lorton once she'd found Hayley, and had forgotten what with everything else being on her mind.

She answered, but allowed him to speak first.

'Is this Teresa Grey?'

'It is. But please call me Tess.'

'Jeff Lorton.'

'Yes. Is there something the matter, Mr Lorton?'

'You could say that. It's Hayley. I know you took her home last night—'

'Yeah, about that,' Tess began, trying to concoct a satisfactory excuse for neglecting to inform him.

'It's not that. I understand you probably had a lot going on and I was the last person on your mind. No, the reason I'm calling is I've been by Jessie's house this morning and Hayley has gone.'

'Gone?'

'As in packed her bags this time and gone for good.'

Tess bit down on a curse. 'Did Jessie know where?'

'Wherever it was you found her last night. Apparently Hayley spent half the evening on the phone to her friend up in Bangor. When Jessie woke up this morning, Hayley had gone. She'd taken her clothes and things, and left a letter telling Jessie not to look for her. Jessie thinks she telephoned her boyfriend to come collect her. It's why Jessie didn't call you first thing, she thought it would be a waste of your time having you bring Hayley home again, only for her to run away at the first opportunity.' Lorton was silent for a few seconds, then got around to why he was really calling. 'I know you're done with this job now, but I just wondered if you'd do me one thing . . .'

'What's that, Mr Lorton?'

'Can you please give me the address of Hayley's friend? Maybe

I can go up there and talk some sense into her, get her to come home.'

'I'm sorry,' said Tess. 'It isn't something I can do. Please, Mr Lorton, the best thing to do right now is to leave Hayley be, allow her to think, and she'll see the error of her ways and come home. If you go up to Bangor, she'll feel as if you're invading her bolthole, and she'll resist all the more.'

'But, Tess, I can't help feeling that I'm the cause of her falling out with Jessie. If I can only explain, then maybe it'll smoothen things between them and—'

'I understand,' said Tess, 'but, I'm sorry, the answer's still no.'

He was about to plead, and Tess didn't want to hear him beg. She didn't wish to alarm him, but the last place she wanted Jeff Lorton going was to Madison Toner's apartment. There were already too many people at risk simply by being there, and it'd only make matters worse if Lorton stumbled into the sights of Dominick or Temperance. Tess ended the call.

Her phone began ringing seconds later. She declined to answer. It rang again, but this time Po's name was displayed.

'Hey,' she said by way of greeting. 'Did you get a car? Great, how soon can you pick me up?'

'Just pullin' up outside the office,' he said. Po had a habit of disregarding the parking restrictions outside the civil building Emma's office was housed in. 'D'you want me to come inside, or are you gonna run out?'

'I'll run out,' she said. 'Literally. We need to get on the road, Po.'

TWENTY-FOUR

'**P**ull over here and I'll walk across.' Arlen Sampson indicated the parking lot adjacent to the underpass of the river bridge.

Temperance swung the van into the lot, and maneuvered it under the overhanging boughs of the trees at its edge. Dappled shadows concealed the van from all but the closest scrutiny. By chance she'd parked in the same spot as Po Villere had the afternoon previously when Tess Grey had first arrived at Madison Toner's apartment.

'Wait here, I won't be long,' Sampson instructed.

Temperance said nothing. She sat expelling sharp spurts of air between her clenched teeth.

Sampson had deliberately come back to speak to the Toners without Dominick. As Blake had pointed out, Dom was useful when a blunt instrument was required, but Sampson needed finesse if he hoped to control the damage already done by the aggressive thug. He hadn't trusted to bring Dom along one bit; leaving him in the van with Temperance he'd probably return to find them locked in a death grip with their hands around each other's throats. Blake might have given the order, but Temperance had taken too much pleasure in carrying it out, and Dom was not the forgiving type. She'd pay for punching him in the nuts, but not without retaliation. Sampson could've driven here alone, but had thought it best to get the woman out of Dom's reach. She understood his motive, though it aggrieved her, because avoiding a showdown with Dom, or any bully of a man, simply wasn't in her nature.

Sampson got out of the van and surveyed the metal fabricator's workshop across the railway line. His gaze tracked from the converted loft on the uppermost floor to the roller-shuttered garages at ground level. A dated model Chrysler was parked with its hood nosing the leftmost shutter. According to the events related about last night, the PI crew had escorted the youths back to Portland but obviously Madison's friends had returned. Unsurprising to Sampson. During Mike Toner's conditioning session yesterday, he'd admitted that his daughter was the brain behind the scam, and that he and one of Maddie's friends had been recruited to assist her with the mechanics of it. Toner, again admittedly, was engaged to do the scut work, while the girlfriend was involved in the social media campaigns designed to draw in the gullible so that Maddie could fleece them of their cash. Without the involvement of the friend, a cog was missing from their otherwise well-oiled machine. Her boyfriend was a loose end that required clipping.

Purposefully, Sampson kept his head down as he paced across the road. If anyone was spying on him from the apartment, he didn't wish to alarm them. He paused to check the railway line. It was single gauge and rarely used, but he'd no wish of being flattened by a train. He stepped over the tracks and went left, towards a dilapidated garden. As he rounded the corner of the building, he came across a youth hunkered on the raised edging stones around the garden's single tree. The youth was engaged in his passion for nicotine, blowing smoke between his bent knees – he was a fraction slow to hear Sampson's approach and the bigger man was almost upon him before his head jerked up. The youth's mouth fell open as he reared back.

'Steady on, son,' Sampson said, patting the air between them. 'You don't have to get up. Finish having your smoke.'

His words had the effect of the youth glancing away from Sampson at the half-smoked cigarette between his fingers. Perhaps he'd expected the return of Dom, so Sampson's appearance disarmed him. However the youth wasn't stupid, he knew what Sampson signified; he was only unsure of what kind of trouble the stranger brought. He dropped the cigarette, stood and ground it out under his sneakers. His nose was only level with Sampson's collar, and he was outweighed by around thirty pounds, yet he squared up, hands tightening into fists. 'Who are you and what do you want here?' The youth jutted his chin menacingly.

Unperturbed by the show of bravado, Sampson looked to where the youth had propped the entrance door open. 'I've business with Mike Toner,' said Sampson. 'If all goes well, there should be zero trouble from now on.'

'So you're with those assholes that burst in last night and threatened Maddie's dad?'

Sampson held out his arms from his sides, allowing his unzipped jacket to flare open. He'd done away with his shoulder holster: it was to show he was unarmed – which he wasn't – but the youth barely took any notice. 'I'm not here for trouble, only business.'

'What type of business?'

'Nothing to concern you, son.' Sampson turned for the entrance, even as the youth skipped past to block his passage. Sampson halted. 'Look, go take another smoke, or go get in your car and take a slow drive. The less involvement you have in this the better for you.'

'My girl's up there, if you threaten her I swear—'

'Don't make threats you can't carry through. Trust me, anything I swear I'll do, I will do. Now go, stay out of this, because you're not helping. I'm only here to make things better.'

'Say's you, man. You still haven't told me who you are.'

'I'm the carrot, son,' said Sampson, and knew from the dumb lack of comprehension he didn't get the analogy of Dom being the stick. 'If you're not going to get out of my way, fine, I don't need to go inside. But do me the favor of going up and letting Mike know I'm here. We can speak privately out here if he prefers.'

Shooting out his palm the youth said, 'Wait here. I'll go tell him.'

Sampson was under no illusion. Once the kid ran upstairs he'd probably suggest that they barricade the door and ignore him until he was forced to leave.

'I'll be right here,' Sampson confirmed.

The youth nodded and turned for the open door. Sampson's footsteps were silent on the pavement. He slapped a palm over the youth's mouth, and bore him into the entrance foyer by force of their forward momentum. It was an unadorned space, blank walls and blind closed doors leading to the twin parking garages. Sampson thrust his captive flat against the wall between the two doors, even as he slipped his opposite arm around his throat. As he cinched his hold tight, he moved his smothering hand to brace his other arm. There was no opportunity to shout, the youth's larynx was already under tremendous pressure and all that escaped him was a panic-stricken wheeze. Sampson readjusted his hold and continued to constrict the captured neck until the youth buckled at the knees, unconscious. Sampson held the stranglehold for a few seconds more, and then lowered the youth to the floor. The strangle had attacked the blood supply to the youth's brain, depriving it of oxygen; as soon as the flow returned the youth would begin to recover. He wouldn't be out for long, but it would take him longer to return to his full faculties, and come up with a considered response.

By then, it wouldn't matter. Sampson left him there and mounted the stairs, taking them three at a time. He was at the uppermost landing before he heard the faint hints of the youth regaining consciousness: it was in the form of a startled bleat, and the scuff of clothing on the floor. The kid still wouldn't know up from down for a few seconds more. The door to Maddie's apartment was on an open latch. Sampson pushed inside. He was halfway down the narrow hall, guided by conversation in the room ahead before a warning shout came from two flights below. The shout brought the conversation to a hushed halt, and three startled gazes met Sampson as he entered the room. He was a stranger to both girls, but Mike Toner visibly deflated before him.

'What are you doing here?' Toner croaked.

Sampson offered an apologetic shrug, aimed a finger back along the hall. 'I would've knocked, but the door was already open.'

Madison Toner started forward, but her father's palm met her abdomen. He guided her behind him, facing Sampson. The man wore an ugly wound on his cheek, and his nose was swollen across the bridge, wounds courtesy of Dom the evening before.

'Why are you here, Arlen? We've done everything we were told to do.'

'I hoped to make some kind of amends. Dom was out of order last night.' Sampson gestured towards Toner's injury. 'That was unnecessary. He was only meant to request payment, to show your good faith, not to beat it out of you.'

Toner touched his face, wincing at the memory more than the pain. 'He goddamn pistol-whipped me!'

His statement wasn't entirely true, as Dom had clubbed him with the butt, but Sampson wasn't about to argue semantics. 'It was unnecessary and uncalled for. You recall how adamant Kelly was that proper respect is adhered to in our relationship? Dom doesn't understand that respect should be earned, not enforced. Sometimes he acts before thinking, and that can mean he can be spontaneously violent. It's not the way I prefer to conduct business.'

Just then, the youth clattered down the hall, red-faced and wild-eyed. He almost fell into the room. Sampson turned sideways so he could see all parties. The youth faced him, breathing raggedly, then his gaze darted to check on his girlfriend. Since he'd entered the room, the purple-haired girl had stood statue-like, one hand fisted at the hollow of her throat. The youth pointed a trembling hand at Sampson. 'I tried to stop him . . . *he fucking choked me out!*'

Toner's back straightened an inch or two. He wasn't the most aggressive man, but neither was he the type to let a kid being harmed go unchallenged. His attitude earned him some credit from Sampson. 'So violence isn't your thing, eh, Arlen? What about choking Jacob, is that the way you prefer to conduct business?'

Sampson observed Jacob for a few seconds. He was red-faced and slightly disheveled but otherwise looked fine. 'Are you injured, Jacob?' he asked directly.

'You choked me!'

'I strangled you. There's a difference. If I'd fully choked you, crushing your windpipe, I seriously doubt you'd be standing here right now. If by chance you survived a choking, I'd say you would be in considerable pain and discomfort, and have difficulty complaining about your perceived mistreatment. How do you feel, Jacob?'

Other than being mildly wobbly on his feet – as much a result of shame, as it was any lingering effect of his strangulation – Jacob was unhurt. Sampson had attacked the sides of Jacob's neck, closing down the arterial feed to his brain until he'd blacked out. If he'd continued to squeeze, the boy would've eventually perished, but Sampson had taken care. Jacob would suffer no detrimental harm whatsoever.

'I'm . . . uh . . .' Jacob's accusatory finger lifted again, but he'd no energy to argue. His hand went to his face, and he rubbed at his forehead as he tried to collect his thoughts.

'I strangled you unconscious so that I didn't need to physically hurt you,' Sampson went on. 'Sadly, it was all I could do in the moment to stop you from running up here and slamming the door.' He returned his attention to Toner. 'I wished to speak with you calmly, without any histrionics, and, as I said earlier, hoped to make amends.'

'What kind of amends?'

'For starters, there's the matter of reimbursing you.' Sampson looked directly at Madison for his next announcement. 'If you check your account, you'll see that the cash you transferred last night has been fully refunded to you.'

A moment of confusion followed, where father and daughter talked hurriedly between them, a note of confusion overriding everything. Sampson caught a number of glances aimed at him. A furrow so deep had formed between Madison's eyebrows it had to be painful.

'Check if you wish,' Sampson told her. 'I'm happy to wait until you confirm it.'

More rapid-fire words were exchanged, then Toner urged Madison towards the home office. Jacob took his opportunity to slip across the room and join Hayley. They too exchanged words, and Sampson noted that any concern for welfare went only one direction: that girl wasn't as invested in Jacob as he was in her, Sampson deduced.

Toner shook his head. 'What's this all about, Arlen? I don't get it. Why have Dom demand the money and then give it back?'

'Like I already mentioned, it was supposed to be a show of good faith. To ensure we all knew where we stood in our arrangement. Mutual understanding breeds mutual respect, yes?'

Toner didn't know how to answer. He nodded simply by rote.

'Good. I'm glad we've cleared things up. Or we will as soon as Madison confirms the money's back in her account.' Sampson raised his voice. 'How're things going in there?'

Madison didn't reply. The sounds of her fingers on a keyboard indicated she was still in the process of checking. Sampson stood silently, waiting. He caught a glimpse from Toner and offered a supportive smile. Toner only appeared dumbfounded by the unexpected turn of events.

'I don't expect us to be friends,' Sampson said, 'but in future we can be civil with each other, right? There's no need for further animosity. I understand how you and Madison must feel, having to hand over half of what you believe is rightfully yours, but it has to be better keeping half than none at all?'

'I guess, when the alternative's being closed down, and having nothing.' Toner replied as if in agreement, but Sampson knew there were words unsaid: being closed down meant permanently, and that meant killed. For all Sampson had presented a more agreeable approach, it wasn't lost on Toner that it was a front adopted by the man, and events could turn horrible again if he stepped out of line.

Coming out of the home office, Madison's demeanor had altered. Gone was the deep furrow between her eyebrows, her features had smoothened into a mask of disbelief. She blinked at her dad. 'It's back,' she confirmed. 'All of it.'

Sampson spread his hands, smiling amiably. 'As I promised it was. That isn't to say that your next payment isn't due in line with the original agreed timetable. Between now and then, Kelly expects you to have raised considerably more funds. Now,' Sampson regarded the elephants in the room, causing Hayley and Jacob to stare back at him in miscomprehension, 'how are we going to handle the unfortunate situation that has arisen? Namely, that your presence here has attracted the attention of a private investigator.'

The couple glanced at each other. Jacob was quivering, his emotions a mess. Surprisingly to Sampson, the girl snapped at him. 'I told you that you didn't have to stay. You can go home now. I won't be going back with you.'

'Hayley, I know but—'

Hayley ignored him. She met Sampson's gaze, and in hers was the red of outrage. 'The private investigator won't be back. She did her job and now I've got nothing to do with her. I made it clear to my mom I won't be going back to Portland, and I told her not to look for me again.'

Sampson nodded at her assertion, although he wasn't as sure as she was.

'I'm telling you,' Hayley said stridently, 'Tess won't be looking for me again. Why would she if she isn't being paid? And before you ask, the answer's *no*. She has no idea about Maddie's insurance scam, I didn't mention it, she never asked me about it, so you don't have to worry about her informing the cops on us.'

For a few seconds Sampson ruminated. Hayley was possibly right, without a paying client, the investigator would most likely move on. Her curiosity might've been piqued by the goings on in Bangor, but there was no profit in digging around further. Knowing full well how the world worked, Sampson decided Tess Grey required remuneration for her time and energy and with nobody behind her with an open cheque book, she'd have to seek work elsewhere. Last night Tess told Dom and Temperance she'd called the police; she hadn't, it was a bluff. Ergo, with no evidence to offer them, it was unlikely she'd contacted them since, or would do so in the future. Sampson turned his scrutiny on Jacob.

'I know Hayley plays an integral part in the scam,' he said, 'but what good do you do?'

'Uh, I . . .' Jacob looked to Hayley, then at the Toners for support, but nobody came to his defense.

'Other than having a crush on Hayley, and being a handy taxi driver when she needs one, I don't see your worth to the operation, son. I mean, look at you, you aren't even handy to keep around as muscle. But still,' Sampson wagged a finger in the air, 'you've profited from the operation, at the risk of blowing it wide open.'

Jacob gawped, unclear of his meaning. Sampson was clear on how Maddie's scam worked. Hayley enticed their young victims through targeted advertisements on the social media platforms, drawing in young and inexperienced drivers with the promise of cut-rate insurance cover. Posing as a broker, Maddie blatantly ripped them off. She input the personal details of older, often but not exclusively female drivers, and an inexpensive vehicle, through various price comparison websites, applying for the one with the lowest tariff. Armed with a quote, she would then replace the bogus information with that of the victim and their car. Nine times out of ten the victim would be won over by the seemingly unbeatable quote and pay up for a year's cover, into one of several accounts unbeknown to them set up by Maddie.

Again with the bogus details, she would apply for the insurance cover, and once she was the recipient of it she'd manipulate the policy certificate and accompanying documents as she had before, and forward these to the happy customer. Shortly after, using the cooling off period offered by the insurance company, she'd cancel the policy, and the cash was refunded to her account. Unless an accident occurred, or the customer was stop-checked and investigated thoroughly by the police, the young drivers remained blissfully ignorant they'd no cover. It was, until now, a foolproof scheme that'd already netted Maddie several hundred thousand dollars. With Jacob, he'd been given friends' rates, where he'd gotten the cheap cover, but Maddie had not subsequently stolen his payment. Sampson doubted the boy knew his policy was worthless when it still existed under the bogus details of an elderly man. It confirmed to Sampson the boy's genuine value to the girls: beyond being Hayley's driver he too was worthless.

'You've got to go, son,' Sampson stated.

'Wha . . . whaddaya mean?' Again Jacob sought support from Hayley, but she turned from him and stood next to Maddie. Both girls eyed him coolly.

'Kid,' said Sampson, 'it's easier for me to see being an outsider, but you don't fit into this scenario. Hayley doesn't want you here, Maddie certainly doesn't. Best thing for you is to save some dignity and walk away under your own steam.'

'No, man! Hayley . . . tell him!'

'He's right,' Hayley replied with a look of disdain for Jacob. She clutched Maddie's offered hand in solidarity. 'It isn't working, Jakey. Truth is, it never did work. I already told you this when you drove me back here this morning. I said you were a friend, but that's all we could be.'

Jacob croaked out a string of pleas, in total denial. Sampson felt sorry for the guy, but he wouldn't let his own feelings get in the way of a result. 'Kid, do yourself a favor. Walk away.'

'No, I'm not going. Hayley . . . please, we can work this out!'

Sampson took a quick survey, and was rewarded by a trio of accepting nods.

'Get your stuff, Jacob. Leave on your own two feet. The alternative is I take you out when I leave.'

Jacob had heard enough. 'Fuck you! And fuck you, Hayley!

Everyone warned me what you were. But I wouldn't listen. I
thought you were better than this. Yeah, well, more fool me.' He
jabbed a finger at Maddie. 'You two are a good match; a pair of
goddamn manipulative bitches, but that's what will ruin you.
Don't come crying to me when you crash and burn, Hayley,
'cause I won't be there to pick you up again.'

Sampson was impressed. He nodded at the kid. 'Well done,
son. Now let's go.'

'Fuck you! Don't come near me. I'm going!' Jacob stormed
down the hall and out of the door. Curses filtered to them as he
descended the stairs. There was an air of relief between the girls
that Jacob was gone; perhaps he hadn't taken Hayley's word for
it before and she'd been longing for a situation like this to get
shot of him. Apparently Maddie had already urged her to send
him packing. Only Mike Toner looked sorry for the boy.

'Can we rely on him to keep quiet about what you're doing
here?' Sampson asked.

'He can't squeal to anyone without landing himself in trouble,'
Maddie said.

'True,' agreed Sampson, and turned to leave.

The problem was, scorned and embarrassed, Jacob might feel
that the price he'd pay for revenge was worth it.

TWENTY-FIVE

Tess didn't trust Jeff Lorton to heed her advice. He wished to explain, to make amends with his estranged daughter, and couldn't do so by staying out of sight and hearing. She hadn't given him Madison's address, but with barely any difficulty he'd likely acquire it from Jessie, and head on up to Bangor on a fool's errand of reconciliation. It was too soon for him to approach Hayley and try to convince her that he was not the deadbeat dad he'd been written off as, and that all would be perfect now that she'd heard the truth direct. She was too confused, too angry, too wrapped up in her own feelings than to give more than a second's passing notice to Jeff's. Showing up at Maddie's place, he would only worsen matters, especially if Hayley learned that Jessie was the one to have sent him. She'd feel doubly betrayed. The girl would most probably respond with a fit of anger and further rebellion directed at both parents.

Tess asked Po to take them back to Maddie's apartment, where they'd be in place to divert Lorton away when he inevitably arrived. Easier done was to contact the guy and talk him out of going through with his unhelpful plan, however each time Tess attempted to call him his cellphone went unanswered. Assuming he'd guessed her reason for phoning him back, Lorton – it seemed – was deliberately avoiding her. Which meant, she decided, he was already en route to Bangor, having again recruited his old buddy Bob to drive him there in his truck. She couldn't be certain, of course, but was unprepared to ignore the probability. Po wasn't fussed at her request, being happy to drive to Bangor as anywhere else. Finding her brooding on the porch that morning, he'd fully expected how his day might play out.

Last night's storm was the first of many forecasted for Maine. Presently there was a lull, the sky mainly blue, although a steel colored band had hovered over the eastern horizon since last time Tess checked. Hopefully they could reach Bangor before the next storm shrieked in. Getting home would be another matter. It all

depended on how long they spent staking out Maddie's apartment. For the journey, Po had brought a sturdy four-wheel drive
GMC SUV; it didn't have the speed of his Mustang but was
better suited to bad weather if they were caught in it.

During the drive, Tess brought Po up to speed on what she'd
learned about Dom, Temperance and the people most likely to
be controlling their actions, Blake and Kelly Ambrose. As Emma
Clancy had, he wondered why anyone at the helm of a successful
enterprise such as BK-Rose would waste their time on blackmailing small potatoes scammers. But he'd shrugged at his own
skepticism. 'I guess some folks are just cut from that kinda cloth,'
he decided.

'It's speculation,' Tess admitted, 'but I think Maddie and her
dad are only the tip of a lucrative iceberg. I've no proof, but
get the sense the property portfolio they manage ties directly
to the victims they're extorting.'

'Maybe,' he said. One way of finding evidence against the
Ambrose couple would be to visit the list of BK-Rose Holdings'
properties and ask tenants outright if they were being leaned on;
sooner rather than later somebody would spill the truth. That
route would have to wait; Tess's priority was stopping further
harm coming to Hayley and her coconspirators. 'Any clue yet
what kind of dirt Maddie's got on her hands?'

'It shames me to admit I haven't the faintest idea.' Tess's
admission wasn't entirely true. She'd figured out that the operation conducted from Maddie's home office involved parting
unsuspecting victims with their cash, but how still remained a
mystery. Whatever her scheme, it had proven successful enough
that she'd had to recruit assistance from both her father and
Hayley, and also attracted the attention of criminals intent on
taking a hearty slice of the profit. She'd wondered if Hayley's
reason for going incognito on the social network sites had more
to do with concealing her criminal activity than avoiding her
adoptive mother. INS: the initials that Tess had discovered listed
alongside Jacob Doyle's other contacts deserved deeper scrutiny,
because now Tess believed it was the disguise Hayley was hiding
behind and could explain what the girl had gotten involved in.

It was just a shame she hadn't gotten to ride back with Hayley
and Jacob the evening before, because during the journey she

was sure she could've prized the details out of them. Now
that Hayley had had second thoughts and returned to help
Maddie, she'd be tighter lipped than during the low point she
was at when she'd abandoned ship yesterday. Jacob was an
easier target to work on; he'd do anything to please Hayley,
within reason, but threatened with possible imprisonment Tess
was certain he'd turn informant. It saddened her to think in
those terms; lovesick Jacob was being used, and she still couldn't
believe Hayley, Maddie or Mike Toner were criminals, not of
the genuine, despicable variety, but people who'd made some
stupid decisions. However, the courts wouldn't see things that
way; all four could be imprisoned, Jacob as a conspirator.

'Whatever Maddie's got going, it's wrong,' Tess said, 'but she
doesn't deserve to be terrorized by armed thugs. None of them
do. You saw her father's face, right? Before Pinky and I made it
inside, that Dom guy had struck him and cut his face open. Not
only that, but when he first arrived at the building, he looked as
if he'd been roughed up before that. Mike Toner's taking his beat-
ings without fighting back and there's only one reason for it; he's
protecting Maddie from them. That tells me that some pretty strong
threats have been made against her in order to control him.'

'As long as they obey instructions, they should be OK,' Po
pointed out. He was playing devil's advocate.

'In good conscience I can't stand by knowing that people are
being scammed out of their money, so I can't let Maddie and the
others get away with this. Either they stop or I will report my
suspicions to the police. But more so, until I can convince them
to stop, I can't turn a blind eye to them being terrorized either.'

'Yeah.' He ruminated. 'I still think we should go direct to the
bad guys. So what if Lorton turns up and tries convincing his
daughter he's not the bad guy? We ain't the ones to referee them
when the inevitable bitchin' and pleadin' match begins.'

'I'm more concerned that he'll arrive at the wrong time and
run foul of Dom and Temperance. They might hurt him to prove
a point.'

'Might not be the worst thing to happen. Maybe if Hayley
witnesses her dad taking a beatin' for her it'll prove he isn't a
total waste of oxygen.'

Tess snorted. 'I can't believe you just said that.'

'Yeah,' he said, frowning. 'Not my finest of ideas, huh? For the record though, I *was* only joking. When I think about it, it'd be best for Hayley to learn why she was really orphaned, and it might change her opinion of her dad.'

For Po, the reasons behind his mother's abandonment of him hadn't come to light until she was on her deathbed. Finally learning the truth hadn't made up for how his life had turned out in the aftermath of her leaving, but he'd forgiven her and that at least unburdened a weight off his soul. Plus he'd gained a sister he'd never known in Emilia. So good had come out of making peace with his mom. The same could be said for Hayley and Jeff given a chance.

'I agree,' she said, 'just not yet. Hayley's head is messed up right now, and unsurprisingly after just finding out her whole life has been based on lies. It doesn't matter that those lies were told with her best interests at heart, they were still untrue. This thing she has going with the Toners; if you ask me Hayley's normally too headstrong and astute a character to get involved in it. Right now she's weak. Mixed-up as she is, it's something to keep her mind off her personal problems. Even the Toners' trouble with Dom and Temperance is a distraction for her. Given time to think things over, I'm hopeful she'll do the right thing and go home. But right now she doesn't want to face up to, never mind accept, Jeff's her dad, and him showing up at Maddie's isn't going to change that.'

'Yeah, but what gives us the right to send Jeff packing?'

'I hope to appeal to his better senses.'

Po grunted. 'Hope for the best, plan for the worst,' he quoted. 'What do you mean?'

'Instead of finding Jeff Lorton, we could be walking back into a return visit from the bad guys. You said before, you thought they'd be back, more determined than ever, and they won't be best pleased to see us again. Or worse, they're happy 'cause we've saved them the inconvenience of comin' looking for us.'

It was Tess's turn to grunt, because it was a genuine concern. 'If we're lucky we'll have Hayley and the others safely out of the way before that happens.'

They lapsed into thoughtful silence. During the journey Tess tried several more attempts at calling Jeff Lorton's cellphone, but it remained unanswered. For the duration Po kept his own peace, undoubtedly by forming a battle plan for what he foresaw as an inevitable showdown sometime in the near future. All the while the next storm front pushed closer. They were on the last stretch of I-95, midway between Newport and Bangor when rain dotted the windshield. Within seconds it fell in torrents. Judging by the depth of puddles already at roadside, this wasn't the first heavy downfall to hit the area. Here the interstate was separated by a wide grassy median, thickly planted with shrubs and trees. They almost missed the drama playing out on the southbound carriageway. Po caught snatches of flashing lights, and emergency workers in high-visibility jackets between the trees.

He slowed dramatically, searching for a better view.

'What is it?' Tess asked.

'Hold up one minute,' he said, as he craned for a clearer view of a car wedged on its side between two scarred trees. Then they were past the accident scene. Traffic was light northbound, but Po had no intention of reversing into it. He touched the throttle again, looking for somewhere to mount the median. A quarter mile on, a single-track access point appeared. It was reserved for highway maintenance and emergency services vehicles only, but Po took it anyway and emerged onto the southern lanes. From there the number of emergency vehicles was more obvious, and even through the downpour Po picked out a fire truck, cop cars and an ambulance. Some traffic had stacked up, but a cop with a luminous baton was directing them past the accident scene. Po drew close to the back of the queue, then crawled the GMC forward.

The car was on its side among the trees. The front was crushed; the roof compacted down to the doorframes. A brief but intense fire had scorched the rear of the car and the surrounding trees, but must have been doused by the previous torrential downpour. Emergency responders worked around the vehicle, but their lack of feverishness told the worst story. Even in that awful state, the car's make and model was known to Po.

He exchanged sickened glances with Tess.

Her hand went to her suddenly pinched throat.

'That's Jacob Doyle's Chrysler,' Po confirmed.

'Oh my god,' Tess moaned. 'What happened here?'

TWENTY-SIX

L ess than an hour earlier, Arlen Sampson had watched in disbelief as Jacob Doyle's car swerved out of control, hit the median and flipped. Shedding tinkling glass and twisted metal it rolled once, smashing the roof flat, before skewing around and performing another one-hundred-and-eighty-degrees twist in mid-air. The car ended up wedged between the boles of two sturdier trees than those it had already crashed through. Steam and smoke billowed from the crushed engine compartment.

Temperance hit the brakes, bringing her van to a juddering halt, as she too reacted to the unforeseen event. Breathing heavily she sat staring at the wrecked Chrysler. 'Holy shit,' she wheezed under her breath. Then she hiccupped out a laugh of disbelief and looked over at Sampson.

He also cursed in surprise, but with more a note of regret than his companion had.

Surviving that wreck would be remarkable, and Sampson held little hope for the youth. In the next instant, sparks popped and fizzed and a soft *whump!* signified the ignition of a fire. Flames wreathed the rear of the car; chemically fueled they were in shades of yellow and green, as noxious as the pitch-black smoke, which engulfed the car. He reassessed his first thought: surviving that wreck would be a miracle.

Theirs wasn't the only vehicle on that stretch of highway. A truck and a car had pulled to the shoulder, and already their drivers had spilled out to try to assist Jacob. Jacob was beyond help, but Sampson decided that appearances were everything.

'Keep the engine running,' he told Temperance, then he slipped out of the van, and after checking he was not about to be mown down, he jogged across the highway towards the flaming wreckage. At the median his shoes sank into the soft turf underfoot and he stepped backwards onto firmer ground. The truck driver had progressed further into the woods, but the heat and poisonous fumes forced him back. The car driver was urgently talking into his cellphone, alerting the emergency services. Other vehicles came to a stop and more people approached. It was human nature to gawp at scenes of misery, and in this modern era to share such misery far and wide; any second now and their phones would be out, not to call for help, but to film the scene. Sampson had no intention of having his face plastered all over the Internet. He turned away from the wreckage and retraced his steps across the highway to where Temperance watched from the van. He approached her window and she buzzed it down.

'He's dead?' she asked needlessly.

Sampson exhaled through his nostrils and frowned deeply.

'Saves us the trouble of shutting him up,' Temperance said.

'Jesus, Tempe, have you no pity? A kid just died here.'

She shrugged. 'It's just the way the cookie crumbles, Arlen. We didn't kill him; his death's on him, so why should I feel anything for him?'

'You've been driving around with Dom too long,' he growled, 'you're beginning to sound like him.'

'I'm nothing like him.'

Sampson refrained from answering. He moved around the hood and climbed back into the passenger seat. 'Let's get out of here before we're asked any awkward questions.'

Other vehicles slowed as they passed the crash, their drivers as ghoulish as those that'd disembarked their cars for a closer look. Temperance pulled out into the slow-moving traffic, so it'd be unobvious they were witnesses leaving the scene. She steadily built speed, while beside her Sampson scowled at his hands folded in his lap.

'Ten minutes ago you contemplated forcing him to pull over and throttling him into silence,' Temperance pointed out. 'We've had a lucky break; Jacob won't be carrying tales to anyone now.'

She was correct. After he left Madison Toner's apartment, he'd asked her to try to catch Jacob. The youth had a few minutes' lead on them, but there were few routes to Portland that he'd have chosen to take, and Temperance rightly elected for the main interstate highway. Sampson saw Jacob as a loose end. It was highly unlikely that any of the others would talk, but the scorned ex-boyfriend had nothing to lose. There was the possibility that

Sampson would have to resort to threats and violence, but he'd also considered trying to sweeten the deal with the promise of reward for Jacob's silence. Only as a last resort would he have strangled the youth into obedience again: yes, Sampson was forced to do shitty things for Blake and Kelly Ambrose, but it didn't make him a shitty person at heart. In one way, he was as much of a victim of use and abuse as the kid, and he felt an affinity with him. Possibly crushed in the wreckage, but still clinging to life, Jacob would've suffered tremendously before the flames or noxious fumes took him.

'Stop the van,' he commanded.

'What?'

'Just stop the damn van!'

Sampson's cheeks bulged. Temperance decelerated quickly, forcing out a car traveling close behind into the passing lane. The angered driver laid a hand on his horn and received a barked curse from her in response. She brought the van to a rolling stop. Before it was at a full halt, Sampson was out of the door and bent double. He vomited between his shoes. The soul wrenching noise he made twisted Temperance's face in revulsion. In the next instant rain thundered down, battering the van's shell, and also Sampson's hunched back. He staggered back to the van, red-eyed and wiping his lips with his sleeve. 'Not a fucking word to Dom about this,' he croaked.

'You're really not cut out for this kind of work,' Temperance said as he climbed back in and slumped in his seat.

'Don't take my empathy for weakness,' he warned. 'I've no qualms about hurting anyone that deserves it, but that . . . that back there was a horrible way for an innocent kid to die.'

Temperance sniffed. She got the van moving again, looking for an intersection to take and return to Brunswick. Highway Patrol would be en route to the crash, and she'd rather they didn't come under scrutiny should anyone have mentioned her van had left the scene. The sooner they were off the highway the better. Soon she turned the van and followed cross-country past an expansive lake called Plymouth Pond, and picked up the lesser-traveled Route 202. It made for a slower journey home, but they'd most likely avoid the law. They were southwest of Albion by a few miles before either of them spoke again.

'Do you think he deliberately took his own life?' Temperance asked.

'I couldn't say what was on his mind.' Actually, Sampson had given it some thought. Not long before the Chrysler had gone off the road it had sped up by increments before finally shooting forward at top speed. By the time the tires hit the soft verge it was traveling upwards of eighty miles per hour. Momentarily Sampson had presumed Jacob had spotted the van tailing them and tried to get away. But he was unaware of their vehicle, having never laid eyes on it, so that couldn't have been the reason for his sudden surge. He pictured the boy sobbing and wailing at being dumped by his girlfriend. Angry and upset, he'd possibly railed against his perceived ill treatment, maybe he was hollering and cursing and beating at the steering wheel as he stamped down on the gas; eyes brimming with tears, he might not have noticed the car was pulling left towards the median, and once the tires dug in to the storm-softened turf it was too late to correct it. Maybe by then he didn't care. Nobody would ever know, but there was the genuine concern that others might suspect foul deeds. Jacob's untimely death hadn't been a lucky break as Temperance had attested; it could prove the opposite.

Make them disappear, if you must, but in a way that does not lead back to us. Blake Ambrose's words resonated in his mind. Despite having no physical hand in Jacob Doyle's death, Sampson couldn't deny he was partly responsible, as it was through him that Jacob had been kicked out by his girl. Why hadn't Jacob taken his advice when he'd told him to go and take a slow drive? If he'd left then he'd still be alive. When news of Jacob's death reached Hayley and the Toners they'd instantly jump to the wrong conclusion; that Jacob's car had been forced off the road.

Sampson instructed Temperance to turn around. He should go back to speak with Hayley and the others, to convince them he had nothing to do with Jacob's demise, before they did something stupid.

TWENTY-SEVEN

Tess trudged to Po's GMC, downcast. She'd thrown on a hooded coat against the rain; the faux fur lining around the hood was sodden, dripping with each step. Her jeans were soaked almost to mid-shin, having slogged through the grassy median as close to the crash as the Penobscot County Sheriff's deputy had allowed. Both she and Po knew the car was Jacob's but she wanted to confirm if he'd had a passenger or not.

'Jacob?' Po asked as she got in the car.

She threw back her hood. Wet eyed, she nodded her head. He'd expected no less.

'Hayley wasn't with him,' she went on.

'That's one thing to be thankful of.'

Just then Tess couldn't feel any relief; Jacob's death had hit her like a kick to the gut. Somehow she felt responsible for failing to keep him safe, despite having been told the crash was purely accidental.

'I spoke with that deputy over there,' she said, indicating a tall woman standing at roadside, her uniform hat pulled low and her jacket collar turned up. The deputy was soaked through, her face grim and pale. She kept the traffic moving in a desultory manner, waving vehicles on with a glowing baton. Tess had informed her she was a retired sergeant from Cumberland County Sheriff's department, and it had won her some leeway to approach the scene. 'I told her I recognized the car, and gave her Jacob's details. Apparently they'd had conflicting information regarding the probable driver, but Jacob's name was one that'd come up already in their inquiries. I told her I was worried that he was traveling with his girlfriend, and she let me go and speak with the fire crew. I didn't see . . . I didn't want to . . . but it was confirmed there was only one male driver involved.'

Po had concluded the same as she had when first spotting the wreck. She'd probed for answers, and the same female deputy had informed her there were no suspicious details surrounding the crash. 'There were witnesses to the accident,' she explained to him, 'a truck driver and a salesman. Both reported that the Chrysler was being driven at speed, it hit a big puddle and the car went off the road and into the trees. No sooner had it crashed than the car caught fire. They couldn't get close to help for the heat and smoke; poor Jacob didn't stand a chance.'

'That's all they said?'

'That's all I could get from the deputy.' The deputy had already extended professional courtesy to its limits by speaking to Tess, and she'd clammed up, recalling the emphasis was now on Tess being an *ex*-sergeant.

'Those witnesses, they didn't say why Jacob was driving so fast?'

'No. Besides, how would they know? You drive fast most of the time, do you need a reason?'

'I drive fast,' he agreed, 'but I also drive to the conditions. Hitting standing water like that at speed, it could'a pulled the steering wheel outta Jacob's hands. The question's why he was driving like an idiot beforehand. Yesterday when we followed him back to Portland, he took things slow and easy, why the change this time?'

'We'll never know.'

Po checked out the huge container truck still parked alongside the highway; the driver must've been asked to wait until a formal witness statement could be taken from him. Po said, 'Stay dry, and I'll be back in a minute.'

Before Tess could answer, he got out of the GMC and jogged through the rain to the truck. She should've spoken with the witnesses herself, but she'd needed a few minutes to come to terms with Jacob's death. She barely knew the boy, but still . . . she *knew him* all the same. She was grateful to Po for taking the initiative.

Ignoring the rain, Po stood, head tilted up. Tess watched a thick, hairy hand emerge from the truck's window, and could almost decipher the conversation by the gestures it made. Po finished up, offered a thumbs up to the driver and was given one in return. He jogged back to the GMC and clambered in, shaking raindrops from his hair. Tess looked at him, lips slightly apart.

'One of the first people at the scene was from a panel van,' Po confirmed. 'The trucker said there were three witnesses there when the car first went on fire. He didn't notice when the guy left, but thinks it was before the cops arrived. I described Dom.'

She could tell there was something coming by the wry turn of his mouth.

'Wasn't him,' said Po, 'unless he's shaved off his beard and stuck it on his scalp.'

Tess's shoulders fell. It was the wrong reaction to Po's words. What did she want, that Dom *had* forced Jacob off the road? Whoever was driving the van, he was probably innocent of foul play, and once he realized there was no hope for Jacob, he'd backed off from the scene and left it to the professionals to clean it up. Maybe, once he'd given some thought to his actions, he'd contact the police and offer up his testimony.

'Wasn't Dom,' Po went on, 'but I think it was still the same outfit. The truck driver says a woman was driving the van, a black woman with cornrows and large, decorative earrings. Sound like Temperance to you?'

Tess wouldn't describe Temperance as black, but yes, she'd African-American blood in her, and casting back her mind, she could picture her tightly plaited hair and ostentatious earrings, of silver hoops and feathers, reminiscent of those Native American Dream Catchers some people hung over their beds.

'They were chasing Jacob?'

'Driver couldn't say. Didn't think so. His truck and the sales rep's car were the first on the scene, the van pulled up after they were already crossing the highway to help. If they were chasing Jacob, they weren't putting much effort into catching him.'

'If Jacob knew they were following him, it'd explain why he might've panicked and driven too fast for the conditions.'

'We can speculate all day long, it won't get us anywhere,' he said. 'D'you want to tell the cops what we suspect, or should we confirm things first?'

'We confirm things,' said Tess, to his satisfaction. It was ever their way.

'What about the other thing?'

'You mean telling Hayley that Jacob's dead? Oh, Jesus, Po, how are we going to break the news to her?'

'That's not our responsibility,' he reminded her. 'It's for the cops to deliver the bad news. No, I meant should we tell the cops where they can find her?'

Tess kneaded her temples, her face cupped by her palms. Finally she decided no. She still wanted the opportunity to get Hayley and the others out of harm's way before everything blew up in their faces. Jacob's death complicated matters for everyone involved, including the bad guys.

'What about Nathan and Adrian?' Po asked. 'They're Jacob's actual next of kin.'

'They have his home address; the cops will inform Jacob's brothers.'

'F'sure,' said Po. 'But that's not what I meant. You saw how hot-headed they were concerning Jacob's relationship with Hayley, how d'you think they're gonna react if they decide she'd somethin' to do with causin' their little brother's death?'

'Yeah,' she agreed. 'They could cause trouble. Last night, they probably gave Jacob the third degree when he arrived home; you can bet they got it out of him that Hayley had coaxed him into joining her at Maddie's place up in Bangor, and when they skipped out this morning that's probably where they'd returned. It's bad enough Jeff Lorton showing up there, never mind the Doyle brothers arriving on the warpath.'

'We should go,' he suggested.

Tess took another look at the accident scene. Emergency response vehicles cluttered her view, but she could see between them to where the medics extricated Jacob's corpse from the tangled wreckage. Thankfully they'd already covered him with blankets before transferring him to a gurney. She looked away. As a sheriff's deputy she'd attended a number of traffic collisions, some of them fatal, some where the victims were in a worse state than how Jacob had ended up, but she'd had no personal connection to the victims then. She'd been able to cope with seeing the terrible wounds by doing her job, boxing away the horror, compartmentalizing what had happened against what needed doing and concentrating on the latter. She must do the same again. 'Yeah,' she said, 'let's go.'

Before setting off, Po had another thought. 'The number of folks possibly convergin' on Maddie's place, things could stack up against us, Tess. I think we'll need help. Do me a favor, will ya? Call Pinky and ask him to join us.'

She did, and Pinky was more than happy to oblige.

'I'm already on my way,' he announced, 'charging to the rescue like the Seventh Cavalry, me.'

In his usual manner Pinky's enthusiasm outshone the severity of the situation. He not only mispronounced the word as 'Calvary,' he'd also neglected to recall that Custer's 7th Cavalry regiment were wiped out at Little Bighorn.

TWENTY-EIGHT

'Is there any way that his death can be connected back to you?' asked Blake Ambrose. His voice was pitched low in anger and Sampson strained to hear him over the rain drumming on the roof of the van, the thrum of the engine and swish of tires on wet asphalt. They were approaching the Bangor city limits, only ten minutes or so from arriving back at Madison Toner's apartment. Sampson would've preferred to keep Blake in the dark about Jacob Doyle's death until he could perform some damage control, but at Temperance's urging had come clean. It was best that Blake was fully apprised of the situation, she'd argued, rather than hearing later where his response might be to punish first and ask questions later.

'The crash was an accident, he hit water on the road and aquaplaned into the trees,' said Sampson, and his next words almost stuck in his throat. He avoided looking across at Temperance. 'It's a lucky break for us, really, because he's one less person we need to shut up.'

'Until his girlfriend starts screaming murder!'

'That's why we're going back to Bangor. I need to convince Hayley Cameron it's in her best interest to keep us out of it.'

'Use the boy's death to terrify her into silence,' said Blake. 'Warn her that's what will happen to her and everyone she loves if she opens her fat mouth.'

'Yeah,' said Sampson, with absolutely no intention of going down that route, 'I'll speak with her, make her understand.'

'Good. Keep me informed with what happens. If it's necessary I'll have Dominick come to Bangor, and he can meet you there.'

'There's no need, we won't have to take anyone to the warehouse this time.'

'You're confident of that? Well I'm not, Arlen. If it comes to it, you will take them to Rockland, if I damn well tell you to take them there. Do you hear me?'

'Yes, Blake, I hear you.' Sampson clenched his jaw. 'But we

won't need Dom. We're almost at Madison's apartment, and I don't want to waste time waiting for Dom getting here. I need to speak with Hayley before she hears about Jacob from somebody else.'

'I'm beginning to think this deal with the Toners is more trouble than it's worth,' said Blake.

Sampson was astute enough to read between the lines. Under no illusion, he knew Blake wasn't suggesting they back off and leave Maddie and Mike Toner to their little scam; whenever something proved troublesome to Blake his answer was to make it disappear – more rightly he'd have his henchmen do the dirty work for him. Sometimes, it had been hinted by Kelly, some of those henchmen had disappeared when necessary too.

'Allow me to try to smooth things over first,' said Sampson. 'I think I opened a rapport with them earlier and can keep them quiet. From what I witnessed Hayley didn't have any real affection for the kid, and was only using him for her own ends' – *the way you use me, you bastard!* – 'I'm sure I can convince her to forget about him, and that it's best to keep our arrangement secret.'

'You're right about not waiting. We can't drag our heels on this, Arlen. If there's any doubt whatsoever we can trust them, I want them all taken to the warehouse.'

Sampson closed his eyes, said, 'Yes, Blake.'

After a moment of silence, he ended the call, as Blake's instruction was absolute. Alongside him Temperance chewed her lips in an uncommon display of worry.

She looked across at him. 'He can't be suggesting killing them all?'

The volume on his phone was high enough that even through the noise of the downpour she'd followed the conversation.

'You'd commit murder for him?' Sampson asked.

'If it came to it, I'd have to whether I wanted to or not.'

'What has Blake got hanging over you, Temperance?'

She neglected to answer.

'Is it worse than what's being asked of us now?'

'I found my mother's rapist,' she said, and didn't need to expound.

'One revenge killing is forgivable, the cold-blooded murder of three innocents is something else entirely.'

'Maybe. But I'd rather nobody ever learns I was the person that cut off my own father's dick and watched him bleed to death.' She held his gaze a few beats before being forced to concentrate on the road ahead. She directed a glance at him and asked, 'What about you, Arlen? What skeleton did they find hidden in your closet?'

His crime wasn't as graphic as Temperance's but a woman had died nevertheless. While Temperance's revenge on her biological father had been premeditated, Mary Rhodes had died through a moment of Sampson's madness. He'd left her bloody, after gasping her last breaths at the edge of a lonely road. In a panic, Sampson had gone to the most powerful friends he knew and thrown himself at their mercy, begging them to save him from imprisonment and his wife Caroline from a life of hardship and heartbreak. Back then he'd no idea the type of people the Ambrose couple really were: he'd thought that they'd connect him with the best legal team to help him avoid culpability in Mary's death, but instead they'd taken steps to cover up his involvement with the woman, period. Their help came with a demand for repayment; for ending Mary Rhodes's life he'd had to give his own in years of servitude to them. Sampson deeply loved his wife, and would do anything to protect her, but he was also a man whose moral center had easily been tested back then; he was not immune to temptation and in such close proximity to her he'd succumbed to Mary's advances, more than once, as he had to those of his friend's wife, Kelly, both before and after he had become her veritable sex slave. On top of the sin of Mary's death, he'd loaded more, and his burden was beginning to drag him down. It was beginning to show in his revulsion for Kelly and in his resistance to Blake's demands.

After a few illicit dalliances with Sampson, Mary Rhodes had suffered an attack of conscience and had wanted to come clean to Caroline; after all she was struggling with the guilt of sleeping with her sister's husband. First she'd met with Sampson, in the hope that they could speak together to Caroline, a united front, to both beg her forgiveness and swear they'd never betray her again. Sampson had only foreseen the ruination of his marriage, and he'd at first begged that she kept their secret between them, next he'd pleaded, and when Mary was still intent on informing

Caroline of their infidelity, he'd panicked and resorted to force. He hadn't meant to hurt her, but his hands had found her throat, and he'd squeezed until she could no longer breathe, and then he'd cast her down and stood over her, screaming how he'd finish the job if ever she opened her damn mouth to her sister: Mary never heard his threat, she was already beyond it. As she landed, her skull had cracked on a curbstone. Sampson had fled the scene of Mary's 'accidental' death, and to this day her case remained unsolved. Sampson's fake alibi – that evening he'd supposedly escorted Blake Ambrose on a business trip to Boston – remained firm, and until now unquestioned. As far as the world, and especially Caroline knew, her sister had died at the hands of a mysterious drifter who'd passed through Maine, and Sampson would have it no other way. He wasn't about to take Temperance into his confidence.

'Who says I've any skeletons to uncover?'

She clucked her tongue. 'Quit the bullshit, man. We both know this isn't you, Arlen. There's something hanging over your head as much there is over the rest of us.'

'If that's the case, then it's for me to worry about. I'm not sharing.'

'I shared with you, don't tell me you're gonna hold my secret over me now.'

He shrugged off her concern. 'There's nothing I want from you, Tempe, except for you to watch my back if and when the shit hits the fan.'

'If?' she intoned, because she was as certain as he was that following Blake's path would guarantee it.

TWENTY-NINE

In the wake of no fewer than three invasions of her apartment in less than twenty-four hours, Madison had finally gotten wise and locked the first-floor entrance door. Tess pressed the button on the intercom. She waited for what felt like an age before pressing the button a second time, this time keeping on the pressure until she was certain anyone inside must have heard. A shaky voice answered.

'Yes? Who is it?'

'Madison? Is that you?'

'What do you want?'

'It's Tess Grey, the private investigator. Again. I need to see Hayley. It's important.'

'Go away. You're not wanted here.'

'Madison, please, it's *very* important that I speak with her.'

'Just go away.' Madison must have ended the connection because the hollow hiss emanating from the speaker stopped.

Tess pressed the buzzer again.

A male voice came on. Mike Toner.

'For god's sakes, there must be somebody else you can harass? Why can't you just leave us be?'

'Mr Toner . . . Mike, please listen to me. Something terrible has happened. It involves Jacob.' It could be hours before the police got around to informing his next of kin, and from there, the bad news filtering down to Hayley. Despite her earlier resolution to leave delivering the death message to the police, there was little else for it. Only, she thought it should be given in person to Hayley, not impersonally over an intercom like this.

'The kid's got nothing to do with us now. Hayley broke up with him . . . he was sent home.'

'Mike, is Hayley in hearing distance? I don't want her hearing like this . . . it's, well, it's pretty bad.'

'Uh, no, she's in the bathroom.' Suddenly Mike Toner understood the gravity in Tess's voice. 'What has happened, Tess?'

'I really need to speak in person with Hayley . . .'

'He's been hurt hasn't he?' Toner's voice had raised several octaves. In the background, there was a corresponding yelp of concern from Maddie who was in earshot. Maybe the girl was less concerned with Jacob's welfare than that the news confirmed another fear to her, that the threats of violence directed at them were being followed through.

'His car might've been forced off the road,' Tess said, 'by the same people we chased from here yesterday.'

'I asked if he's been hurt? You wouldn't be here if he hadn't. How bad is he?'

She didn't answer, and her silence said everything. Toner groaned in dismay, and Maddie could be heard squawking for Hayley. Tess said, 'Please, Mr Toner. Let me come up and speak with Hayley. I'd rather she hear in person than like this.'

'Yes, uh, you're right. You should come up.' There was a faint buzz, followed by a click as a lock disengaged, and Tess pushed the entrance door inward.

Throughout the conversation Po had lurked silently behind her. They'd already agreed she would go up alone if they were granted access to the apartment. He'd guard the entrance. Thankfully they were the first of many people that might arrive, and it was best if Po was in position to deter anyone else from entering. 'If you need me, holler,' he whispered.

Tess nodded, chewed her bottom lip, then set off up the stairs. She dragged her heels for the first few steps, before deciding the sooner this was done the better. She reached the second floor slightly out of breath, her pulse beating in her ears. There was no time for gathering herself; Toner was already in the open doorway, Maddie slightly behind him, her hands cupped over her mouth. Tess had formed the impression that Maddie was a cold-hearted bitch who cared only for lining her pockets, but she wasn't immune to grief after all. Tears tracked down her cheeks, and she dropped her hands to clench her shirt in both fists. Hayley stood mid-way down the hall, and whatever Maddie had told her had already bleached the color from her features. On seeing the apprehension on Tess's face, Hayley wailed and crumpled at the knees. She sat down hard on the floor. Mike Toner practically ushered Tess in, until she was crouching alongside the girl in the hallway. Tess reached and took the girl's shaking hands in hers.

'No, no, no,' Hayley moaned, 'don't say it's true.'

'I'm sorry, Hayley,' Tess said, allowing the weight of her words to impart the truth.

Hayley wailed louder. Maddie and Toner crowded in, each offering their sympathy. A spark of anger ignited in Tess; if it weren't for them and their damn criminal scam, Jacob wouldn't have been sucked into their sphere and would still be alive. She scowled briefly at them, but it was as pointless as aiming her anger at the puddle that'd spun Jacob's Chrysler off the highway.

'Wh . . . what happened to him?' Hayley sobbed.

'He lost control of his car,' Tess began.

'He was forced off the road?'

'It's unclear. But the police think he was driving too fast for the conditions and skidded on water. I'm sorry, Hayley, Jacob was beyond help. If it's any comfort, I think he died instantly and didn't suffer.'

'I . . . I sent him home,' she croaked. 'He wanted to be with me, but I sent him home.' Hayley's eyes grew huge as she stared up at Tess. 'You've got to believe me, I sent him away because I didn't want to involve him in *this* anymore. I . . . I liked Jacob a lot, and well . . . he didn't deserve to be hurt. *He didn't deserve to be killed!*'

Toner and Maddie had backed off a few feet, huddled together in urgent debate. Tess again scowled at them. She raised her voice so they heard. 'None of you deserve to be hurt, but can't you see where this is headed?'

Toner hushed his daughter as he moved towards Tess. She dragged on his elbow but he shook loose. 'You said his car was forced off the road by the ones who were here yesterday. Now you're saying Jacob hit a puddle and skidded . . . which is it?'

'He was driving too fast because they were following him,' she said. Her words were pure conjecture, but she wanted Toner to realize that none of them were safe from a similar fate as Jacob's. 'He might've panicked and lost control—'

'He was upset when he left, angry at us, angry at Hayley for sending him away,' said Toner, reaching for another – possibly correct – explanation for the crash.

'That's why I can only say that he might've been forced off the road. But it's a possibility, isn't it? That Dom guy wasn't playing around here, he's definitely capable of doing somebody harm, right?'

'Except Dom wasn't here when Jacob left,' Maddie butted in, 'it was that other guy, the more reasonable one.'

Toner grimaced at her for speaking out of turn. She'd just fallen into Tess's trap of offering information she hadn't previously known. Tess monopolized on it, again offering supposition as hard truth. 'We know Temperance was driving the van when Jacob crashed, but not who her male passenger was. He was here when Jacob left?'

'He came to make peace between us, after the way Dom and Temperance acted yesterday,' Toner explained. He was conscious of saying too much though, reddening by the second, now he was beyond the initial shock of Jacob's demise.

'He have a name?' Tess demanded.

Toner was reluctant to admit anything more; fear had loosened his daughter's tongue though. 'He's called Arlen,' said Maddie to an answering groan from Toner.

'Arlen?' Tess echoed, looking directly at Toner for more.

'I don't know his second name,' he said, and Tess believed him. She thought back to the list of employees and associates of Blake and Kelly Ambrose she'd compiled for later checking, and one in particular who'd featured prominently: Arlen Sampson.

Tess didn't leave Hayley's side, but she concentrated on Maddie. 'You said this Arlen guy was reasonable? Do you still think the same way about him now that Jacob's dead?'

Maddie said nothing. Her blanched features had a greenish tinge to them. Tess aimed a finger. 'It isn't too late to stop this going further. You have to stop whatever it is you're doing and come clean to the cops. Otherwise you'll never be safe from these people, or their kind again.' Tess shook her head, as if tamping down disbelief. 'What on earth have you got going that it's worth an innocent life, Maddie? What if the next to die is Hayley, or your dad, or *you*? Will your dirty little scam still be worth it?'

'Whoa, whoa,' said Toner, hands raised pleadingly. 'No one else is going to die. Jacob's death was probably an accident;

from what you've said he wasn't rammed off the highway or nothing.'

Tess stood. She ensured she was staring directly at the wound on his cheek. He'd cleaned it up since last she was there, but the cut was still undressed, a puckered gash, alongside his swollen nose. His left eye had grown bloodshot. She looked him up and down. He was wearing a clean shirt and jeans, his third change of clothing in quick succession. 'Twice you've been beaten by those thugs that I know of,' Tess said. 'How can you stand there and try to play things down? You're not helping either of these girls by pretending they're not in genuine danger. Mr Toner . . . Mike . . . do you love your daughter? No, don't answer, because it's obvious that you do. Whatever you're involved in, it has to end. You're a decent guy, I can tell. This has never sat happily with you, but you've gone along with it for Maddie's sake. Well, even more for Maddie's sake, you have to be the one that stops it now. You must tell the police everything; those people have to be stopped from hurting you, your daughter or anyone else. If they're arrested they can't hurt anybody, can they?'

'Can't they?' Toner glanced around in mild panic. 'What about us? We'll also be arrested, we'll go to prison just the same and what's to stop them getting at us then?'

'It's unlikely any of you will be imprisoned. I can't promise you anything, but I'll speak on your behalf, and I've connections with the District Attorney's office in Portland. Maybe a deal can be arranged, your testimony in exchange for bringing down a criminal gang.'

Toner wasn't buying it. Neither was Maddie. Truthfully, Tess would promise anything that might get them to see the light. In all likelihood they would all face prosecution whether they gave evidence against the extortionists or not, their only hope of lighter punishment would be to work with the state against their persecutors. She changed tactics. 'When I promised earlier to leave you be, to keep quiet about what was going on, that was on the understanding that Hayley and Jacob went home safely. Things have changed now and so has my promise.'

'Jakey's dead,' Hayley intoned, as if punctuating Tess's unspoken warning.

'If I have my way, I won't allow those people to hurt anyone

else,' Tess said firmly, 'and if that means having you all arrested
and placed in protective custody, then that's the way I'll do
things.'

Two important points struck Tess almost simultaneously. In
Jacob's phone contacts he'd listed INS, and she'd taken it as an
acronym under which Hayley's details had been hidden, but now
she realized it was an abbreviation, and Pinky had hit the mark
when suggesting it could simply mean 'insurance.' At the scene
of Jacob's crash, the deputy had stated that there had been some
initial confusion regarding the identity of the driver due to
conflicting vehicle ownership information. Maddie's scam
involved using bogus details in order to obtain cheaper driver's
insurance, she'd bet, and Jacob had been the recipient of one of
those fake policies. She said, 'Even if I say nothing to the cops,
or you say nothing, it won't matter because you'll be arrested.
Now that the police are investigating a fatality, they'll follow
every lead. Jacob holds a fake insurance policy' – she nodded
at the look of surprise on Maddie's face – 'and it won't be long
till it leads them back via Hayley to you. Whichever way you
look at things, your scam's finished, and it'll be far better for
you all if you take the initiative and assist the police with their
investigation. Help them to take down the real bad guys and I'll
bet the cops will look on you all more favorably.'

Maddie began weeping. This time her grief wasn't for Jacob,
but for the death of all her plans and dreams. Toner pulled her
into his embrace, trying to hush her, but also muttering to
her that they should do as Tess said. Out of their earshot, Tess
exhaled in relief. She turned to Hayley again. The girl had buried
her head between her knees and wept softly. Tess aimed her words
at Toner, 'I'll give you a minute or two to speak. Then we should
get these kids out of here, before anyone else turns up.'

Without releasing Maddie, Mike Toner regarded Tess with
glistening eyes. He mouthed his answer – 'Thank you' – and she
realized he'd been searching for a safe way for his daughter out
of this mess, and she'd offered a lifeline.

She returned to the landing, and ensuring a turn of heart wasn't
afoot, where one of the girls or Toner might slam the door behind
her, she looked over the railings, seeking Po. There was no sign
of him. Possibly he'd stepped outside to take a smoke now that

the rain had seemingly diminished. 'Hey down there,' she called softly.

There was no answer.

'Po?' she said a little louder. 'Po, are you there?'

She didn't want to raise her voice further. For one she might alarm Hayley, Maddie and Toner, and even the slightest switch in mood could send them down a different route than she'd just talked them into; also, being the only domicile within hundreds of yards, they'd avoided alerting anyone nearby to trouble within the apartment, but that might change if she began hollering for Po. She wanted the cops involved but on her own terms. She took out her cellphone. Po's number was on speed dial. She listened to his phone ringing, but there was no corresponding echo from below. Where had the fool man gotten to now? Her thought was fleeting, and unfair, because Po was no fool, and he wouldn't have deserted his post without good reason. She was about to hang up, and rush to gather her charges together, when he finally answered.

'Po?' she asked into the hollow sound of an open line.

It was not Po's voice that answered.

Almost wearily, Arlen Sampson said, 'If you want to see your man alive again, you'll do exactly what I tell you.'

THIRTY

In prison, a convict either develops the instinct to sense trouble and react to it, or they end up a victim. During his interment Po's senses had saved his hide more than once when his fellow inmates had targeted him for extermination, and he still bore the scars on his forearms from when he'd fought off an attacker intent on taking his eyes with a makeshift knife. Even these days, years after his release from Louisiana State Penitentiary, Po felt the need to stay sharp, because he might no longer be confined but an attempt on his life was still as possible. Therefore he was conscious of the stealthy approach of the man despite the blustering wind rattling the roller shutters at the front of the building and patter of rain on asphalt.

Concealed in a sheath in his right boot, Po carried a blade. It was a multipurpose tool of his trade as a mechanic, but also a weapon of defense when necessary. He was tempted to draw the knife, but didn't. Without first laying eyes on the one approaching he could accidentally threaten an innocent passerby, Jeff Lorton, or maybe even a cop sent to investigate the sudden frequent comings and goings of strangers in the usually quiet neighborhood. Up until now a police response to Maddie's apartment had been avoided, and Po, for one, didn't wish to be the cause of one now through imprudence. Nevertheless, he shook out his arms, and presented himself in the doorway to block the entrance. If Dom's ugly mug were the one presented to him, he would punch first and ask questions later.

Whoever was approaching, their senses were on high alert too. They scuffed to a halt. The rain beat down, but Po was sure he could hear breathing. They had to be standing very close to the entrance, perhaps with their backs pressed to the wall next to the jamb, listening. It was not the action of an innocent bystander, but could still be misconstrued: maybe Jeff Lorton had arrived and was building the courage he needed to face his daughter. Po didn't think so, but neither should he reach out, grab the skulker by the neck and drag him onto his blade. Not yet.

'State your business, bra,' Po said.

The scrape of a sole on the ground was the only hint his voice had caused alarm.

There was a measured few seconds of silence, before the man responded. 'I only want to talk.'

'You're the guy from the van, right? The one who made sure Jacob Doyle was dead before you left the crash scene?'

'That's not how things happened.'

'Are you armed?'

'No.'

'I am. Show me your hands.'

'I'm here to explain what happened to Jacob, not to fight.'

'Show me your hands,' Po repeated, 'or put 'em up. The choice is yours.'

The man stepped away from the wall, and faced Po from the safety of a couple of yards' distance. Directly behind him stood the single forlorn tree under which Jacob used to shelter. He held up his empty palms. Po gave them only a cursory glance before his gaze tracked to other obvious places for a concealed weapon. The man made his search easier by holding up the tails of his coat, then pulling open his lapels showing there was no holstered gun under his armpit in the manner of Dom's favored carrying position. 'Happy now?' the man asked.

'Happy's not a word I'd choose under these circumstances.'

'Yes, the kid's unfortunate death is a sad state of affairs.'

'Depends on your perspective. From yours it's one less witness to shut up. From mine, it means the heat's about to come down on you and your bullying pals.'

'Maybe you're right on both counts, but the kid's death saddens me all the same. It shouldn't have happened, but it did; I want you to know I didn't have anything to do with it.'

'You had a different reason for chasing him?'

'I planned on speaking with him again, appealing to his best interests to keep out of our way, and if that didn't work, I hoped to appeal to his pocket.'

Po stepped outside. The shower had all but stopped in the last few seconds. The man retreated a step. 'Is that how you hope to keep the rest of us silent, with a promise of reward for keepin' our mouths shut? Sorry, bra, but if you knew my partner, you'd know no amount of gold would buy her.'

'What does that say about you?'

'I don't need your dirty money. I just need you to leave these folks alone.'

'If it were up to me, pal . . .' said the man and shrugged.

There was no hint of deception in the man's eyes. But Po had faced up to many opponents lacking the stomach for what they were forced into doing on another's behalf, yet they still did their bidding all the same.

'You're your own man,' said Po, 'you could walk away. Blake and Kelly Ambrose are finished; this is your opportunity to get away before the shit comes down on them.'

At mention of his bosses the man involuntarily flinched in regret. 'The Toners mentioned them by name, did they?'

'They didn't. They didn't have to. My partner is a private investigator; *she* works things out.'

'Unfortunate,' said the man.

'Unfortunate for them.'

'Unfortunate for *everyone*.' He breathed out his next words, sounding truly regretful. 'This is out of control, no longer something I can put right again.'

'So why waste your time and mine? Walk away, bra. Don't make me your enemy.'

'I've heard about you, Villere. You've an admirable reputation.' He left things at that. It was enough for Po to judge the man as a formidable opponent. He'd shown no sign of fear or trepidation at his admission, and neither had he boasted about how he was the tougher guy. It meant that he was in control of himself, and believed also of the situation.

There was the faintest scuff of a shoe on the floor. Coming from inside the building it shouldn't be cause for alarm. But the man's calm demeanor – too calm – triggered Po's response. He began to twist towards the person sneaking up on him, but Temperance was not about to be caught lacking as she had when Po captured Dom. This time, she'd snuck in under the roller shutter, gaining access to the lobby behind Po through the garage's access door to spring an ambush on him. In an instant her knife tip was a hair's breadth from his jugular. If he moved to grapple her he'd skewer himself. She hissed a sour exhalation of victory into his face. Po returned his attention to the man. He'd drawn a pistol, most probably from a holster concealed in the hollow of his spine where Po couldn't have spotted it, despite professing he was unarmed and him lifting and opening his jacket.

'Don't move,' the man warned, still seemingly as indifferent as before, 'and don't try warning your partner.'

'You goin' to shoot me out here in the open, bra? You'll have the cops here in minutes.'

Temperance again hissed in his face. 'It'll only take me a minute to go up there and slaughter everyone. What's to stop Sampson shooting you? Oh, yeah! Me. I could slit you from ear to ear before he has to pull that trigger.'

Po sniffed in disregard. He held no immediate fear of her blade; the guy – Sampson – he was the one in charge. Po discretely cocked an elbow – a swift jab to her solar plexus and then let's see how she'd manage to cut his throat. Sure, he might be encouraging a shot from Sampson, but he doubted it. If he were supposed to die by their hands, he'd already be dead. Nevertheless, he relaxed his elbow. Another thought had come to him, a better way to move things forward.

'What now?' he asked.

From her belt, Temperance pulled out a small cotton sack. Po regarded it with a curl of his lip. 'Really?' he asked.

'Really,' she snapped as she dragged it over his head. Her blade shifted so it stroked the nape of his neck.

'Good, now follow my voice,' Sampson ordered.

Po walked, but had no need of Sampson's instructions, or the occasional nip of the blade in his skin, to walk around the front of the building. The van wasn't parked outside the roller shutters this time, but at the far end of the building where the realtor's signs were. After a door was yanked open, Po was forced to kneel on the van's door ledge.

'Hands behind your back,' Temperance instructed.

Duct tape was wound repeatedly around his wrists.

He felt his captor root around at his belt, and then pat down his legs. She found the blade secreted in his boot sheath. 'Nice,' she commented, and for the first time in a voice that didn't hold pure enmity.

'Take care of it, I'll be needin' that back later,' Po said.

'Don't worry, I'll make sure it goes in the same hole in the ground you do.' Her snarl was back.

His cellphone began ringing.

Sampson rooted around inside Po's jacket and found the phone in his shirt pocket. Po heard his grunt of surprise at who was calling.

After only a moment's reflection Sampson answered and said, 'If you want to see your man alive again, you'll do exactly what I tell you. If you involve the cops, the FBI, anybody, Villere will die screaming. Do you believe me? Good. Then listen closely. Hang up, keep your phone turned on, and wait for further instructions.'

Sampson ended the call. Po's cell wasn't returned to him. He was pushed inside the van and forced to lie belly down. Sampson knelt beside him. 'Let's hope your partner cares enough about you she does as she's been warned,' he said.

Tess, Po knew, loved him so fiercely she'd follow him into hell if she must. She wouldn't involve the police; she wouldn't tolerate their interference in getting him back safely.

THIRTY-ONE

Tess hurtled through the drizzle to the parking lot where Po had left his GMC. He had no reason to return to their car without her, the same way that Arlen Sampson had no reason to falsely claim that Po was his hostage. But she must check. Her reaction was the natural response of one who cared deeply for her partner, and was driven partly by denial, but mostly due to the lot offering a good vantage point for looking both directions. Broad Street and Front Street merged a little distance from her, then paralleled the Penobscot River a good distance: there was no sign of Po or his abductors along its entire length. In the opposite direction Broad Street took a dogleg turn and swept beneath the underpass: it was more likely that Po had been taken that way as it gave more direct access to the main routes out of Bangor. She checked what she could see of the traffic on the river bridge, but there was no saying that Po's abductors would use that road out of town. Her first instinct was that he'd been snatched and taken to Blake and Kelly Ambrose. She'd concluded their center of activity was in Brunswick. The temptation was high to leap in the GMC and hurtle directly to a confrontation with them.

Mike Toner jogged across the road towards her. He was blowing hard from the unexpected race downstairs. Steam rose from his head even as everything else in the vicinity dripped.

'Is it true? They've got him?'

Tess's expression told him everything.

'Oh, crap,' he groaned, his hands snarling in his damp hair.

Tess looked both directions again.

'Where in Brunswick would they take him?' she asked.

He shook his head, fingers still tugging at his hair.

'Think, Mike! Where would those people take him?'

'I know where they took me,' he admitted. 'It wasn't in Brunswick, though.'

'Where?' Tess got up almost in his face.

'Rockland,' he said. 'The same place they snatched me from. They were waiting for me at the harbor and forced me into their van. We didn't drive that far.'

'You're certain about that?'

'Yes. I was taken to some deserted building. I got the impression it was on the headland to the north of the harbor; when I was loaded back in the van to be returned to my truck I was blindfolded, but I could still hear the surf crashing and boats thumping against a wharf.'

'They took you to a deserted building so they could beat you?'

'To torture me,' he emphasized, 'out of sight and hearing of any potential witnesses. It's my guess they'll do the same with your fella.'

Thinking furiously, Tess conjured a mental map of the Maine coast but couldn't quite recall where Rockland was. She still had her cellphone clutched in one hand. She checked the screen for fear she'd missed a call during her frantic run from the building. If she rang Po's number again, would Arlen Sampson answer? Would informing him she knew where he was going put Po in immediate peril, or would Sampson realize the game was up and release him? Her latter thought held no credence. She stabbed in Pinky's number.

'Yo, pretty Tess!' he answered.

'How far away are you, Pinky?'

'From Maddie's place? Half an hour at most, me.'

'Po's been taken?'

'Say what?' Pinky's demeanor changed instantly.

'He's been taken.'

'Those motherfuckers from yesterday?'

'Yes.' She didn't correct herself. Pinky knew only of Dom and Temperance, not yet that Sampson was another player in the game. 'They have him hostage, and have warned me about involving the police if I want him back alive.'

'The wise thing to do would be to call the cops.'

'Of course it would.'

'But you're not gonna, you.'

'Of course I'm not.'

'Give me ten minutes and I'll be there.' It was exaggeration, but Tess pictured him flooring the gas and racing towards Bangor at high speed – she didn't want him to lose control on the slick roads the way Jacob evidently had.

'No, wait. Don't come here. Do you know how to get to Rockland?'

'I don't have the first clue, me.'

Tess sought Mike Toner for clarification.

'There's no quick route across country. From here you need to follow the Penobscot till you hit the coast, then follow Route 1 through Belfast and Camden. It's a ninety-minute drive at the best of times, in this weather . . .'

'Belfast, you say?' Pinky had overheard Toner's directions. He had no idea he was only a mile or so shy of where Jacob Doyle recently died, or that the intersection he was approaching was the one taken from the scene by Temperance and Sampson earlier. 'I just saw a sign for Belfast, me. Someplace called Plymouth, too. Will that road get me there?'

'It will,' Toner confirmed, 'and at about the same time as us if we leave here now.'

'Sounds like a plan, Tess,' Pinky announced. 'I'll call you when I'm approaching town and we can meet, us. We'll travel together from Belfast, yeah? If you hear from those fuckers in the meantime, you let me know, y'hear?'

'See you there,' she said and ended the call. It was better that she kept any calls short to avoid missing her next instruction from Sampson. She stared at Toner.

He squirmed.

'What did you mean by *us*?' she asked.

He looked over at the GMC, as if it were obvious. 'I'm coming with you. You need me to show you where they've taken your partner.'

'No, it's too risky.'

'You'll never find him without me.'

'You said you were blindfolded when you were there.'

'Rockland isn't exactly a big city, hell it's hardly a town, and I've lived and worked there for the past three years. I've a good idea where it was I was taken to. I think the point of me wearing the hood was to encourage fear rather than conceal where I was.'

'You need to stay here and be with the girls,' she went on.

'The girls will be fine without me. I'll make sure they lock

up and don't answer the door to anyone. After all,' he eyed her
with meaning, 'your plan for calling the cops has changed, right?'

'I still need you to come clean with the cops, but you're right:
I don't want you to do it right now. Not while they still have Po.'

'Yeah, I kind of figured.' He looked back at the building.
'Maddie's not a bad girl, you know. Yeah, she's doing wrong
with this insurance scam she's got going, but it's only about the
money. It isn't personal. She'd never deliberately seek to cause
anyone harm, same as I can't stand by now and see your partner
hurt because of us.'

'Let's not waste time moralizing.'

He wagged a finger between them. 'Pot calling the kettle
black.'

She understood. It was fine working outside the law when it
suited her, but not for him or his daughter to do the same?
'There's a difference. I'm willing to break the law to save a life,
it trumps scamming vulnerable people out of their hard-earned
cash.' She waved away another response from him. 'To be honest,
Mike, I don't really care what Maddie is doing now, only that it
has brought us to this. Jacob dead and Po in danger of being
next. Now if you're coming with me, go and tell the girls to lock
the doors. Warn Hayley that her father, Jeff Lorton, might show
up, but she must not open the door even to him. I'll bring over
the GMC.'

He did as instructed while she headed across the parking
lot. She was three paces short of reaching the GMC when realization struck, eliciting an uncommon curse from her. Po had the
only set of keys! While Toner was upstairs she'd fully intended
driving off without him, now her plan was scuppered. Angered
by her lack of foresight she still approached the vehicle in the
hope he'd left the keys in the ignition: it wasn't like Po but she
must check. The car was locked and going nowhere.

She cursed again, heading back towards the building. She had
no wish to place Toner in direct danger, but she'd accept a lift
from him to Belfast to rendezvous with Pinky. Once there, she
would demand he return to the girls' sides. As she approached
the roller shutter, she noted that it stood open about a foot
above the ground. It hadn't looked like that earlier, and it struck
her that access via the shutter was the way in which Sampson or

Temperance had gotten the drop on her partner. No, she thought, Po was too counter-surveillance savvy to allow either foe to creep up on him so easily . . . Oh! *The reckless idiot!* They hadn't gotten the drop on him, he'd allowed them to take him hostage, knowing fully well that it'd lead him and – because she'd follow – Tess to the main villains of the piece. He'd let himself be snatched in order to infiltrate the bad guys' lair and usher in what he saw as an inevitable showdown with their enemies.

Tess heaved the roller shutter open.

Toner's pickup truck was an old workhorse, but it'd get her where she needed. The keys weren't in the ignition and not in any obvious hiding spot behind the visor or glove box. The access door to the lobby stood ajar, again showing the route of Po's ambusher into the building. She went through it and craned to look up the two flights of stairs. Toner was still up there, giving instructions to the girls. She danced from foot to foot, eager to get moving, but it was important that the girls understood the seriousness of the situation and didn't leave themselves vulnerable. When he appeared again, Maddie followed Toner down the stairs. He'd pulled on a coat against the weather.

'We're going to have to use your truck,' Tess announced before he'd made it halfway down. 'Po had the keys for the GMC when he was grabbed.'

Toner slapped at his jeans pockets: he'd changed out of the soiled trousers he'd been wearing yesterday. He cursed, raised a hand in apology and ran upstairs again. Maddie continued down. 'I've come to lock the door.'

Tess thumbed towards the garage. 'After we leave, make sure that the roller shutter and this door's secure too. Your dad told Hayley her father might turn up?'

'He won't get in, I promise. Tess, I, uh, I wanted to apologize for . . . well, you know?'

'Acting like a selfish bitch?'

Maddie grunted in surprise, but after a moment's reflection she nodded in agreement. 'I'm genuinely sorry about what has happened, and I know it's entirely my fault. If anyone's to blame, it's me . . . not Hayley, not my dad. Please, Dad's adamant he's coming with you, but please promise that you won't let him get hurt. He's already suffered enough because of me.'

It wasn't a promise Tess could make. Instead she said, 'I'll do my best.'

'Thank you, that's all I can ask for.'

'In return, all I ask is for you to do the right thing,' Tess said.

'We've talked things through, Hayley and I. Helping you is the only right thing to do.'

Tess studied her for any sign of deceit. Maddie stared back, clear-eyed.

Toner returned, taking the stairs at speed. He clattered into the lobby, immediately noting the way the women appraised each other.

He stumbled to a halt, holding aloft his truck's keys. 'Got 'em.'

Tess reached and squeezed Maddie's upper arm. 'Remember what I said; lock everything after we leave.'

Maddie went to her dad. She hugged him, whispered, 'Be careful.'

Toner kissed her on the forehead, said, 'Lock up behind us, I'll be back in no time, OK?'

Maddie wasn't ready to release her hold, and Tess couldn't bear the delay any longer. 'Come on, Mike, we have to get moving.'

Within seconds they were in the truck, and Toner reversed it out of the garage. He pulled a tight turn to avoid the rail track, and swept past the building. Behind them, Maddie watched from the open garage, but as Toner took a left, she reached up and unfurled the shutter. Toner sped through the dogleg under the bridge. Tess sat with her cellphone cradled on her thighs, watching the screen. Her instructions had been to keep her phone on, to await further instructions: she wondered if Sampson had made the error of also leaving Po's phone switched on. If she'd her laptop with her, she would've been able to patch in remotely to Emma Clancy's systems and launch a program from where she could triangulate the location of Po's phone. Hell. These days, with the phone's GPS locator switched on she could easily do it from her phone, but Po – suspicious of such tracking devices – had his disabled. In future she would demand that he kept the damn thing switched on, as would she, to avoid situations like this one.

She glanced over at Toner. He had his jaw set in determination as he drove. For now he was her tracking device, and she was grateful. He took her down roads she'd never have found, cutting minutes off the journey time, and they entered the small town of Belfast within the time he'd estimated. Pinky had gotten there ahead of him, and waited at curbside just after the road spanned the tongue-twisting Passagassawakeag River. Pinky stood alongside his Volvo SUV, his normally dark pallor a noticeable few shades lighter, his eyes wide and partially bloodshot: he looked as fraught with concern for Po as Tess felt. Pinky hugged her when she went to meet him.

'How'd Nicolas manage to get himself snatched?' he demanded.

'That's the thing, Pinky. I think it was a deliberate act.'

'Oh? Right. I see.' Some of the pressure was released from behind his bulging eyes as he snorted out a laugh. 'Should've known that rogue was up to one of his tricks.'

'It would've been better if he'd brought us in on his plan,' she said.

Pinky's mouth stretched in a long-suffering grimace. 'That's Nicolas for you. He probably kept it quiet knowing full well you'd hear nothing of it.'

'There is that,' she agreed.

'You heard anything from the bad guys yet?'

'No.' She hadn't genuinely expected a call, because Sampson and Temperance would have been mobile too, and possibly not too far ahead of them. 'I don't expect they'll call for an hour or more yet.'

Pinky aimed a finger at the highway. 'While I was waiting for you, I did some checking, me. We stay on this road and it takes us down the coast to Rockland.' His next words were directed at the pickup truck. 'What we doing about him?'

Summoned by the attention, Toner stepped out of the cab. 'You ain't leaving me behind,' he announced. 'Even if you drive off together, I'll only follow. I told you Tess, I want to help, and I mean it.'

'I've no intention of leaving you behind,' Tess said, because contrary to her earlier decision she'd come to appreciate Toner's knowledge of the district. 'Pinky can follow you. I'll travel with him from here, Mike.'

Toner eyed them both, suspicious of a double-cross, but finally conceded *why would Tess lie?* She wished to travel with her friend in order to concoct a plan for freeing Po. He nodded in agreement, slid back into the driving seat and readied to leave.

'You trust him not to warn the bad guys we're coming?' Pinky asked.

'He'd give his life for his daughter,' Tess said. 'Right now he wants only to protect her, and thinks helping us is his best way of doing that.'

'Unless he thinks selling our lives for hers is a fair price.'

THIRTY-TWO

Anyone seeing Dom on his drive to Rockland would be forgiven for thinking they were looking at a crazy man. He drove with his nose angled towards the windshield, his bristling beard split by his clenched teeth in a wide, demented grin. He still smarted from the punch in the testicles he'd taken, but he'd all but forgotten his seething hatred of Temperance in anticipation of what was coming. Maybe Blake had reconsidered punishing him, and for sending Sampson off to put the situation to rights, because Sampson had royally fucked up. Now Dom was back on the job. He'd show Blake who could really be relied on in a pinch, and it wasn't that whining punk Sampson, or the high-yeller bitch Temperance, who was good for nothing but driving, mopping up piss, and – if, no *when*, he had his way – going down on her knees and blowing him.

'Yeah, bitch! Try punching me again with my junk bouncing off your goddamn chin!'

Anyone hearing Dom's disgusting proclamation would have to reconsider, not only was he crazy but they'd realize they were witnessing the passing of a completely deranged sicko.

He couldn't care less.

For starters the road was deserted for most of the drive up the coast, and when passing through the tiny conurbations clustered up against the highway, he ensured he kept his thoughts silent for his own amusement. He was inordinately happy, an emotion uncommon to him. He had Sampson to thank and the irony was sweet; through Sampson's mishandling of the job his vaunted superior was about to hand Dom vengeance on a plate.

Dom glanced in his side mirrors, stirring again the memory of yesterday evening when Nicolas Villere had made him flee after disarming him. Shrouded by the pouring rain, the tall southerner had watched him leave, seemingly unmoved by Dom's promise they'd meet again. More than he'd been annoyed at Temperance's sneaky punch, or at Blake elevating Sampson so highly, was that he'd been forced to run away from his enemy. He'd soothed his bruised ego by telling himself he was evading the cops, not running from Villere, and now he'd get the opportunity to show just how little he feared Villere or his blade.

'Yeah. See you real soon, asshole,' Dom crowed, emphasizing the timescale.

He entered Rockland, taking Park Street almost to the same spot where he and Sampson had met Mike Toner off the fishing boat. That had been a little more than thirty hours ago, but to Dom felt a whole lot longer. He picked up Maine Street north, past the ferry buildings and the pier and several boat yards at Lermond Cove. Everything dripped from the most recent shower, scintillating diamonds of light shining everywhere, but all beauty was lost on Dom: beauty to him was in the crimson of spilled blood, the purple of bruised flesh. His destination wasn't far. Just before the North End Shipyard he took a right turn, slowing down when he spotted workers at a nearby boat maintenance shop but they were too busy to be distracted by his appearance. He drove to the deserted building where he'd almost throttled the life from Toner yesterday. He hid the saloon car out of sight of anyone coming or going from the shipyard.

The building was included in BK-Rose's property portfolio. Its previous tenants had tried unsuccessfully to run it as a seafood restaurant, but this had been in a town already brimming over with longer established seafood outlets. Entering the ground floor, Dom could make out the layout of the dining room; some of the tables and chairs still gathered dust in ungainly stacks against the back wall. Faded menus and chalkboards carried the ghosts of meals past. There was a bar, complete with beer taps, but none were hooked up to barrels – Dom knew this for a fact, because he'd checked – and the only liquor bottles were those that'd been recycled as candle holders.

He moved through the dining room towards the back. Out there was a fully equipped kitchen, now unused, and empty storerooms – one of them contained walk-in freezer and refrigeration compartments, that Dom preferred to avoid because of the stench of rot and decay it held. Beyond the storage area was a short service vestibule to the back door. He unlocked it in anticipation of the van's arrival. Temperance would deliver her hostage to the rear door to avoid the possibility of anyone witnessing Villere's arrival.

Dom poked his head outside. The restaurant's service yard backed very close to the sea; waves sloshed back and forth against the rocky outcrop and among the wooden pilings of a nearby jetty. The wind blowing in off the harbor parted Dom's thick beard. He spat between his teeth, then grinned openly at the next weather front forming a mountainous bulwark on the near horizon. Upstairs, with plans for a live music venue, the last owners had soundproofed one large room; it was the room where Dom plied his trade. Ordinarily the sounds of torture didn't filter beyond the walls. But he welcomed the coming storm, because by the time he was done, he wanted Villere screaming for mercy and the storm's ferocity would help muffle them.

He checked his wristwatch. Sampson and Temperance weren't due to arrive for another twenty minutes. All good, it gave him time to prepare a proper welcome for their hostage. He left the door unlocked, and backtracked through the vestibule to the single set of stairs. He went up, flicking on a light at the top. He was in the short hallway containing the bathrooms. He took a leak. His attention was drawn to the mirror he'd caught Sampson staring into yesterday, and he wondered what the fuck the man had seen in the grimy glass. Dom saw only his own smug grin. He left the bathroom. At the end of the hallway was the soundproofed room. Beyond it a couple of storage rooms Dom had never visited. Opposite the bathrooms was the room that Kelly employed as an office whenever she visited. She liked it because it was the only room on the upper floor with windows and gave a view over the harbor town. In there, concealed in a desk drawer, Dom kept a few tools wrapped in a chamois. They weren't for completing maintenance chores on the building: he opened the chamois on the desk, disgorging a pair of leather gloves, a set of brass knuckles, a leather sap filled with coarse sand, and lastly a pair of gardener's pruning shears. In the past he'd utilized the knuckleduster and sap to good effect, unfortunately the shears had been employed merely as a threat. This time he intended using them, whether given permission by Sampson or not.

'Yeah,' he said aloud, as he held up and studied the slightly tarnished shears, 'let's see Villere pick my pocket with none of his fingers attached.'

He made a couple of test clips with the shears, and snarled in satisfaction at the meaty clacks they made each time.

He dragged a chair to the center of the soundproofed room. Because Kelly wasn't joining them for this round of torture, there was no need of the desk that was primarily used to safely separate Kelly from her victims. Along with some rolls of duct tape, he set out his tools on a small plinth to the side of the door. Villere would be ushered inside hooded and would not see what was in store for him until Dom chose to show him. Keeping a victim ignorant until the last moment was always Dom's preferred method; he loved each fresh look of desperation as the next torture instrument was brought into play.

He filled a bucket with cold water and set it aside.

A tough guy like Villere, he might withstand the blunt force trauma of Dom's brass knuckles and sap, he might even endure the removal of a finger or two, but Dom was yet to find anyone able to tolerate prolonged waterboarding.

He worked his hands into the gloves, then fisted them on his hips. Observed his preparations for a moment and nodded in satisfaction. Turning for the hallway, he crept a hand under his jacket and felt the butt of his pistol. He'd reloaded it after having it taken away by Villere. Villere would be blind, tied up and guarded by Temperance and Sampson, but Dom wasn't about to take any chance of his gun being liberated again. He drew it from its holster and also set it on the plinth with his other tools.

From below he heard the squeak of door hinges and the soft thud of feet. The building thrummed as a gust of wind pummeled through it. Familiar voices filtered up to him. He grinned nastily as he strode down the hall.

'Dom?' Sampson called up from the dining room.

'Up here. Ready and waiting.'

Temperance was first to appear at the foot of the stairs. Her features were set as she trained a steely gaze on Dom, awaiting a nasty comment no doubt.

'Hey, come on up. You bring me a gift. All is forgiven, my girl.'

'I'm not your damn girl,' Temperance growled.

She stepped forward, and into the vacated spot Nicolas Villere stumbled. He was hooded, hands secured behind him. The southerner paused a second, head tilting as he tried to make sense of his surroundings. From behind, Sampson shoved him forward with a gruff warning to 'Mind the step.'

Temperance aided Villere's cumbersome march up the stairs with a fist bunched around his jacket collar, tugging him upward. Sampson prodded Villere with his pistol. With each step Villere took, Dom swayed from foot to foot in anticipation. As the trio neared the top of the stairs he backed down the hall, flourishing his arms in encouragement to join him in the room, his torture chamber.

Within the hood Villere's head tracked left and right.

'Sit him down,' Dom commanded, relishing being in charge.

Temperance pushed Villere down into the chair.

Dom would prefer his captive's arms tied to the arms of the chair, but it'd have to do the way he was. He tossed a roll of duct tape to Temperance. 'Secure him best you can.'

She needlessly warned Villere to stay still as she began binding him: Villere should know he was going nowhere without being shot by either of the men. She wound tape around his chest and the back of the chair. She then bound his ankles to a chair leg apiece. She moved to remove the hood.

'Not yet,' said Dom.

Over the gloves he fixed the brass knuckles.

Then, without warning, he practically ran at Villere, winding up his fist. His punch slammed Villere, connecting – Dom approximated – on his right cheek. Villere slumped.

'Some fucking tough guy,' Dom growled.

'Good start, asshole,' Sampson observed. 'How we meant to get our message across to him when he's unconscious?'

'What message? Oh, wait. Didn't you hear? The plan's changed, Sampson. This motherfucker doesn't leave here alive. He's going in a barrel and dumped from the next boat out to sea.'

'Is that your plan, Dom?' Sampson stood directly in front, holding his gaze.

'I take it you haven't spoken with Blake recently?'

'Blake wants Villere dead?'

'He said I should teach him a lesson first for fucking with Blake's business, and then I should bury him at sea.'

'I need him alive and conscious for when I speak with his partner,' Sampson said slowly, as if explaining to a dullard. 'We need her to comply with instructions, and she won't do that if Villere's already dead.'

'So I'll wake the fucker up. Don't worry, Arlen, I don't intend killing him quickly. He'll be around long enough for you to trick his girl here. In fact, it'll be more fun if we get her, do her in front of him, before I finish Villere off for good.'

'Blake thinks that murdering a couple of private eyes is the way forward? Has he completely lost it?'

'He wants them killed as a warning to anyone else who thinks he's to be messed with.'

'This is insane!' Sampson looked to Temperance for agreement, but she dropped her chin and wouldn't meet his gaze. 'You knew about this? It's why you snuck up on him like that? I should've known you were in position too soon.'

'Dom called me just after you got out of the van,' Temperance admitted. 'He said Blake's order was to bring the PI's here to Dom. When I heard you talking with Villere, and I spotted the shutter wasn't locked, I saw my chance.'

Sampson shook his head in disbelief. 'That's why Blake sounded so pleased when I called him after and told him we had Villere; he thought I'd done as ordered. Why didn't he disagree when I told him I planned convincing Tess Grey to leave us alone in exchange for her man?' He pointed a finger at Dom. 'Because it was unnecessary, right? He'd given you different instructions and knew they'd be followed.'

Dom wafted him away like a bad smell. 'If you don't have the stomach for the job, leave me to it.'

Sampson glared, chewing his bottom lip. Finally he came to a decision. 'I have to call Tess Grey with instructions. Wake him up, Dom, for when she asks for proof of life.'

'Sure,' said Dom. He slammed his augmented knuckles into Villere's midriff, jolting him awake as he gasped for breath.

Sampson fished Villere's phone from a pocket and brought up Tess Grey's number.

THIRTY-THREE

Pinky followed Mike Toner's pickup truck down a slipway off Rockland's Main Street, and Tess asked him to draw the Volvo alongside the truck so she could converse with him through their open windows. They were parked on a hard-pack patch of ground just above the rocky shore of Lermond Cove, mostly obscured from view by the trees that butted up against the beach. To their right a launch ramp was submerged beneath the high tide, and a long narrow jetty was in danger of being pulverized by the tumultuous ocean. A boat yard behind them was deserted, those working there having taken shelter inside a workshop from the latest incoming storm.

'D'you see that building there?' Toner indicated the nearest spur of headland a few hundred yards to the north. On it were clustered several buildings and dozens of dry-docked boats in various states of repair. He was more specific, 'That old one with the tin roof and the tree growing up the back wall. I'm positive that's where I was held.'

Tess studied the structure. It was set slightly apart from the rest of the shipyard, squatting on an ancient concrete platform that stretched over the sea along one side. A wooden pier ran cater-corner to the building, ending with a gazebo-type structure. At ground level the windows were opaque, and it was a moment before she realized plywood boards had been nailed over them. On the second level there were large picture windows, but they reflected the moody sky and she couldn't tell if she was watching the clouds shift, or people inside. The place looked abandoned, in a state of disrepair, but looks could be deceiving. At the rear of the building, adjacent to the sea there was a service yard, and in it were parked two vehicles, concealed from the rest of the shipyard by a tall timber wall. One was a dark blue saloon car, the other a panel van. Even from a distance Tess was certain the van was the one used to snatch Po, but it wasn't enough.

'I need to take a closer look,' she announced.

'If we drive any closer we could alert the bastards,' Pinky said.

She indicated the beach. 'I'll go that way. On foot. Wait here, I'll only be a few minutes.'

Pinky reached across and grabbed her elbow, stopping her from getting out. 'I'll go.'

'No, Pinky. No offense, but you're too noticeable. With my hood up, I'll pass for a local walking on the beach.'

'Take a look around you, Tess. D'you see any other locals walking the beach? In this weather they've more sense, them.'

'Then I'll pass for a reckless tourist.' She squeezed him a smile.

He acquiesced, releasing her elbow. But he said, 'Wait up. You'll need this.'

Tess had to scrunch back in her seat as he leaned awkwardly and flipped open her glove box. 'Reach up inside there,' he said.

Tess did as asked. Her fingers touched the grip of a pistol secreted in the dashboard.

'You brought a gun?' she asked. 'I thought you'd put guns behind you?'

'I've put trading in illegal arms behind me,' he corrected. 'I'm still of the old saying that it's better to have a gun and not need it than need a gun and not have one.'

'Fair enough.' Ordinarily Tess would employ her grandfather's old service revolver in a situation like this one, but it was locked safely in its strongbox back at Po's house. She unclipped the pistol from its hidden mounting. She held it on her lap alongside her cellphone, checking the workings and magazine.

'It's a CZ-75 chambered for nine millimeter Parabellum rounds in a sixteen rounds double-stack magazine,' Pinky began.

'Yeah? Save me the sales pitch,' Tess said, and aimed a smirk at him. 'I'll take it.'

'If I hear shooting, I'm coming in, me,' he told her.

She shoved the gun away in her coat pocket. 'Like I said, I need to take a look around first. If there's any shooting it won't be me doing it.'

'More's the reason I'll be coming in then.'

'Fair enough,' she repeated. She squeezed out between the Volvo and pickup truck. Toner's forehead shone with a layer of sweat. He was risking a lot by assisting her, and could even regret making the decision he had back in Bangor. 'You should go back and get the girls out of the apartment, take them somewhere until it's safe to show your faces.'

'I'm not leaving, Tess,' he answered. 'Whatever happens next, unless all of these guys are taken down, rounded up or whatever, my daughter's life's in danger. If they win, there's no safe way of coming back from this for us, because they won't allow us to live knowing they were the ones responsible for killing you and your partner. They'll want to shut us up permanently, your friend Pinky too, and anyone else they think is involved.'

He was probably correct. 'OK. Sit tight here then. I'm going to get closer; once we know Po's here we'll decide what we're going to do about it. If anything bad happens, listen closely and do as Pinky says.'

Toner checked with Pinky, who nodded sagely. 'You heard her, you.'

Tess left them, moving close to where the trees grew at the high-tide line. The surf bubbled almost at her feet, foaming and swishing between the large pebbles and occasional boulder. Raindrops slanted sideways. She pulled up her hood, could feel the comforting weight of the pistol in her pocket. Her cellphone she kept in her hand, risking dropping it in the surf as she negotiated the driest strip of land available. Mid-way to the shipyard, she'd to clamber over a fallen tree. She was stepping over the trunk where it had been rubbed to a silky sheen by the countless backsides of beachgoers that'd rested on it, at her most unsteady, when her phone rang. Straddling the trunk, she plopped down on it, checking her screen. Po was calling. More correctly, his captor was.

'Tess Grey?'

'Who else?'

'You obeyed my instructions?'

'No cops,' she answered, 'and I've waited for your next instruction. I've upheld my side, now you must do something for me. I want to speak to Nicolas.'

'You're not in a position to make demands.'

'Am I not? Unless I hear his voice right now, the gloves come off. I will have to believe the worst, and there'll be no stopping me calling the cops then, or from hunting down every last one of you.'

Unmoved by her threat, Arlen Sampson said, 'Give me a minute. I'll let you hear him.'

'No, hearing's not enough. I want to speak with him, to check Nicolas is all right.'

'I can't promise you that.' Sampson moved the conversation away from his hostage with a demand of his own. 'Tell me where you are.'

Tess thought quickly. He must have heard the surf crashing behind her. 'I'm still in Bangor,' she lied, but added a layer of believability to it. 'The Toners kicked me out of their apartment – they want no involvement with me or Nicolas, especially not now – so I'm across the road with our car, you know, in that parking lot alongside the river?'

Sampson grunted in response.

Tess thought about mentioning the wind blowing through the trees, the rushing of the storm-swollen river, as an excuse for the surf, but thought she'd be overdoing it. To keep up the charade though, she added, 'You expected me to be somewhere else? How can I go anywhere when the only set of keys for our car is in Nicolas's pocket? Actually, by now you probably took them from him, so you know I'm telling the truth. I'm standing in the rain, freezing half to death, but I don't suppose you care?'

'Frankly, no, I don't care.'

There was a note in Sampson's voice that told a lie. Tess tried to capitalize on it. 'What do you hope to gain from taking Nicolas? If it's to ensure my silence it's bound to do the exact opposite. If a hair on his head has been harmed I'll scream bloody murder. You strike me as an intelligent person; surely you know this can only end one way, and it's with you all in prison?'

'If that's true, it's important you listen to me, so we can come to some kind of compromise.'

'Here's the compromise. Let Nicolas go, and turn State's evidence against Blake and Kelly Ambrose.'

'Sorry, Miss Grey, but what you ask is impossible.'

'The first or the latter?'

'Both.'

'Then I can't imagine there being any compromise between us.'

'Things have happened that do not sit well with me . . .' Sampson began.

'Good. You should feel ashamed.'

'But they are what they are,' he finished.

'Release Nicolas, leave the Toners and Hayley alone, and I give you my word—'

'Don't make empty promises you've no intention of keeping.' He exhaled heavily. 'Miss Grey, I know a little bit about you and your partner. You've both proven determined and resilient in the past. There's no way that either of you will back down. Take your man here . . . Nicolas; are you telling me that if he's released he won't immediately come back at us seeking revenge?' Sampson paused briefly, allowing her to consider his question, but not expecting a reply. He went on. 'You're going to do everything in your power to stop us, and that's admirable in its own way. You should. And you should do it quickly.'

'What do you mean?'

'Perhaps this will galvanize you.'

He must have adjusted his phone, or perhaps opened a previously closed door, because she could hear other voices, and the repeated solid whack of a blunt object impacting flesh. Faintly she heard Po curse his abuser for being a coward.

'Po? Po!' There was no possible way her fiancé could hear her. She turned her attention back to Sampson. 'What's happening? Do not touch him. Goddamn you, I'll—'

'You'll make haste here. If you hope to save Nicolas, you shouldn't waste any more time, just get here.'

'Where's here?'

'Come off it, Miss Grey. Don't take me for a fool. We both know you're not kicking your heels in a parking lot in Bangor.'

Frowning, Tess looked towards the ramshackle building only a couple of hundred yards ahead, wondering if at that moment Sampson was watching her from behind one of the picture windows. If he were, he didn't admit it.

'I'm about to leave,' he continued. 'Dom and Temperance will entertain Nicolas until you arrive.'

'Wait! What are you—'

'I'm leaving,' he repeated. She could hear footsteps descending a staircase. 'Don't try stopping me, it will be time better served saving Nicolas's life.'

Sampson ended the call.

In the distance, Tess spotted a figure emerge from the building. It was the first time she'd laid eyes on him, but she knew the man marching towards the blue saloon car was Arlen Sampson. What was he up to? Was this a devious attempt at drawing her into a trap? She couldn't quite grasp his reasoning; it was as if he wanted her to stop Dom and Temperance, and had given her an opening to do so. What was his motive though? If he thought it'd buy him her silence, he was wrong. Sampson started the car and sped from the service yard.

Torn with indecision, Tess rose up from her tree trunk perch, intending to rush towards the building in a blind assault, but it'd be rash. Instead she vaulted back over the fallen trunk and dashed towards Pinky and Toner. Already, concealed by the trees between them, Sampson's car flashed by her, headed for an unknown destination.

Pinky scrambled out of the Volvo, taking her urgency for something else as she rushed back along the beach. He scanned the area behind her, and towards the distant building, seeking a living enemy.

'Get back in the car,' Tess hollered as she bounded towards him.

'What's wrong, Tess? Is it Nicolas, is he—'

'Right now he's still alive, but I don't know how long that's going to last. Come on! Get in.'

Pinky went headlong into the driver's seat, while Tess danced between the Volvo and pickup for the passenger door. Toner assaulted her with questions, but she was almost deaf to them. She took a chip out of his truck's paintwork as she flung open the Volvo's door and scrambled in. She pointed in the direction of the shipyard. 'Get us there now.'

'What about me?' Toner called.

'If you're coming, come, but you'd better keep up, you,' shouted Pinky, throwing the Volvo into drive and hitting the gas. He powered up the slipway, and Pinky – recklessly – didn't halt to check for traffic. Luck was on their side, and he took a squealing turn onto the main road without hitting another car and headed north. Behind them Toner's pickup truck roared in pursuit.

THIRTY-FOUR

P o had been forced to reassess his plan to go willingly as a hostage to the bad guys' lair. It hadn't garnered him access to Blake and Kelly Ambrose for starters, and had earned him an unnecessary beating in the meantime. Recognizing the error wasn't his finest moment, he scolded himself for being an impulsive fool. Tess had warned him that one day his impetuous nature would get him into the kind of trouble he might not be able to get out of. He must get free and turn the tables on his captors.

The hood over his head was a hindrance. It muffled noise, but Po could still sense he'd entered a larger, open space. He tried to form a mental image of his confines, seeking an escape route. He'd no way of knowing that the vestibule behind him was the only regular way in or out, a reason the restaurant owners' plan to expand as an entertainment venue had been turned down because it had failed fire safety regulations.

Through the hood's tightly woven mesh, he could barely make out their shadows as Dom and Temperance moved around him. They were indistinct, giving no hint of limbs or speed of movement. He took half a dozen blows to his head and neck from Dom, none of which he could avoid or try to absorb because he didn't sense them coming. The hood offered meagre protection, dulling the blows a little, but the edges of the brass knuckles still bit through it to split his skin. Blood washed from a severe nick above his left eyebrow and another cut on his left cheekbone. Po's lips were swollen and a tooth had been chipped. His tongue felt lacerated, probably from biting it with his chipped molar, and he tasted copper in the back of his throat. It didn't deter him from cursing Dom, or goading the thug into punching a little harder.

'Man,' Po laughed after Dom's latest assault, a punch to the back of his head that admittedly left his skull tolling like a bell, 'is that all you've got? My grandma used to whup me worse when I was a boy.'

Dom laughed in response, evidently enjoying his victim's macho bullshit. 'Buddy, I haven't even broken a sweat yet. You wait, you'll see. Tempe, gimme that from over there.'

'Get it yourself, asshole.'

'Watch him then.'

'Why? He isn't going anywhere.'

'Fuckin' watch him, bitch. Don't want him wrigglin' outta those bonds and spoilin' our fun.'

'Our fun?' Temperance's voice was brimful of disbelief. 'You gonna kill him, Dom, just kill him and have done. Where's the fun in any of this?'

'You need to ask?' Dom laughed again. Po heard a swishing noise and wondered what fresh torture he must endure.

Dom exploded a hand grenade alongside Po's left knee. Despite himself Po croaked in agony and tried to draw his legs up defensively. The pain in his knee was white hot. Po could visualize the raw agony washing through his brain. He could *taste* it. No, it was the shock playing havoc with his senses. The sharpest, most intense hot pain subsided quickly, replaced by a different kind: this a cold burning sensation that shot down his shin bone, and almost all the way up his thigh to his groin. It was a second or more later before Po understood what had happened. No grenade had been detonated; Dom had rapped Po on the outside of his knee with a sap. He could bear the punches to his head and torso, but this had come out of left field, unexpected and direct to a cluster of exposed nerves, bone and cartilage. 'You yellow son of a bitch,' Po growled at his tormentor, 'for that, when I get loose, I'm gonna bring you a world of hurt.'

'Is that right? You hear him, Tempe?' Dom chuckled. 'We'd best make sure he doesn't get loose, eh?'

'I didn't hear him cursing me, Dom,' said Temperance, 'it's you he's carrying a boner for.'

'You positive about that, girl? I'm sure I heard him say somethin' about a yeller bitch?' Dom moved fast. The sap landed on Po's right elbow, eliciting another shout of agony. 'Hey you,' Dom chided, 'let's have less of the racist and sexist bullshit from now on.'

Po had no idea what went on between the two next, except he heard Temperance snort and exclaim, 'My fucking hero.' Dom laughed as if it were the funniest thing he'd ever heard.

'Get that bucket, will ya?' Dom said, once his laughter was under control.

This time Temperance didn't rebel against his command. Po heard her lift the bucket, a metallic squeaking and slopping of water accompanying the action as she lugged it closer. It clunked down heavily alongside the chair. Before he could consider it any longer, Dom had moved in behind him. Fistfuls of the hood were dragged tightly backwards, and the rough cloth scraped his facial wounds raw again. Po fought the hood for a moment, but his neck muscles were no match for Dom's arms and shoulders. His head was craned backwards over the headrest.

'Come around here,' Dom told Temperance, 'and take over for me. C'mon, Tempe. You've seen me do this plenty times.'

The material of the hood cut into Po's throat. He could still breathe, and he suspected there was reason, rather than mercy, behind the way Dom had pulled it. There was some fumbling, and a momentary lessening in the pressure as Temperance took charge of it. After tugging it tight, she pushed her weight against the back of the chair in order to control him. Dom bent and grasped the bucket, and Po knew what was coming. He held his breath. Prepared to tolerate hell. Prayed, *Tess, I hope you're not far away.*

Dom sloshed water over the hood.

The cloth was sodden, and icy water poured over Po's features. He had his lips tight, but water invaded his nostrils and earholes. That was tolerable, but not for long. Po couldn't hold his breath forever.

Dom upended the bucket further.

More water flooded between the cloth and Po's skin. He exhaled sharply to clear his nostrils, but that compounded his fight to hold his breath. As the icy tide ran down over his chin, he chanced taking a quick gulp of air, but Dom must've been watching closely for such a response. He dashed more water directly over Po's mouth. Po inhaled water. He gasped, spluttered, and a rarely experienced panic engulfed him. He squirmed against his bindings, and when he found no space for movement, his body wrenched forcefully.

'Now that's what I'm talking about!' Dom crowed. 'Hold him, Tempe. Here I come again.'

More water flooded inside the hood. A ragged moan escaped
Po as he fought to expel water from his throat. Pressure built
behind his swollen eyelids, as if his head would explode. His
feet drummed on the floor.

For a reason unknown to Po, Dom dropped the bucket and it
clattered about his feet. Water sloshed over the floorboards. Po's
drumming soles now splashed droplets everywhere.

'What?' Temperance wondered.

Dom had moved aside.

'Where's the fucking fun in watching him drown in a sack?'
Dom responded. 'I want to see the fear in his eyes, I want him
to beg for mercy, I want him to watch as I take every last one
of his fingers and toes. You hear me, Villere? I'm gonna fucking
leave you with nothing but bleeding stumps.'

Temperance took Dom's words as a fresh instruction. She
pulled the hood off him. Po ignored her, craning his neck so he
could glare directly at Dom. He could feel the heat of hatred
emanating from his eyes. Dom grinned back at him. He held
aloft a pair of gardener's shears. He snipped the air a couple of
times in malevolent promise.

'Come near me with those, and I swear to God . . .' Po grated
out. Blood-flecked frothy water spilled from between his lips and
he hacked out a cough.

'Take off his boots,' Dom said.

'You take them off.' Temperance moved aside. Po knew by now
that the woman had a vicious streak, but what Dom planned for
him repulsed her. He wondered what she'd witnessed in the past
– perhaps an act by her own hand – that made the blood rush from
her features and leave her dusky features a few shades lighter.

Taking off Po's high-top boots wasn't the simplest of tasks
for Dom. When Temperance secured his legs she'd wound the
duct tape around his ankles and the chair legs; to get at the laces,
Dom had to first negotiate the tape. He took the easiest path.
Kneeling, he jammed the blades of the shears under the laces
and began cutting, and when he reached the tape, he sheared
through it as well, then the last few remaining loops of lace. He
wrenched the boot sideways, loosening it and then yanked it
free. He tore off Po's sock. He spied up at Po, 'Ready for your
pedicure, Villere?'

Po curled back his toes, squirmed his ankle to free it from Dom's grasp.

'Quit moving,' Dom warned, 'or I might accidentally nick you.'

Temperance looked as if she was ready to run. Her head snapped around like a startled bird. She said, 'Where did Arlen get to?'

She elicited a grunt of scorn from Dom. 'Told you, he hasn't the stomach for this stuff. By the looks of things you haven't either. Get over here, girl, toughen yourself up, why don'tcha?'

Ignoring him, Temperance paced towards the hall. She gave it a cursory check, and her gaze alighted on the bathroom door.

'Probably chucking up again,' Dom said. 'Forget him, after today I doubt he'll be one of the gang. Tempe, get the fuck over here and hold this asshole's leg, will ya!'

Out of Po's sight the woman must have shaken her head.

'Fuck you then,' Dom snarled at her, 'I'll do it myself.'

He snatched Po's foot into the crook of his bent thigh, grabbing and twisting his toes apart, choosing the smallest. He grinned maliciously at his victim as he forced the steel blades either side of the digit. 'You stole my wallet, from me, now I'm gonna take somethin' of yours, Villere.'

He began to close the shears, taking his time, relishing the tremor of anticipation that flooded through him.

From below the explosion was terrific. A shudder went through the entire building, the corrugated tin roof warping and flexing. The room rocked and the floor shifted, and Dom toppled backwards onto his butt. The floor slanted away from him, he tumbled, and Po slid after him, until his chair twisted around, toppled and he crumpled backwards.

You couldn't have timed things better, Tess, he thought.

THIRTY-FIVE

I t wasn't solely Tess that Po had to thank for saving him from amputation, Pinky had also played his part. And in his fashion, Mike Toner had too. He'd supplied the means for the distraction when handing over the keys of his pickup truck to Pinky.

'You do have insurance on your truck, right?' said Pinky.

'Yeah, it's covered.'

'Legitimately?'

'Use your freakin' Volvo if you prefer.'

'Nah, this'll do nicely,' said Pinky as he'd settled his weight in the truck's driving seat. He adjusted the seat's position, clearing more legroom. He started the engine, gunning it a few times and feeling the surges of power. 'You'd best get going, Tess, I shouldn't waste any more time, me.'

Jittery with anxiety, Tess nodded at him and set off at a jog, his CZ-75 held down by her right thigh. Pinky waited until she'd made it past the front of the building and had disappeared into the service yard. He hit the gas a third time and the exhaust belched smoke. There was no hint that those inside were aware of him revving the truck.

Mike Toner waited alongside him, one hand grasping the window ledge. Pinky looked at him, this time with mutual respect. 'Follow me inside,' Pinky said, 'but not before you pick up a weapon, you.'

'That reminds me,' said Toner. He dipped his arms over the raised sides of the flatbed and came up clutching a steel wrench as long as his forearm. 'This should do, huh?' He took a few test swings.

'OK, Tess has had enough time to get inside,' Pinky announced with a wink. Toner stepped aside, hefting his makeshift weapon.

'You're positive you were held upstairs?' Pinky asked.

Toner only shook his head. He'd already told Pinky how he'd been manhandled up and down the stairs inside; it hadn't been a figment of his imagination.

'It's just I'd hate to make a foolish mistake, me,' said Pinky as he gunned the engine again. The truck came with a stick shift and clutch. Pinky rammed the first into gear, and lifted his foot off the other. The truck bucked as it launched forward. Pinky aimed it up the incline towards the abandoned restaurant, his mouth clenched in a grimace. 'You'd better not be loafing around on the ground floor, Nicolas,' he whispered behind his teeth.

Pinky avoided the near corner of the building where it would be at its most structurally sound, instead directing the hood of the pickup a few feet to its left, where part of the wall was weakened already by the inclusion of a window. The plyboard covering didn't add much strength or integrity against a speeding truck. It smashed to shards, the wood around it to splinters, and the truck kept on going, ramming completely through the wall and inside.

Surprisingly the windshield survived the impact, although the hood and fenders buckled up, and parts of them tore away. Pinky kept his foot on the gas, slewing the steering wheel to the left. The back of the truck clipped the corner support even as the front hurtled through an upright column supporting the floor overhead. Finally the truck came to a bruising halt and Pinky shook lucidity back into his head. A quick check showed a gaping hole in the building, and an unnatural tilt to the ceiling, but it wasn't enough for him. Pinky threw the stick into reverse, and felt the tires judder and skid as they found traction on splintered planks. Then the truck rocketed backwards and again he swung the steering, this time angling the flatbed for the back wall. The wall exploded outward, casting broken boards and glass out over the surging tide. Luckily he halted the truck before it took a similar plunge into the cove. It teetered, held in place by jagged remnants of the wall. Pinky piled out of the truck, and into the dust clouds and falling detritus he'd caused. He checked around for a weapon, but couldn't see anything that hadn't been shattered by the truck, and then recalled Toner had tools in the back. He rooted around, had to throw aside handfuls of splinters and chunks of wood, but came up with a prize: a weighty claw hammer. He turned with it clutched in hand, just as Toner was silhouetted in the brand-new doorway Pinky had opened for him.

'Let's go,' he said and moved across the empty dining room. He had to avoid broken planks and some stacked furniture the crash had disturbed; chairs had toppled across his path. Toner came forward at an oblique angle to him, seeking an exit from the room. He used his wrench as a pointer to indicate a door, beyond which Pinky supposed they'd find the stairs.

Tess had had a feeling that when he abandoned ship, Arlen Sampson had left open the outer door, and Toner had added to the supposition saying he believed the staircase was accessible from it. By now Tess should already be upstairs and Po's captors reeling from experiencing the building buckle under their feet. It had to be assumed that Dom and Temperance were armed, and with more potent weapons than a handyman's tools, but at least Tess's gun should level the field. Pinky didn't slow as he rushed for the stairs, the hammer clutched as though he was a vengeful god of thunder.

The building creaked ominously.

Something shifted, cracked loudly and the upper floor dipped towards the demolished corner. Shouts rang out from above, male and female voices, and some that were hard to define. Already Tess had engaged the enemy. Pinky flashed his eyes at Toner, jerking his head, urging speed. He plunged into a short vestibule, found the stairs and went up, his broad frame filling the space, elbows brushing the walls. Behind him Toner followed at pace: in protection of his daughter the man showed a complete turnaround from the bullied and brutalized man who'd last spent time here.

A gun fired.

Feet drummed. A woman yelped, before gathering herself for a fight and her next vocalizations were angry shouts of challenge.

More shouts erupted, and feet scuffled. Something crashed and something heavier hit the floor. The shouts were a combination of curses and counter curses.

Pinky spilled out from the top of the stairs into a hallway. Doors to either side were resolutely shut. He ignored them, rushing forward, trying to define friend from foe as several figures jostled in the half-light. The room hadn't survived the collapsing of the building. The floor tilted away from Pinky, one part of it having fully collapsed in the short time since he'd left the dining room. Dust swirled everywhere.

Pinky took stock in little more than an instant.

Tess was upright, in a catfight with Temperance. Both women

had a fist locked in the other's hair, while their free hands punched and ripped. Tess kneed her opponent between the legs. Temperance returned the favor, aiming for Tess's abdomen to wind her. There was no sign of the CZ-75, but so too had Temperance's knife been lost in the scuffle. Deeper in the room, Po grappled with Dom. Po was hindered by the remnants of a chair clinging to him on ribbons of duct tape. He was encumbered by the backrest of the chair that drooped from a loose band of tape around his chest: it got under his feet and almost tripped him. Po had to take a second to kick free, but there was a broken chair leg attached to his left ankle and it got caught. Dom capitalized on Po's lack of motion, swinging a clubbing right hook at Po's head. Po staggered under the blow. Even in the dusty twilight, Pinky saw the glint of metal on Dom's knuckles and he chose his move.

Over his shoulder he hollered at Toner – 'Get her the hell off Tess!' – and then he charged forward swinging the hammer overhead. Dom saw him coming, and the trajectory of his next punch was disturbed as he flung out his hand to grasp at the haft of the hammer. Pinky took delight in the way the hand missed and the blunt steel head buried itself an inch in the soft flesh of Dom's forearm. It was only a pity the hammer hadn't landed between the son of a bitch's eyes. As Dom backed away, cradling his injured arm, Pinky met his friend's eyes and was shocked at Po's bloodshot sclera and the dazzle of shock in them. Po, he thought, was only upright and moving on instinct.

But no, that wasn't true.

Po's mouth curled in a lopsided smile, and he took the moment's respite to wrench the chair leg free of his ankle, then shucked out of the tape looped around his chest. The other parts of the broken chair fell away. Po said, 'I've got this from here, Pinky.'

Po carried gaping wounds on his face, his left elbow looked swollen and he favored his right leg. He was drenched and grimy. Just then, Pinky thought a strong wind would knock him over.

'You sure you don't want me to kick his ass, you?'

'Thanks, but I owe the bastard big time.'

Po moved towards Dom, limping discernibly, but undeterred, and it was only then that Pinky noted Po's other foot was bare.

He had no idea the extent of what punishment Dom had put Po through, but he sure was going to pay for it.

THIRTY-SIX

As she'd hoped, Arlen Sampson had left the service door unlocked. She only fleetingly wondered where he'd gotten to, and if this was some elaborate trap in order to catch her, and in the next space was thankful to him for giving her clear access to Po's prison. She'd earlier warned that he'd get no grace from her, but just then she would've kissed him fully on the lips for the opportunity to save her loved one.

With the pistol before her, she ducked inside the building, heading quickly for the foot of a set of stairs. Toner had been adamant she'd find Po upstairs, and he was right judging by the voices that filtered down to her.

She heard Dom's gruff request. 'Tempe, get the fuck over here and hold this asshole's leg, will ya!' He quickly followed up by cussing the woman out and claiming he'd do it himself.

With no idea of Po's predicament, other than it could be anything but good, Tess quickly stole up the stairs. She advanced down a hallway, her eyes on Po, who was bound to a chair, his back to her. Initially she couldn't see Dom, or Temperance who must have been lurking to one side of the doorway or the other. Then she spotted movement, and understood that Dom was kneeling directly in front of Po. 'You stole my wallet, from me,' he crowed, 'now I'm gonna take somethin' of yours, Villere.'

She couldn't see the clippers he began closing around Po's little toe, but she saw Po fight his bindings to escape whatever was in the sadist's mind. Tess took the last couple of hurried paces over the threshold, was about to shout at Dom to halt, and that was when Pinky exploded through the ground floor in the pickup truck.

Tess jostled for balance. Pinky had warned her his distraction would be loud, but she hadn't expected him to almost bring down the roof. As it was, the entire building shuddered, and an impact wave buckled the roof. Underfoot the floor shifted, and she saw Dom topple backwards and slide along the tilting floor. She lunged, to grab at Po, but he slid after Dom, his chair skewing around and toppling. He had no idea how close she was to saving him, but then he never was one to wait for rescue. Po kicked out with his one free – bare – foot, using the freeing of that leg in order to twist against his bindings. The chair was torqued out of shape, but it wasn't enough for him. He fought around onto one knee, then threw his shoulder at the floor. The chair fell to pieces, but the sundry parts were still attached to him by lengths of duct tape. Po pushed up to his feet, wrenching and twisting his wrists and the ripping of his bonds was a shriek to match the one of rage that left his throat.

All of this had taken seconds at most. Down below, Pinky was tearing through the building in a second attempt at razing it. Beyond Po, Dom had found his feet, and he pushed away from a sudden chasm that appeared in the floor, gasping in dismay that he'd almost fallen through it. The big man came fully upright, searching for Po and his gaze barely alighted on Tess before he snapped a look to her right.

It was scant warning, but Tess began to turn in that moment, just as Temperance leapt at her from the dimness of the near corner. The dusky-skinned woman's face was contorted in a shout of challenge, one that Tess answered as she snapped out a hand to grab Temperance's wrist. Lucky that she did, because Temperance's knife was aimed directly at the side of her neck. Temperance grabbed Tess's opposite hand too, pushing the CZ-75 aside. Deeper in the room Po and Dom yelled challenges and clashed, but Tess had no time to watch them while fighting for her own life.

The floor collapsed at the far end of the room, a thunderous avalanche of planks, support beams and furniture, and dust billowed everywhere. Tess tasted pulverized wood on her lips, and she'd to screw her eyelids to avoid the blinding cloud. She wrestled Temperance away, back towards the corner the woman had launched her attack from, and they thudded against a wall. Tess's gun went off, a sharp crack between other cracks and snaps. Temperance yelled and in desperation wrenched the gun free of Tess's grasp. Thankfully it spilled from her fingers too and was instantly lost to them both. Tess battered her opponent's hand against the wall repeatedly, until her grasp loosened and

Temperance dropped the knife. Still in a hand on wrist struggle, they waltzed free of the wall. Tess attempted to trip Temperance, but the woman was too wily, and too wiry, to succumb. In the next second, Temperance wrenched out of Tess's clutch and grabbed a fistful of Tess's blonde hair. She yanked Tess off balance and punched at her face with her other bunched fist. Tess felt the impact on her right eyebrow, and a sharp pain ricocheted around her skull. Angered, she entwined her fingers in the other woman's hair, hanging tightly to a bunch of thin plaits, and for a few seconds they circled around each other, feet splayed, yanking down on the trapped hair while throwing punches like ice hockey combatants.

Tess was furious. This was not a fight she wished to prolong. If only she'd caught Temperance as sweet as she had Nathan Doyle the day before, and knocked the bitch unconscious in the first few seconds! The problem being, she knew her lucky knockout of Nathan was just that, and providence wasn't smiling on her a second time.

You want to end things, Tess, then damn well end things!

She arched her back, jabbing upward with her knee directly into Temperance's crotch. It wasn't a finishing blow as it could be with a male opponent, but hurt savagely at any rate. Temperance responded with a knee to Tess's belly, but she'd kind of expected it, had hoped that Temperance would follow her lead. While the woman had one leg in the air, Tess looped her right arm under it, yanking upward so that Temperance windmilled her arms, off balance. She'd released her grip on Tess's hair as she fought to stay upright. Tess also released the captured plaits, but barely moved her fingers more than a few inches. As she released the trapped leg, she grabbed one of the flamboyant earrings and tore it, and part of Temperance's earlobe free.

Temperance screeched in rage and shock, but Tess could care less. She threw a kick into the woman's nearest shin, and an elbow into her face as Temperance buckled forward. As the woman fell to her knees, Tess aimed a clubbing punch at the nape of her neck that should have put her down for minutes. However, Temperance was tough, and enraged, and the blows hurt but didn't finish her. She reared up again, and to Tess's horror, with Po's knife clutched in her hand. Temperance ripped up at Tess's torso.

The steel wrench swung by Mike Toner snapped the bones in the knifewoman's forearm.

Tess backpedaled, watched her would-be slayer sink down with a moan of agony as she cradled her broken arm across her abdomen. Then she glanced at Toner, whose face was rigid with determination as he shoved Temperance over onto her side, and then swept away Po's knife with the sole of his shoe. He stood over her, threatening her with the large lug wrench that he shook in dire warning. Temperance paid him little heed; she wept at the pain she was currently experiencing.

Breathless, Tess tore her attention from the woman to Pinky who she saw batter Dom's arm with a hammer. Po was partly obscured by his friend's bulk, but even through the swirling wood dust, she could tell he was hurt, but alive. A lump the size of a baseball formed in her throat, and she opened her mouth to call him, but then he shucked loose of the chair parts and duct tape and she knew he wouldn't hear. His attention was solely on Dom, and would be until the thug no longer posed a threat to anyone.

THIRTY-SEVEN

D om had discarded the sap when he selected the garden shears as his next torture implement. He'd lost those as he fell and then scrambled away from the hole opening under him. He still wore the brass knuckles on his right fist, and though Pinky had struck him with the hammer, it hadn't caused lasting damage. Dom was mostly fit and strong, whereas Po had been beaten repeatedly, he limped and had one arm wedged against his ribs for support. Blood loss must have weakened him. Dom probably felt he was the tall Cajun's match in a fight under usual circumstances; injured the way he was, Po wouldn't last seconds.

Dom rubbed his forearm vigorously a few more times, then grinning in a rictus, he curled his fingers, beckoning Po towards him.

He didn't know Po Villere.

Like a wild thing, Po was at his most dangerous when he was injured. Ordinarily he would fight with a sense of honor and morality, and if there were rules of engagement would stick to them. Gaining the upper hand, he'd be merciful with his opponent. Here the circumstances were different; here he'd fight as if his life depended on it, because it did. Any blow from those augmented knuckles could shatter his skull, killing him outright or leaving him forever maimed, so here the fight was not dictated by honor or morality and with a single rule: kill or be killed.

Pinky was at Po's back, so Dom had no way of getting past him to the door. His only way out if he chose it, would be via the collapsed floor that now gaped two or three feet wide in places. He'd bet Dom wasn't for risking a drop into the void below, for fear he'd end up impaled on a broken support beam. Po limped forward, forcing Dom to crouch or go backwards. He chose the former.

Po formed loose fists. There was little sensation in his left leg from when Dom struck it with the sap, but it felt stable enough.

His other leg was fine, but the jagged splinters strewn across the floor were lacerating his bare foot. Rather than numb, his abused elbow was swollen, on fire with nerve pain. He shook it out, though it made little difference.

Maybe he should have allowed Pinky to kick Dom's ass.

No, he'd made his abuser a promise and meant to keep it. 'Welcome to your world of hurt,' he grated as he moved to close the distance.

Dom lunged, throwing a punch at Po's body.

Po sucked his gut back, and jabbed the point of his left elbow down into the meat of the bearded man's forearm. It struck at much the same spot as Pinky's hammer had a minute ago. The pain that flared through Dom's arm was commensurate to the worst pain ever! Dom cried out, shrilly. His arm went entirely numb, and he withdrew it protectively, cupping it across his abdomen. Ignoring the resulting pain in his elbow, Po swung and battered the knuckles of his right hand an inch or so above Dom's outer knee. The big man staggered, and Po steadied his feet as he watched fear well in Dom's eyes.

With Dom's arm and leg injured, they were almost on a par for the remainder of the battle. The knuckleduster gave an unfair advantage, but only if Dom could land it. Time, Po decided, to level the field a little more, and bust up the thug's face as a match for his own. Po sprang, throwing straight punches, piston-like, at the bearded chin and face. He avoided the bald dome of the skull, because there the bone was generally tougher than any fist. Instinctively, Dom threw counter punches, but they lacked strength or direction. They didn't trouble Po. He swayed his upper body, avoiding Dom's clubbing fists. Then he planted his weak leg, stepped into a kick and thrust his bare foot into Dom's midriff. Dom went down on his butt, skidding on the down slope. He panicked, slapping at anything he could reach before gravity could snatch him through the hole in the floor.

Po took a moment to check over his shoulder. Pinky clutched the hammer still, looking as if he'd happily take over and bash in Dom's skull. Po squeezed him a reassuring smile. 'I've got this, brother,' he promised.

He searched for Tess. She was in the open doorway to the hall, one hand braced on the jamb, unsure of the floor's integrity.

She was right to be wary. Under his feet it bounced and sprang with each step. They met gazes, and Tess tried to imbue her love for him across the intervening space; he wanted her to know he regretted not bringing her in on his plan to bait the bad guys in their lair. Thankfully it didn't matter now; she was here, she was unhurt, all was as well as it could be . . . for now. Another quick glance showed him Mike Toner standing guard over the downed woman, and right then, Po had no idea who'd put her in her place.

Scrabbling noises alerted him. His attention snapped back to his opponent. Dom, on hands and knees was scuttling, trying to get around Po. Po checked his destination and spotted an overturned plinth. There was a rag of chamois leather next to it, and Dom's sap. Was that what he hoped to get his fingers on? His brass knuckles had proved ineffective against a mobile Po; did he truly think an extra few inches of reach would turn the tide of the fight? Po was tempted to let Dom reach it, but Pinky was having none of it.

'Nuh-uh, no way, no how, you cowardly piece of crap!' Pinky moved with alacrity uncommon in a man of his size, to snatch up the sap and shove it away in a pocket. He backed away, allowing Po the stage again. Dom looked undeterred, he continued scrambling on all fours, and it was a second or so more before Po spotted why. The man had another weapon in the room that had gone unaccounted for. His pistol. It must have fallen off the toppling plinth and slid further down the decline before wedging against a warped floorboard.

Po lunged to intercept Dom. The floor gave another heave, and something beneath it gave way. The surface dropped from under Po's feet. He skidded, with no control of his destination, and checked up against Dom. Dom turned the pistol he'd managed to grab on Po and pulled the trigger.

Skill rather than luck saved Po's life. He struck with the side of his hand at the barrel just as the gun fired, and the bullet went through his deltoid muscle as opposed to his throat. The wound could prove serious if the bullet had struck bone, or one of the major nerves or arteries serving his arm, but in that second Po gave it no concern. He grasped down on the barrel of the pistol, shoving it aside, as he jammed his stiffened fingers in Dom's face. He hoped to blind the shooter, if not permanently he'd make do with temporarily: enough time at least to disarm him would do. Po didn't try any fancy move, merely levered back and up on the gun barrel, trapping Dom's index finger against the trigger guard, and wedged it against metal – because he still wore the brass knuckles – and the gun couldn't be trained on Po again. Dom's finger was being crushed and his ragged scream hinted at his agony. He might have been relieved when Po reversed the pressure and easily stripped the gun from his grasp. His relief would be measured in nanoseconds, because in the next instant he'd understand how woefully outmatched he was by the man he'd have made his victim. Dom cried out for leniency as Po drew back his hand to land another blow to his bruised face.

'Buddy,' Po growled, 'I've only just gotten started with you.'

He slammed Dom under the chin, and the beard did nothing to lessen the blow. Dom's teeth clacked together, and his eyeballs rolled in their sockets. He sagged. Po shoved him away and Dom reached for the wall for support. It wasn't near. He fell on his side and began rolling, loose-limbed and senseless. The hole in the floor beckoned. Po was tempted to let him fall.

He handed back Dom's pistol to Pinky, then limped after the unconscious man. Now that the heat of the battle was waning, his moral center was reaffirming its control over him. He couldn't let the man fall to his death, to land impaled like a fish on one of the broken shards below. He grabbed Dom's jacket before he reached the precipice and tugged him away.

'You're a better man than I am, Nicolas,' Pinky told him. 'I'm not sure I could be so merciful, me.'

'I only want to beat on the fucker a little more.'

Po waited a beat before offering a smile at his joke.

Pinky exhaled sharply, then, raising his eyebrows, he offered the hammer.

Po ignored the gesture, as Pinky knew he would. Pinky tossed the hammer away, but slipped Dom's pistol into the safety of his belt. Po grasped Dom's jacket tighter and dragged him back towards the entrance hall. 'See if you can find any of that duct tape, will ya?' he asked of nobody in particular.

Mike Toner and – more importantly to Po – Tess had their prisoner under guard. Unbeknown to him, Tess had discovered where the CZ-75 had fallen during her struggle with Temperance, and recovered it. She only loosely aimed it at the woman, but Temperance didn't appear fit to launch an escape attempt: blood leaked from a torn ear, and she cradled an arm, her features ashen and slick with sweat. Po threw Dom down near the door. The floor creaked ominously.

'Whose idea was razing the building to the ground?' he asked.

Tess aimed a nod at Pinky, who had already thrown up his hands.

'Guilty as charged, me!'

'It was a bit extreme.'

'As was your ridiculous plan to act as bait,' Tess added.

Pinky answered for both men. 'But you have to admit, it got results.'

'It could still get us all killed,' Tess remarked. 'Let's get out of here before the rest falls down.'

Between Tess and Toner, they jostled Temperance up between them, Tess aiming a dire warning in her good ear about what would happen if she tried anything stupid. In fairness, Temperance barely had the will or strength to support her own weight. Toner had to assist her as she began the descent.

Dom was twice the woman's weight, and neither Po nor Pinky fancied helping him down. They each grabbed an ankle and dragged him along the hall, intent on pulling him down the stairs on his back – if his skull happened to bounce off every step on the way down, then so what?

Nobody had answered Po's request to find the duct tape. Therefore, Dom wasn't yet secured. Neither was he as unconscious as he pretended. As they reached the top of the stairs he suddenly kicked out, pulling away from Po. Pinky still had his fingers on his ankle, but was in a bad position, wedged by the doorjamb, and Dom was able to yank his foot free. He began scrambling to escape, coming up to his feet by clawing at the walls. A door flew open under his touch and he tumbled inside the room. Po went after him, followed seconds later by Pinky.

They were in an office of sorts, with a desk and chairs and large windows. Dom tried to put the desk between them, and Po suspected there could be a hidden weapon in one of the drawers the man clawed at. He didn't wait to find out. He vaulted the desk with one hand propped on top for support, and kicked out with both feet. Dom took the impact high on his chest, and was thrust backwards. All that was there to cushion him was a window. It shivered under his weight, exploded outward and Dom flipped through the gap with a cry of terror.

Po had to steady himself after sliding off the desk. In the moment he had given neither his injured arm nor busted knee a thought, but the agony blossoming in each were swift reminders. He staggered to where Pinky was already leaning out over the windowsill.

'Is he dead?' Po asked.

Pinky said, 'He's got a head like Humpty Dumpty, him.'

Po peered down, grimacing. Dom hadn't fallen too far. It was far enough that when his skull struck the concrete it had shattered as easily as an eggshell. Pinky was correct, there'd be no putting Dom together again.

'Hmmm,' Po murmured. 'This might take some explaining to the cops.'

'What's to explain? Distraught at the thought of going to prison, he took the coward's way out, him.'

'I'm not sure that story will wash,' said Po.

Pinky studied him up and down. Po, bloodstained and bruised, with only two fully working limbs between four, looked fit to drop. 'Nicolas, there's not a cop on earth would believe you had the strength to knock a big dude like him out of a window.'

THIRTY-EIGHT

There was no escaping lawful process for any of them now. Blake Ambrose's instruction to Dom to torture and murder their hostage was a step too far to come back from. Handled differently they might have gotten away with Villere's disappearance, but there was no possible way of covering up the crime when his partner, and those around her, all knew who'd snatched him. Even if Blake sent his minions on a rampage of death and cover up, targeting anyone with a connection to Villere, Tess Grey, the Toner family and friend, or to Jacob Doyle, there was no possible way to shut everyone up in time. This had begun as a simple ploy to bully compliance – and their profits – out of a couple of small-time scammers, and it had devolved into chaos. Who could have guessed that a private investigator's search for a rebellious girl would throw them all together on a collision course of violence and death?

Arlen Sampson believed in karma, and that when it came around to bite you on the ass it was with the ferocity of a junkyard dog. Never had he intended to hurt his sister-in-law. Why hadn't he agreed to go with her to Caroline, to admit their infidelity and beg his wife's forgiveness? It would have been difficult, no doubt, and also for Caroline but he believed now she'd have understood why they'd succumbed to base lust, and that it didn't diminish either of their love for her. He could have won her trust again, and their lives would have been so much fuller with Mary Rhodes still in it. Instead he'd allowed his fear, and self-pity, to direct him down a path to hell. When Blake and Kelly helped him conceal his involvement in the accident, he should have known what he was letting himself in for. He knew they were despicable human beings, and that their wealth had been built on other people's misfortune. How could he have ever trusted he'd be treated any different?

At first, Sampson's role in their protection racket had been minimal, but sadly he'd proven too good at his job, and from then on had been pushed into acts that were destined to shrivel his soul. He'd forced compliance from victims, by threats and by deeds, and if it wasn't with the same level of sadistic pleasure as Dom, or with the seething hatred of humanity displayed by Temperance, it was in a form of self-harm, and at the penance he thought he owed.

If it weren't for the simple fact he'd be convicted alongside them, Sampson would admit he was relieved that Blake and Kelly were about to get their overdue comeuppance. For him there was no escaping what was coming and if not for Caroline he'd welcome the punishment. His wife shouldn't be made to suffer for his wrongdoing. Her future shouldn't be blighted by his lies, his sins, his actions. She should be allowed to go on in blissful ignorance, not be tormented by the knowledge that the man that supposedly loved her had cheated and killed, and gone on cheating afterwards. It wouldn't make a difference that he'd been pressurized into his couplings with Kelly Ambrose either, for they were as a direct result of his previous unfaithfulness towards his wife, and couldn't be excused. There was no hiding the depths to which he'd wronged Caroline, not once the police arrested them and they were taken in for questioning; each would throw the other under a bus if they thought it'd win them some leniency. He wouldn't put it past Blake to hand him over in a bargain plea, Sampson's killing of Mary Rhodes trumping the conspiracy charges leveled at him, or for Kelly to swear her husband was so controlling that she'd feared to go against his will; as proof of her loveless life she'd admit to seeking intimacy from another man: Sampson. He wouldn't put it past her to make out she was a victim of his, a monster whose morals were so low he'd slept with his wife's sister then killed her to keep his secret. Sampson's character would be synonymous with shit. By the time they were finished, he'd be the major evil behind all this, practically the devil incarnate.

No, Sampson thought, as he stared at his reflection in the car's rearview mirror, *I'm not going to allow it. I'm not your scapegoat in this; I'm no longer your slave.*

The decision had come to him before he'd even arrived with Villere and delivered him to Dom for torture. At first he'd still been torn by indecision on how he'd proceed. However, on discovering that Blake had handed over Villere's fate to Dom, superseding any hope Sampson had for making peace between them and the private investigators, he'd concluded enough was enough. For a few bare seconds he'd considered freeing Villere, but to do so he'd have had to fight Dom, and perhaps Temperance, and though he'd no love for either it would be regretful to have to kill them. They had their own ways of exhibiting their displeasure, but they were as much victims of circumstance, and of the poisonous Ambrose couple, as he was. Karma would catch up with them; it needn't directly be by his hand. He'd offered the task to another.

He wasn't stupid. In no version of reality would Tess Grey wait idly by for his instructions, she'd be hot on the trail of her abducted lover. When he'd telephoned, she'd tried to lie about her location, but he could hear the crashing sea, and suspected that she was nearby, poised to launch a do-or-die attempt at saving Villere from Dom's clutches.

She could be karma's agent of retribution.

He'd hastened her along as he'd abandoned Dom and Temperance to their fates, even leaving a door unlocked for her. 'I'm leaving. Don't try stopping me, it will be time better served saving Nicolas's life.'

His warning about not trying to stop him had twofold reason. Tess's time would be best served freeing her partner, rather than getting in his way. He'd something equally important he must do if he was going to save Caroline from excessive heartbreak. Finding that Dom had left the keys in the saloon car's ignition, he'd driven away, and had no idea what the outcome at the abandoned restaurant would be. It didn't matter; if everyone involved killed each other then it was out of his hands, and control; the thing he wanted most was to hear his wife's voice. He hadn't seen Caroline in two full days, and though it wasn't unusual in his role of a BK-Rose employee, every long minute they'd been apart ate at him. Yesterday evening they'd spoken briefly when he'd been forced to ring her, to explain Blake had ordered he stay over for the duration of the storm, and he was certain she'd been suspicious. Earlier today, before his first visit to Maddie Toner's apartment, prior to Jacob Doyle's death, he'd made excuses again to his wife about having to work. Her answers had been curt, angry, but mostly she'd been hurt and he couldn't blame her one bit.

Once he'd gotten clear of Rockland and was well on his way down the coast towards Bath, he pulled over at the roadside and dug out his cellphone. He wanted to speak to Caroline, to tell her how much he loved her, and reassure her that from here on things would be different. He wished he could promise her things would be better, but he couldn't.

He'd brought up her number, but before hitting the call button he'd glanced at his reflection in the mirror and become overwhelmed by the tsunami of emotions he'd been holding in. He'd dropped the phone between his knees, grasped the steering wheel in both fists, and screamed at the Mirror Man until he was breathless and too weak to support his weight. His head tipped forward, forehead on the horn, and he'd been unaware of its blaring until he again lifted his face and stared through the rain-blistered windshield towards Bath.

He delved between his knees for his phone. The screen had gone dark. He didn't bring up Caroline's number again. Instead he started the engine and drove on.

THIRTY-NINE

'The cops will be here any second,' Po cautioned, 'we should get outta here.'

'We can't go,' Tess replied, waving a hand at the partly collapsed building. They were standing at the base of the slope at the entrance to the shipyard, Po resting his backside on the fender of Pinky's Volvo. Other people milled around in the distance, having emerged from the workshops at the sounds of destruction. One or more of them must have called the police by now. 'We have to explain ourselves, Po, not run away like criminals.'

'So what about the Ambrose couple, not to mention this other dude, Sampson?'

'They won't escape.'

'We can't be certain. We should go after them now, hold them till the cops can get there.'

'Po, you should be in hospital, not thinking about chasing more bad guys.'

He flexed his injured knee, hiding the pain that shot through him. 'I'm good to go.'

'You're good for the junkyard, you,' Pinky piped in.

'I've been in worse shape than this,' said Po, and he was correct. One time that he'd assisted Tess in defeating an enemy he'd ended up stabbed in the gut by a knife, a wound that'd almost proved critical. On another occasion, due to a feud between Po and the Chatards, the disgruntled family had set upon him with pickaxe handles and baseball bats to his body. 'Just let me find my other boot and we'll hit the road.'

'I grabbed your boot.' Pinky tossed it down. 'Don't know how you're going to keep it on with the laces cut through.'

'Nothin' a little duct tape won't solve,' said Po.

'You'll be needing this too.' Tess offered him his knife. 'Mike took it off Temperance after she tried to gut me with it.'

'If I'll be needin' it . . .'

'You might want to throw it in the sea before the cops arrive,' she suggested.

He shook his head. A fresh trickle of blood erupted from the largest cut on his face. Tess closed her eyes slowly, taking deep breaths.

'Po, you need to go to an emergency room,' she said.

'This wasn't my wisest plan ever, and I've paid for my stupidity. But my injuries are superficial. Once I get cleaned up, you'll see.'

'Po, you were shot!' Tess cried.

As if reminded of the fact he frowned down at the bloody mess on his shoulder. 'Oh, this little scratch? The bullet took a chunk outta my hide, but didn't hit anythin' important.' To prove the point he worked his shoulder in circles, and even managed to hide the pain this time. Then again, it was likely his sore shoulder was the least of his pains and easily concealed.

'You killed a man,' Tess went on, but could see he had a ready-made answer.

'The fall killed him. He was running around and fell out of a window in a derelict building, nothin' I could do to save him.'

Tess pursed her mouth. She hadn't witnessed Dom's demise, but suspected there was more to it than Po or Pinky were prepared to admit for now.

'You need to explain that to the cops,' she repeated, 'otherwise they might conclude differently.'

'They can conclude whatever they want; I'll put them straight once things are over with. C'mon, Tess, I know it goes against your grain, but so does the slightest possibility of those other punks making a run for it. That Dom guy, he was a grade-one asshole, and Temperance is a vindictive bitch, but they're small fry compared to the Ambroses. They're the ones you really want to put behind bars.'

Mike Toner drove towards them, behind the wheel of Temperance's panel van. He pulled to a stop alongside the Volvo. In the rear compartment, in an act of sweet irony, Temperance had been secured. For the moment she was silent and well behaved, more concerned with getting her broken arm fixed than the imminent jail time she faced. Dom's corpse lay where it had fallen; though Tess had made the effort of protecting it from view by throwing a tarpaulin she'd found over it, pinned down at the corners by chunks of broken wood.

'You guys still here?' he asked through the open window. 'Go on, get yourselves gone. Sampson's still loose. What if he decides to make a try for the girls?'

'I don't think we need worry about him going after Maddie or Hayley,' said Tess. 'The sense I got from speaking with him, he isn't fully committed to his job anymore, and wants nothing to do with hostages or torture.'

Toner had more experience of Arlen Sampson than any of them, and when he nodded at Tess's summation it was perhaps because he'd come to the same conclusion. Understandably, he was still worried for his daughter's safety though. Nothing should be taken for granted. 'If none of you are going, I want to return to Bangor to check on them.'

Tess said, 'You don't need to. Once the cops get here, you can have them send over a patrol to collect them.' She checked with Po and caught the slow blooming of a smile; he'd cottoned on that she was bending to his train of thought. 'Mike, will you please stay here with Temperance and explain everything to the police? We're going after Blake and Kelly, and I fully expect we'll run into Sampson too.'

'You want me to try to buy you some time?' he asked.

'It's best that you show that you're fully assisting them from the get-go. It's important that they understand who the good guys are, and they don't waste any time chasing us. By all means, tell the cops what we're up to and that we'd appreciate some help to arrest them.'

'Won't that put the cops on your asses immediately?'

'We are in Knox County here, Brunswick's in Cumberland County. Knowing how cross-departmental bureaucracy works it'll more than likely slow them down. On the drive down, I'll contact my boss who works with the Portland District Attorney's office and hopefully get her to vouch for us so there isn't a roadblock waiting for us.'

Po had wormed his bare foot into his boot. It waggled loosely when he took a test step. 'Hey, Mike, you got any duct tape in there?'

Toner rooted around in the front of the van. 'Temperance has a veritable serial killer's kit on hand here,' he announced, and tossed a roll of fishing line to him. 'Will that do for a lace, instead?'

Po cut off a length with his knife, and was about to set to lacing his boot. The act of bending and trying to coordinate his hands showed his wounds were more troubling than he'd let on.

'Gimme that and sit back down,' Pinky commanded, and took over securing Po's footwear.

Their ragtag little bunch had begun to attract more attention. Some of those that'd emerged after Pinky attacked the building with the pickup were growing bolder, or nosier. Two men approached, one of them speaking into a walkie-talkie – probably relaying information to a colleague in contact with the police on a telephone.

'Guys,' Tess warned as she spotted more people approaching. There were houses across from the shipyard's entrance, a nearby seafood shack and various business premises; people had spilled out of them to investigate the drama in their midst. 'If we're going I suggest we go now, before the locals get the wrong idea and try to stop us.'

Po elected to ride in the back of the SUV, and when Tess offered to join him, he shook his head gently and said, 'I could use a little more movin' round space, y'don't mind?'

What he really meant was he didn't want her fussing over him for the entire drive down to Brunswick.

'Mike,' Tess said as she went to get in the Volvo's front passenger seat, 'take care around her. She's a dangerous woman.'

Toner glanced in the back. 'I've got this under control, Tess. Temperance isn't going anywhere except to jail. If she gets too noisy, she can see what wearing a sack over her head feels like.'

She was reasonably certain she could hear Temperance swearing at Toner before she closed the door fully. She hoped for his sake that the police would arrive soon and take the vile woman off his hands, but not before Pinky had gotten them clear of Rockland's main street.

Pinky drove through the small crowd gathering at the entrance to the shipyard. They looked bewildered, shocked and a little excitable. Some people craned to get a look at them, and Tess covered the side of her face nearest with an upheld hand. Pinky, by comparison, rolled his eyes and stuck out his tongue at them. Somebody in their wisdom thumped the car with their fist, for a reason unfathomable to Tess. Maybe they felt it their duty to show displeasure at those who'd brought violence to their small town. Hopefully their self-righteousness wouldn't extend to the rest of the locals and Toner would be left in peace until the police showed up: it'd be bad if the crowd read the situation wrongly and descended on the van to break free his prisoner. In defense of his daughter, Toner had proven his resilience and toughness; she trusted that his prisoner was in good hands.

They took the harbor road through town and avoided any incoming law enforcement officers, although a firefighting crew shot past in the opposite direction, using their sirens to clear a path, even though there was little traffic about. Pinky took them onto Route 1, and soon they were passing Waldoboro, Damariscotta and approaching Wiscasset on the western bank of Back River. During the drive, Po tried cleaning his injuries with a packet of wipes handed to him out of the glove compartment but he still appeared rougher than Tess would've liked. She occasionally checked on him while talking animatedly on her cellphone with Emma Clancy.

At one point Tess thought Emma would refuse them help, but her future sister-in-law was only exhibiting caution. Once Tess had narrated the events since coming across Jacob Doyle's wrecked car and Po's subsequent kidnapping and torture, Emma showed a similar determination in bringing Blake and Kelly Ambrose to justice; she even admitted that after their brief conversation about BK-Rose she'd done some digging of her own and thought there was much the couple had to answer for. She also told Tess where she was more likely to find the couple, not in Brunswick, but a few miles nearer her present location at their home north of Bath in Sagadahoc County. Emma promised she'd mobilize the police to meet Tess there, after a reasonable time had been allowed for Tess to arrive first, but without raising suspicion she'd been stalling.

Pinky took his new directions without comment, and soon they passed through Woolwich and were astride the bridge over the Kennebec River. A minute after that and they were heading through Bath's historic town center, only minutes from arriving at the Ambrose family home.

The final approach to the Ambrose house was along a single-track road. Huge puddles had pooled at the grassy verges. The inclement weather was holding its breath, gearing up for another imminent squall. The waters of the river were choppy and reflected the bruised heavens. When it hove into view, the ostentatious house and outbuildings looked out of place on the riverbank. They also appeared empty. The stormy weather had brought an unnatural gloom to the afternoon, and not a single light burned behind any of the windows or even above the entrance door at the top of a grand set of steps. Next to the house the doors to a drive-in garage were wide open, one swaying on the breeze, and the interior was as deserted as the house appeared. Maybe Sampson had alerted Blake and Kelly Ambrose to expect trouble and the couple had flown the coop. Perhaps he'd delivered a warning in person, and then joined them in another car to whisk them away to safety, and that would explain why the saloon car Tess watched him leave Rockland in had been abandoned at the foot of the entrance steps.

Maybe, she thought, with a growing sense of discomfort, Sampson's reason for coming here was for a different reason entirely. Which wasn't to say the Ambroses were gone, just that the house was lifeless because nobody alive remained inside.

FORTY

Not long ago, Arlen Sampson got out of the saloon car and trudged up the steps, observed by Kelly Ambrose from the front door. The red-haired woman stood with her fists digging into her plump hips, as she scolded him silently. Her scorn would have had more effect if he'd given her any notice. When he met her on the porch, she thrust a palm against his shoulder, forcing him to stop and register her presence. 'What are you doing here, aren't you meant to be handling the mess up in Bangor?'

'I was. Dom's taken control of it,' he replied. He began to move past but she interjected in his space, refusing to move.

'What do you mean? I thought Blake wanted you to take charge.'

'Blake changed his mind and ruined everything.'

'He didn't tell me.'

'He didn't tell me either, Kelly. That's why I've come here, to check exactly where I stand with Blake these days.'

'You know exactly where you stand.' She folded her arms over her chest, petulant. 'You do exactly what you're told. No arguments and no complaints.'

Sampson snorted and brushed past her.

'Hey!'

Ignoring her, Sampson entered the house and halted in the wide vestibule. He glanced around, checked upward to the head of the stairs, and the suspended landings to either side.

He felt Kelly at his back but refused to look at her. He could hear her heels rapping on the flooring as she shifted, trying to decide what action she should take.

'Is your housekeeper here?' he asked.

'What? Why? What are you up to, Arlen?'

'We need to talk. You, Blake and I. There's some tough decisions to make,' he answered, 'and they're not for the ears of anyone else. If she's here, send Marianne home.'

'Mrs Perez left hours ago. But that's beside the point.' Kelly again got in his face. He could smell her breath and it was unpleasant, tainted by gin and something sour. 'What gives you the damn right to walk in here and try ordering me around?'

'How does it feel when the shoe's on the other foot?'

'What?'

He turned from her, brushing her question off and began walking towards Blake's home office. Kelly squawked in anger. She grasped at the sleeve of his jacket. He pulled free.

'Arlen! Stop right now! You'd best explain yourself before I—'

He snapped around. She was following so close behind that she almost crashed into him. She took an involuntary step backwards, one hand going to her throat. Her cheeks had flushed red in the past few seconds; her eyes looked startled. 'Before you do *what* exactly?' Sampson challenged.

'You are forgetting your station, Arlen,' she countered, but there was little conviction in her voice. She'd seen Sampson upset before, and even angry enough to be rebellious, but this time there was something in his demeanor that was frightening.

'Forgetting my fucking station? Listen to yourself, Kelly. Who the hell do you think *you* are,' he threw up a hand, indicating her grand home, 'the lady of the goddamn manor? I've got news for you: you're a gold-digging slut with delusions of grandeur. It's about time you realized your fucking station. Now get out of my way . . . I want to speak with Blake. It's time he heard a few home truths, too.'

'Wait . . . what? What kind of truths? Do you mean—'

'That when he's away my usual station is between your legs?' he asked viciously.

She croaked in dismay, and grabbed at him with her manicured talons. It was a grasp of desperation. 'Arlen! Please! Keep your voice down.'

Again he snorted and yanked free. He turned again for Blake's office. Over his shoulder he said, 'Don't worry, Kelly. If I have anything to do with it, nobody will ever know how you used me. It's so shameful it makes me sick to the stomach.'

Abruptly she went from fearful to enraged. She rushed to get past him, clawing at his shoulder to move him aside. In the doorway to the first sitting room Sampson rounded on her, the fingers of his left hand snaring her throat. He shoved her against the doorjamb. Her toes danced above the floor, her heels taking her weight. Sampson thrust his face into hers, bathing her with his hot breath this time. 'Shut your goddamn mouth and listen to me. For years I've done what you commanded; I've terrorized and harmed decent people that didn't deserve it; I've been forced to do the most horrible things on your behalf. Well it ends here and it ends now, Kelly. Do you hear me? You constantly demand respect, and that's the most ironic bit about all of this. Ha! You have no respect for anyone or anything.' He again indicated the house, and her entire privileged life in particular. 'This isn't enough for you, it never will be. You always want more. You always *demand* more, and you won't stop. Why the fuck should anyone ever respect you, Kelly? Respect should be a two-way exchange, but you've no self-respect and nothing to give back. Neither you nor Blake care about respect, all either of you care about is *making demands*. Well, I'm here to tell you *no*. No-fucking-more.'

He released her throat. She sunk at the knees, gagging. She could choke to death for all he cared. He left her there, and moved deeper into the house.

'Blake?' He called out loud enough that he should be heard from any room in the house. 'Blake, where are you? Show yourself.'

Blake said nothing.

Perhaps he'd heard Sampson's exchange with Kelly, and was still trying to absorb the enormity that his wife had cheated on him, with one of the lowly slaves no less. Sampson would have laughed at the bitter irony if not for the fact he burned with shame at the admission. He stormed into Blake's office, expecting to find him seated in his customary place. He wasn't there. Kelly stumbled into the room behind Sampson. He ignored her ragged gasps of anxiety.

'Where's Blake?' he asked.

Kelly shook her head. Obviously she'd expected her husband to be seated at his desk. There were two tumblers of gin and tonic sitting on the desk, each of them only half drank. That was where she'd probably left him when first she'd heard

Sampson's arrival and gone outside to investigate. She abruptly spun on her heels and rushed out of the room, calling her husband's name.

Sampson followed.

As he arrived in the grandiose hallway, he found Kelly running up the stairs, clawing at the bannister for stability. Sampson took the stairs three at a time and caught her on the landing nearest her bedroom.

He doubted she expected to find Blake there, but from his experience of her boudoir, Sampson knew that was where Blake kept his gun in a safe-box. He caught her by her hair, fisting a bunch of it and dragged her to the floor. 'Let's not do anything stupid,' he warned her, 'yet.'

Kelly shrieked at the top of her lungs.

Blake appeared from concealment below. He must have secreted himself in one of the other first-floor rooms, while he eavesdropped and plotted the right moment to show his face. He appeared less concerned at his wife's rough treatment than Sampson expected, but then again, perhaps not after what he'd heard. Sampson hauled her up, and shoved her so she faced Blake over the railing.

'Blake?' Kelly bleated. 'Help me!'

Blake ignored her plaintive cries. He directed his words at Sampson, smiling. 'You seem a bit annoyed about something, Arlen. Why don't you come down here and tell me all about it.'

'Where were you just now?'

'I was making a telephone call,' said Blake.

The man was feeble, sickly, but he hid his condition well behind the same sanctimonious mask he often wore during business dealings. Sampson knew it was a facade, that Blake's reset demeanor was sour and grumpy.

'I guess it wasn't to nine-one-one.'

'You know me better than that,' Blake said, and snorted a brief laugh. 'No of course not, Arlen, I was calling an associate of mine. He'll be here shortly . . . you should leave.'

Sampson wasn't concerned. He understood what Blake implied; this associate was one of those professionals he occasionally needed the services of. It was supposed to throw fear into Sampson's heart . . . it didn't. Blake had not had time to call for help from anyone, let alone to request a professional killer whose services would be routed via several middlemen.

'Nice bluff, but it's bullshit.' Sampson propelled Kelly towards the stairs. 'Get down there.'

She went down tentatively, as afraid of Blake as she was Sampson. Blake barely looked at her; his attention was fully on Sampson as they descended. Kelly didn't go to him, but around him, and for the briefest moment Blake's gaze shifted to her. She dropped her face and refused to meet his scrutiny.

'You're right, of course,' Blake admitted as Sampson reached the bottom of the stairs. 'I wasn't calling for help; I don't believe I need it. You're upset and acting out of character, I can see that, and can even understand it. But here's the thing, Arlen; it doesn't matter. It doesn't change the situation between us one bit. I still own you, unless of course you're prepared for the truth to come out. How will Caroline react once she learns you were screwing her sister, then strangled her to death when she wanted to come clean?'

'It will devastate her,' Sampson admitted. 'But that's what makes her a good, decent human being. Everything that you and your slut of a wife aren't.'

'Kelly's a slut? Oh, you're referring to that thing you thought you had going on behind my back? Arlen, I didn't take you for stupid, please extend the same level of intelligence to me. What? You thought I was unaware of Kelly's infidelities? And yes, I'm talking plural. I was fully aware she was sleeping with you, and with Dom for that matter. Why wouldn't I when it was with my blessing, and at my instigation? Look at me, Arlen. I'm not the virile young man I once was, and I'm the first to admit it. Sex does not appeal to me any longer, but my wife is young, with a young sexual woman's needs . . . have I denied her anything else she has ever demanded?'

Sampson said nothing.

Kelly though made a small noise of surprise, and then triumph flared in her eyes. Blake's admission was an unexpected 'get out of jail free' card, and she hoped to capitalize on it. She placed her hands on his shoulder, leaning close to him. 'Blake, I would never have—'

He snapped up a palm, and she stumbled back. 'Quiet. Don't say another word.'

She scowled now, and Sampson smiled slowly. It hadn't occurred that Kelly was as much a slave to her husband as they'd made everyone else in their employment. Unlike all the others, though, he couldn't feel any sympathy for her. Not when she was complicit with her husband and probably a keen instigator of his vileness.

Raising his eyebrows, Blake demanded a further answer to his previous question.

'Caroline will never learn what happened with her sister.' Sampson stared at Blake, challenging him.

'That's for me to decide, not you.'

Shaking his head, Sampson said, 'I've been an idiot. All this time I've lived in fear of you turning me in, when all along you couldn't. How could you, Blake, when it'd also implicate you? You helped me cover up my part in Mary's death, and you gave me an alibi. If the truth ever comes out, you are guaranteeing your own imprisonment.'

'That'd be the case if ever you'd used my alibi. There's only Caroline who believes you were away on a business trip with me when Mary died, the authorities never called you on it, did they?'

The police had never investigated Sampson. It was easier for them to conclude that Mary was the victim of a murderous drifter.

'I don't need to tell the police about you and Mary, I only need to tell your wife. I'll retract your alibi,' Blake said smugly, 'after all, she only heard it from you, right? She never heard it from me, Arlen. I wonder how Caroline will react. Do you think she will keep your secret then, or want justice for her dead sister?'

'If I go down I'll take you both with me. If I'm arrested, I'll come clean about everything you've had me do for you.'

'My legal team will rip your testimony to pieces, and show you for a desperate liar trying to divert your own guilt.' Blake snorted, and Sampson could tell Blake actually believed it.

'That might've been the case before, but not now. You've just had a private investigator tortured by Dom, possibly murdered. There isn't a legal team in the world that'll save your ass from prison.'

'I'll disown Dom. He's known to be a violent irrational man. His actions are his own. Who is to say otherwise?'

'The investigator's partner.'

'Well, if my instructions have been carried out, and she has fallen into the trap, she won't be an issue.'

Sampson again said nothing, and sudden understanding struck Blake. For the first time his sanctimonious mask slipped. 'You were supposed to lure her to Rockland, and have her disposed of too.'

'Yeah well, your instructions got a little confused when you put Dom in charge.'

Blake shifted uneasily. His eyes darted to Kelly, and she too was turning pale and sickly looking.

'What did you do, Arlen?' Blake asked.

'That's the thing, Blake; once Dom took over I didn't do a damn thing.'

Blake swore, and it gave Sampson great satisfaction.

'Actually,' he went on, 'that isn't entirely true. Once Tess Grey knew where to find Villere, I got out of there and might have left the door unlocked on my way out.'

'You did what?' Blake suddenly cast about in a mild panic. He shot an instruction at Kelly. 'Call Dom. I want to know exactly what is going on up in Rockland.'

Sampson didn't stop her from taking out her cellphone. She rang Dom's number, listened, growing more concerned by every ring that went unanswered.

'Try Temperance instead,' snapped Blake.

'You're wasting your time,' Sampson said. 'By now it's over with. Whatever has happened, it's not good. You may as well face it, Blake. You and Kelly are finished. There's nothing now you can say that will force me into obeying you again.'

Blake threw up his hands. 'You son of a bitch,' he snarled. 'How does betraying us help you? If we're arrested, I swear to god I'll tell everyone about you and Mary.' He pointed a trembling finger. 'You'll pay for everything you've done, Arlen.'

'I don't expect to escape justice. What goes around comes around, Blake, and I knew that one day my sins would catch up with me.' He nodded at his own resolution. 'I'm going to pay for my crimes, sure, and so are you two, but that isn't to say Caroline has to suffer for them.'

From behind his back he drew his pistol.

'See, the thing is, the only ones apart from me that know what happened to Mary is you,' said Sampson, 'and once I'm done here, you won't be around to tell anyone.'

Almost as if heralding their doom, the power went out and the house fell into gloomy twilight. Twin flashes from Sampson's pistol lit up the faces of Blake and Kelly, and it brought him some satisfaction that their final expressions were of abject defeat.

FORTY-ONE

Tess approached the Ambrose house warily, Pinky's gun in hand, but kept low. She was prepared for conflict but hoped to avoid it if possible.

All around her branches rattled and knocked, the wind dirged and the swollen river raged towards the sea. The house itself was too quiet. It had the feel of a mausoleum about it, at odds with everything else.

The stormy weather was having an effect, even if the latest squall hadn't hit yet. High winds must've taken down the power lines because there wasn't a hint of light inside the house, or in the neighboring dwellings that she could glimpse across the river.

She went up the steps, rapped on the door and then moved aside. She raised her weapon alongside her shoulder.

'Arlen Sampson,' she called loudly.

Sampson didn't answer.

Tess checked on her companions.

Po had gotten out of the Volvo despite her request for him to stay put, and he'd moved adjacent to her so that he could check the saloon car. It was probably a good idea. Who knew if Sampson was inside and would pop up from hiding once they got past the car? After surviving the battle at the collapsing restaurant it'd be a bad show if they were now cut down in an ambush. Pinky had also left the car, but was at a loss where to go. He stood at the car's hood, hands by his sides so he didn't represent a threat, but ready to hurl himself up the steps at Sampson if the situation degenerated into violence.

'Blake Ambrose?' Tess again rapped on the door. 'Kelly?'

Po limped to the foot of the steps.

Tess shook her head at him, but he ascended them anyway.

'I don't like this,' she whispered.

The cuts on Po's face and his bloody shoulder were a reminder that none of these people were to be underestimated.

'Maybe we should wait till the cops get here,' she went on.

'Your call, Tess,' he replied, but she could sense he was on the verge of pushing inside. At least, for now, he hadn't yet drawn his knife.

She thumped her hand on the door again. 'Arlen Sampson,' she called again, 'if you can hear me, we need to talk.'

She sensed Sampson's presence on the other side of the door, the way she had Po's wish to storm the house. She could picture him standing there, listening but not yet responding. Was he armed? Po had told her that it was Temperance who'd snuck up on him at Maddie's apartment, but Sampson had shown his hand by drawing a concealed pistol from behind his back.

Tess said, 'We're not here to fight with you.'

Po's expression pinched, but he kept his opinion to himself. Tess had relayed how Sampson had made it possible for her to come to his aid, making it somewhat unnecessary for Pinky's over-enthusiastic distraction. If Sampson hadn't ushered her to action when he did, Po might not have survived, or if he had it would've been with fewer digits. Po was obliged to give Sampson an opportunity to explain himself.

'I don't believe you want to fight us either,' Tess added.

'I don't,' came back Sampson's muffled voice, 'but I won't let you stop me.'

'Are Blake and Kelly inside with you?'

'You don't have to worry about them, they aren't going anywhere.'

'What have you done, Arlen?'

'I've done something that needed doing. It should've been done a long time ago.'

'Are they dead?'

'I think I made myself clear enough, Miss Grey.'

'If you murdered them, I can't let you leave.'

'Then it's unfortunate; we *are* going to fight.'

Po interjected. 'Suits me, bra.' He held up a hand to Tess for permission to go on. She shrugged at him, he was going to whether she gave it or not. 'If you want a fight, why don't you come on out and meet me like a man this time? No guns, no knives, just you and me.'

'It'd be unfair.'

'I promise to take it easy on you.'

Sampson grunted in laughter. 'It'd be unfair on you. You're hurt.'

'Dom thought the same thing. He was wrong.'

'About that: I want you to know something, Villere,' said Sampson. 'It was never my intention to help kidnap you. Temperance was taking her orders from Blake, and when she ambushed you, I was equally surprised. You might say that the situation got out of my control.'

'You still drew on me.'

'What would you have done if I hadn't?'

'Who knows?' Po wasn't about to admit he'd willingly gone along as a hostage, intending drawing all the bad guys into a single neat trap for when Tess arrived with police reinforcements. He knew now that not only hadn't his plan worked as he'd hoped, it had been risky to the point of stupidity.

'I take it things didn't go well with Dom?'

'Depends on your perspective. Dom's dead.'

'Can't say I'm upset by the news. What about Temperance?'

'On her way to jail.'

'At least she didn't die. Temperance isn't as bad as she likes to make out.'

'Believe me,' said Po. 'She ain't a nice person.'

'Try walking a mile in her shoes, you might have a different opinion. Sometimes people do bad things because life dealt them a bad hand.'

'Amen to that,' said Po, without extrapolating.

'I'm coming out,' said Sampson.

Po reached towards Tess, but she indicated she was ready. She aimed her gun as the door cracked open.

Sampson's weapon appeared too.

Po was on high alert, ready to grab at the gun given a chance, but Tess was certain that Sampson wouldn't shoot unless provoked. She cautioned Po, and indicated they should step back. They did, though she kept the CZ-75 trained on the opening door.

Sampson emerged. Although he and Tess held their guns on each other, it was without rancor.

'Blake and Kelly are done with, they won't hurt anyone ever again,' Sampson stated.

'You shot them in cold blood?' Tess asked.

'Are you prepared to do the same with me?'

'If I must.'

'Sorry, but I don't believe you.'

'I will if I must,' Tess repeated.

Sampson nodded. He didn't lower his pistol.

'I stopped those monsters,' said Sampson, 'because they needed stopping. Is what I did any different to what you guys have done in the past?'

'We've never killed in cold blood.'

'Neither have I. I was red hot with fury when I shot those bastards.'

'But now you're cool?' asked Po.

'I'm cool.'

'Good,' said Tess. 'Then you're probably thinking straighter.'

Sampson nodded behind him. 'I knew exactly what I was doing, and wouldn't change a thing now. Other than I wish I'd stopped those monsters years ago.'

'OK, you've done the world a service. It's done now, so I need you to put down your gun,' Tess said.

He shook his head. 'It isn't going to happen. You'll try to stop me and I can't let you. There's something I need to do first.'

'I can't let you hurt anyone else.'

'If that's what you're worried about, don't. I don't intend harming anyone. Hear me out and I'll make you a promise. I'll give up without a fight, but there's something important I need to do before I surrender.'

'I can't let you go. The police are on their way here; don't make things any worse for yourself.'

'I'm going to jail,' he stated, 'no way around that now. But before I do, I need to speak to my wife.'

'You'll get your telephone call,' Tess said.

He shook his head. 'I need to speak to her in person.'

'Unless your missus turns up here in the next few minutes, it ain't gonna happen,' Po interjected. 'It's like Tess just said, she can't let you go. You've just confessed to murdering two people, it's her duty – and mine – to hold you till the cops arrive.'

Sampson ignored him, instead concentrating on Tess. 'I understand this puts you in a predicament, but I'm calling you on a debt you owe.'

'She doesn't owe you a goddamn thing,' said Po.

'I made it so you could be saved,' Sampson replied. 'If I'd not left calling Tess when I did, how do you think your day would've turned out?'

'I'd've found a way to save my own ass.'

Tess wasn't so sure he would've. Only Pinky's ramming of the building had thrown Dom off balance, and given Po the opportunity to break loose of his bindings; she hadn't been in position to save him from having his toes amputated. If not for Sampson's urgent warning she might even have dithered longer on how to approach the situation, and who knew how much damage Dom might have done to Po by then.

'Why's it so important you speak with your wife now?' she asked.

'I might never see her again.'

'You'll get visitin' rights,' Po said snarkily.

Sampson grunted in mirth. 'Logistically, I'm unsure how that could work out.'

Tess had no idea what he meant. She exchanged a glance with Po, but he appeared no wiser. By the time her attention shifted back to Sampson the tableau had changed. His gun was no longer pointed at her but directly at Pinky. She flinched, and aimed at Sampson's heart.

'Take it easy there,' he cautioned.

'Don't do it,' Tess warned him.

'I can't think of another way,' Sampson replied. 'If you don't get out of my way I'll be forced to shoot your friend.'

Pinky held his empty hands aloft. 'I was beginning to feel insulted at being left out of the conversation. Now I'm not that bothered, me.'

Sampson kept his pistol trained on Pinky. 'Nothing personal, buddy. I know we've never met, but I'm fairly sure you're a good guy, so I'll apologize now if I have to shoot you because your friends won't grant me a last request.'

'Shoot him,' Po growled, 'and I'll cut your heart out and eat it raw.'

Tess noted Po's blade had slid from where he'd concealed it in his sleeve: his warning might sound over the top, but if he harmed Pinky, Po would at least try to cut out Sampson's heart.

The alternative was she'd have to shoot Sampson dead first, and would the instant Sampson tried to carry out his threat, and he knew it. She didn't believe he'd go through with it, but neither would she risk Pinky's life like that.

She lowered her weapon. When it wasn't enough to appease Sampson, she placed it on the floor and slid it aside with her foot.

Po frowned at her, remaining poised to lunge at the barest hint of pressure on Sampson's trigger finger.

Sampson eyed him, without ever losing track of Pinky.

'C'mon, Villere,' said Sampson. 'Put down the knife. You've already proved you're a tough guy, but if you come at me it's only your friend here that's going to get hurt. I actually find it reassuring that you'd kill to protect someone you care for. We're not too different in that respect.'

Po exchanged looks with Tess again. She nodded for him to stand down.

'It needn't have to have been like this,' Sampson said as he moved between them and down the steps, gun permanently trained on Pinky. 'I was going to suggest you follow me and I would surrender to you once I'm done, but I guess you couldn't do that, not without feeling the heat from the law yourselves. So we're going to have to do things another way.' He directed his next words at Pinky. 'Get in my car, big guy. You can drive.'

Pinky squinted at the saloon car, then at Tess and Po. Tess reassured him with a barely discernible nod. He moved for the car. Sampson said, 'Keys are in the ignition. Get her started, buddy, and please . . . no funny business.'

'That's a shame,' Pinky muttered, 'seeing as "Funny Business" is my rapper name.'

Sampson again grunted in laughter. 'I think me and you are going to get along just fine.' He appraised Tess and Po once more. 'Please don't force me to shoot your friend. Oh, by the way, I expect you to follow me, but just in case we get separated I'll have your buddy ring you and let you know where you can come arrest me.'

'What's this all about, Arlen?' Tess tried, wondering at what the hell was really going on in Sampson's mind.

'I love my wife,' was all he said, before sliding into the back

of the car, taking the seat directly behind Pinky. He kept the gun
trained on the back of Pinky's head until the car swung around
and was heading down the track towards Bath.

They didn't wait for more than a heartbeat before Tess snatched
up her gun and chased Po down the steps towards the Volvo.
Thankfully, Pinky had left the ignition fob in place. Without
consultation Tess took the driving duty, Po's injuries relegating
him to the passenger seat this time. Tess drove after the saloon.

'We could've taken him,' Po said.

'We could've,' Tess said.

'But you felt you did owe him for my life?'

'What do you think, Po?'

'I'm flattered.'

She squeezed him a smile.

'You think we can trust him?' Po asked.

'I think he meant what he said. Especially that last bit about
loving his wife.'

'Yeah,' said Po, 'I believe that too.'

FORTY-TWO

There was no losing track of Sampson and Pinky on the short drive between Bath and Brunswick, most of it on the open highway that took them into town past Brunswick Executive Airport. Pinky kept his speed to the posted limit, and made no rash or injudicious maneuvers, and thankfully didn't earn himself a bullet in the spine. Tess stayed a respectful distance behind, closing down the gap only after the heavens opened and the battering rain made seeing anything more than fifty yards ahead impossible. When taking routes across town, Pinky always gave warning of his intention to turn by way of the saloon car's blinkers. They were led through town, past the sprawling campus of Bowdoin College, into the residential suburbs on the south side and into a district clearly dedicated to retirement communities and residential care homes.

Tess's cellphone rang for the umpteenth time since they'd left Bath. Having taken charge of it while she drove, Po checked the screen and said, 'It's Emma again.'

Without asking he declined the call.

'I hate ignoring her calls like this,' said Tess. 'Especially when she'll be worried to death that something bad has happened to us.'

'This doesn't qualify as being bad to you? Pinky being held at gunpoint by a murderer?'

'I asked for her help, and now I feel bad for cutting her out like this.'

'It's best we do. She's probably communicatin' with the cops who by now have probably found the Ambroses and want to know where the hell we are. If she's kept in the dark, she can't later be criticized for stalling them.'

'I know. But still . . .'

'Maybe I should turn this thing off,' he said. He didn't need to remind her that the police would soon triangulate her phone signal to identify their location. The thing was, switched on or off it wouldn't make a difference as they could still locate it, and she'd no intention of having him chuck it out of the window.

'What if Pinky calls?'

'Does it look as if we're gonna need directions?'

She shrugged. They drove past several medical practices specializing in dental and orthodontic procedures, and various senior rest and rehabilitation homes. They approached a residential health center, and Po said, 'Maybe you can drop me here and pick me up on your way out?'

He was trying to make light of the situation, but he was concerned for Pinky. She was worried for their friend's welfare too, but was also sure they'd done the right thing in going along with Sampson. By taking a hostage, he'd offered them a way to help him without them being viewed as co-conspirators. Sampson was determined to speak in person with his wife, and had they tried to hinder him somebody would have needlessly died, most probably Pinky, followed soon after by Sampson. Allowing Sampson a little leeway, on the promise of his surrender afterwards, was always risky, because this could be Sampson's elaborate plan of escape. Plus, there was a more frightening prospect that she had to consider. What if Sampson's reason for seeking out his wife was for a similar reason to why he'd gone to the Ambrose house? What if Sampson planned on killing her, and then himself in a murder-suicide? There was no way possible that they could allow the man to be alone with his wife whether he made a plea for privacy or not.

The saloon's blinkers came on, indicating a left turn. It took the corner into a short dead-end street. Tess followed, and drew to a halt outside the entrance to a sprawling low-level building in a self-contained walled compound. Pinky had taken the car through the open gate, which remained unsecured. He stopped in a designated visitor parking space. Next to it was an ambulance equipped with an automated lift so wheelchair passengers could board.

Tess exchanged looks with Po.

She'd caught the relevance of Sampson's earlier reply to Po's suggestion that his wife could visit him in prison. 'Logistically, I'm unsure how that could work out.'

A sign at the entrance to the building confirmed her suspicion: *Assisted Living Residence.*

'D'you think Sampson's wife could be some kind of health care professional?' Po pondered as he scrutinized the sign. 'Or that she's an old gal and he's her toy boy?'

She didn't qualify his jest with a response.

Sampson got out of the back seat of the car. Pinky must've rolled down the window to listen as Sampson spoke. The pistol he'd earlier used to threaten his hostage with had disappeared, but that didn't mean that Sampson was unarmed. Tess immediately pulled the Volvo up alongside the saloon and shut off the engine. She caught a glimpse from Sampson over the top of his car.

'You're going to demand that you come with me, huh?' he asked.

'I am.'

'Me too,' said Po, but Tess asked him to wait with Pinky.

'No way, no how,' he answered and began hauling his stiff frame out of the Volvo. Tess got out and rounded the vehicle. She got between him and the car.

'I don't think we'll all be allowed inside,' she told him, 'and dare I say it, you might attract undue attention. Stay here with Pinky and I'll keep an eye on him, OK?'

Po nodded at her wisdom. He was unhappy with her request, but didn't kick up a fuss. Tess wasn't the type to require her hand held.

'The first hint of trouble and I'll be comin' in, an' I don't care what kind of damn attention I attract.'

Tess tapped her jacket pocket, indicating where she'd secreted the CZ-75. 'There won't be any trouble. Look.' She tilted her head towards the back seat of the saloon, where Sampson had discarded his pistol.

'Hmmm,' said Po, and it was enough to show she'd appeased him.

Quietly, she added, 'Give us a few minutes then call the cops.'

She moved around to where Sampson waited.

'The clock's ticking down, I assume?' he asked.

'Let's go.' She allowed him to take the lead.

The automatic door swished open and Tess followed Sampson inside the building. It was homely in a sense, but there was also an undeniable air of institutionalization about the place. The lobby was decorated with comfortable seating, flowers in vases, pictures on the walls, but the reception desk and various signs behind it were reminders this was no normal residence. As with any hospital she'd ever visited the atmosphere was clinical, redolent with a faint chemical smell and a mild charge of electricity that stirred the short hairs on her neck. The place cast back Tess's memory to when her father had spent his final days in a hospice before succumbing to cancer; the melancholy she felt now subdued any nerves she'd experienced while following the self-confessed murderer inside.

A portly woman was seated behind reception. She had rosy cheeks that contrasted with her white hair. Over trousers and a pullover sweater she wore a tabard, the name of the private institute embroidered above her left breast. She also wore a name badge: Marjorie. Sampson didn't need to read it to greet her; he was obviously a regular visitor.

'Hi, Arlen,' Marjorie responded to his personable hello. She gave Tess a cursory smile too, then raised her eyebrows in question.

'This is Tess,' Sampson said. 'She's a friend. It's OK if she visits Caroline with me.'

Sampson posed his words, not as a request but a given fact. Marjorie didn't react other than to smile again, and offer Tess a clipboard with a list of visitor signatures on it. 'I'll need you to sign in,' she said, then after a mock grimace, 'rules are rules, right?'

Tess used the attached pen to scrawl her name and approximate time of arrival on the log sheet. Marjorie again offered a smile as she accepted the clipboard back. Immediately she settled down to whatever paperwork she'd been working on before their arrival. It was obvious to Tess that Sampson's was a very familiar face, and that he was intimately familiar with his environs. He said, 'Thanks for everything, Marge,' and then walked away before the receptionist reacted to the finality of his words.

Tess followed him down a corridor. They passed rooms in which resided patients requiring different levels of care, but all of them acutely. Some reminded Tess of chain hotel rooms, others hospital suites, and again of the room in which her dad died. She shivered inside and out.

'Caroline requires round the clock care,' he elected without a prompt. He wasn't seeking pity, but perhaps some understanding of his recent actions. 'If I was able I'd have her at home with me . . . but, well, that wasn't possible while the Ambroses had me on a leash. I couldn't spend the time I wanted with her, because of *them*. It was different when Caroline's sister was here. She helped me with Caroline, but' – he cleared his throat – 'something bad happened to her. It shames me as a man, and as a husband, that I'm not here for her all the time.' He stopped, faced Tess, and she could see genuine regret in his posture. 'I won't be ever again.'

Again there was no subtext to his words; simply he was stating how he foresaw his future. For a moment Tess forgot he'd done despicable things and pitied him as much as she did the wife he was going to be forced to abandon. She didn't respond, mostly due to the catch in her throat. They walked on.

He said, 'Caroline fell from her horse. We actually wed right here, with a minister conducting the ceremony, and her sister Mary and a nurse as witnesses. It might shock you when you first see her. But be under no illusion, she's fully aware, and in full control of her senses. All I ask is that, for her sake, you let me tell her what I've done my own way.'

'I'm only here to ensure you fulfill our bargain,' Tess reassured him.

'She'll hear soon enough about my arrest, but we don't need to do it in front of her do we?'

They were approaching the final room at the end of the hall. Unlike the others they'd passed this one's door was different. It had a viewing window. Tess said, 'I don't need to be in the room with you as you say goodbye. If anyone arrives, I'll do what I can to stall them until you're done.'

Again he halted, and his features flushed pink as he regarded her. 'I've done some bad things I shouldn't have, but believe that I'm ashamed of them more than anyone. I'm sorry for what happened with the Toners, and especially that poor kid Jacob, and I'm sorry your man was hurt. I don't expect your forgiveness, so won't ask for it, and you probably aren't seeking gratitude, but I want to thank you, Tess. It takes a special kind of person to do what you've done for me.'

'Like you said earlier, I owed you one.' After a pause, Tess reached and gripped his forearm, giving it a supportive squeeze before he entered Caroline's room.

'Your debt's repaid, and I'll pay mine,' he promised.

He went inside.

Before the door swung shut she briefly saw Caroline open her eyes and smile in delight as Sampson entered. Feeling slightly voyeuristic, Tess adjusted her position so she could watch through the door's viewing window. The woman lay on a hospital-style bed, her upper torso strapped to and slightly raised on a plastic backboard that molded to her contours. All kinds of medical contraptions surrounded her, and she was hooked up to most of them by wires and tubes. There were feeding tubes in her nostrils, an oxygen mask fitted loosely over her mouth, and a catheter in her throat. On a hinged arm alongside her left cheek there was some kind of control pad from which protruded a joystick and a thin sip and blow tube. Next to the bed stood a sling by which she could be lifted and turned by her carers. She was no expert, but Tess knew that Caroline Sampson had suffered a terrible trauma that had paralyzed her from the neck down.

Sampson sat on a chair next to the bed, bending at the waist to lay a hand gently on Caroline's forehead. The woman had limited movement to turn to him. Tess watched her press her cheek to his palm; there was such affection between them in that simple gesture that tears pricked Tess's eyes. He was not going to press a pillow over her face, nor hang himself with one of the trailing wires: his love for Caroline was too strong. Whatever the Ambroses had forced Sampson into doing she couldn't hold it against him when he felt he must obey them to protect her. She turned away from the window, allowing them a few minutes privacy, knowing that Sampson was correct. It'd be a long time, if ever, before he would be able to touch and speak in person with Caroline again.

FORTY-THREE

The burial of Jacob Doyle was held under pale blue skies, with breath misting from the mouths of mourners as they paid their last respects. The recent storms had passed, replaced by the chill of an early winter. Standing around the grave, the attendees shivered despite their heavy coats, scarves and gloves. The sudden drop in temperature plucked those leaves spared by the storms from the surrounding trees, and they drifted lazily to the ground, a shimmering backdrop of reds and yellows and all colors in between. Some leaves fell on Jacob's coffin as it was lowered into the earth, to join a wreath placed upon it by his siblings.

Tess couldn't equate the two broken figures with the angry guys she and Po had scuffled with only a couple of weeks before. It was obvious that the tough love they showed their youngest sibling was love all the same; the price of losing him was grief. Jacob's death had diminished them somehow; they looked as brittle as the falling leaves. At one point she'd feared that the brothers might react to the news of Jacob's death by blaming Hayley Cameron, but as far as she could tell there'd been no obvious rancor from them. Hayley attended the funeral, supported by her dad Jeffrey Lorton and adoptive mom Jessie Cameron, but stayed back a respectful distance from the frontline mourners. Recognizing the sacrifices that Mike Toner had made for his daughter, Hayley had come to value the idea of embracing her own father who might just one day fight for her too.

Neither Madison nor Mike Toner were present. Currently they were both remanded on pre-trial detention, whereas their co-defendant Hayley had been granted bail, her bond paid for by Jeff Lorton. Of the three, Mike Toner faced considerable time in prison, having taken the lion's share of blame when it came to organizing and running the insurance scam, claiming Maddie and Hayley were manipulated by him into helping him get rich quick. Also, and no less surprisingly he'd taken the heat

for some of the events that subsequently occurred at the abandoned restaurant in Rockland. To spare Pinky involvement, he'd
sworn that he was the man to drive his pickup into the building,
and also to have chased Dom to his accidental death when the
thug tried to jump to freedom through a window he broke. On
what to charge Toner with on these matters, the prosecuting
attorney was still trying to make up his mind, because they
occurred during Toner's brave attempt at saving the life of Nicolas
Villere, who at the time was being brutally tortured by Dom and
Temperance Jolie. Remarkably Temperance hadn't attempted
to contradict his story, because when it came to it, she genuinely couldn't recall who had done what to who after her arm
was snapped in the free-for-all. Tess suspected that these latter
crimes would be waived in favor of throwing the book at both
Toners for their fraudulent activities instead, but still regretted
she couldn't do more to have them released on bail. Emma Clancy
was also hoping to influence her contemporaries in Bangor, with
a view to having the Toners' detention reviewed by the right of
habeas corpus: they were unlikely to commit a further serious
crime, interfere with the investigation or attempt to flee justice so
they should fit the bail criteria.

After he'd finished in Caroline's room, Arlen Sampson
surrendered to Tess, who handed him over to the detectives Po
summoned to the care home. Sampson made a full and frank
admission to his part in kidnapping Po and to the murders of
Blake and Kelly Ambrose, and lastly to the second kidnapping
of Pinky that'd allowed him to make it to his wife's side. There
would be further crimes he'd confess to in the coming months,
those involving blackmail and assault, but nobody – including
Tess and her comrades – would ever learn of his infidelity with
and subsequent accidental killing of his sister-in-law Mary
Rhodes. Though he'd said his goodbyes to Caroline, he'd spared
her any more torment than she was already in by keeping his
awful secret – anyone else that ever knew was dead.

Capital punishment was abolished in Maine almost one
hundred and fifty years ago, so he wasn't facing a death penalty,
but multiple life sentences were in his future; the fact he made
a deal to stand state's evidence in the investigation into the
criminal activities of BK-Rose Holdings LLC might chop a few

years off his sentence, but more importantly to him, he'd requested compassionate visiting rights to Caroline's bedside: Tess sure hoped that his demands would be met.

Tess, Po and Pinky escaped punishment. Though there was suspicion that their parts in Dom Burgess's death, the reckless destruction of property and later allowing Sampson to escape immediate justice at Bath, wasn't all it seemed, it was not in the public's interest to either investigate or charge them. Instead Po and Pinky were recognized as victims and Tess as both their rescuers, and the arrestee of a double murderer. They were fortunate not to have joined Arlen Sampson at Maine State Prison but Tess hadn't gotten off scot-free. Emma Clancy had metaphorically torn a few strips of hide from her during a telling off about trust and lawful process, but all delivered after a knowing wink and nudge had passed between them.

As the ceremony ended at graveside, Tess linked her elbow with Po's. A fortnight after having his knee smashed by Dom he was on the mend, but it still ached having stood on it in the cold for too long. He limped as they walked slowly from the grave, surrounded by similarly slow-moving attendees. Pinky, a looming figure in a voluminous black overcoat and wearing sunglasses, looked like a bouncer on the door of the roughest nightclub in town. He had kept a respectful distance behind the family and friends group nearest the grave, but now moved to meet them. He'd driven them first to the chapel in Standish and then on to the graveyard as they followed the hearse to Jacob's final resting place, and had waited to take them home. They murmured greetings, but another person retreating from graveside distracted Tess. She excused herself from Po's side and walked to intersect Stacey Mitchum's path.

Stacey and Jacob hadn't dated long, but Tess was aware that the girl liked him more than he'd reciprocated. She looked devastated, her face pale and eyes wet as she trudged solemnly away. It took Stacey a moment for Tess to register in her vision, and a moment longer to place the face. Tess offered her a sad smile of condolence. Fresh tears spilled from the girl and Tess placed an arm around her and held her while she shook with grief. Though they were relative strangers, Stacey accepted the comforting hug. When she'd gotten hold of her emotions, she dabbed at her face with her sleeve, and said, 'If Jacob had stayed with me, he'd still be here.'

'It's not your fault, Stacey. Don't blame yourself.'

'I don't.' The girl checked around and her gaze snapped on Hayley, who was now standing at the grave, looking down into its open maw. Stacey's face lit up a scarlet shade. 'She's responsible for Jacob's death. I ought to go over there and say something . . .'

'It won't help,' Tess cautioned her. 'You are hurting, but so is Hayley. I've spoken to her a few times since Jacob's accident and she's genuinely heartbroken.'

'She used him. Why does she care?'

'Sometimes,' said Tess, thinking with a twinge of melancholy of Caroline Sampson lying paralyzed in her Brunswick assisted living home, 'you don't know the true extent of love until it's no longer there. Hayley has had a short sharp shock, and I think it will impact on her for the rest of her life. I'm betting that from now on she's a different girl to the one you once knew.'

Stacey considered for a moment, and Tess watched the anger, and some of her grief, wash out of her. 'Maybe you're right.'

'I'm rarely wrong,' she said, then allowed a smile to creep in place. Stacey laughed gently, and it made Tess feel better. Stacey's unhappiness had always felt like a loose end to Tess, since she somehow felt partly responsible for pushing Jacob into breaking up with her and running back to Bangor. Bringing a smile back to the girl's face was good for her own soul.

Together, they walked away, following Po and Pinky out of the graveyard.